"A smooth, slick ride back in time with tension that never lets up . . ."
—Amy J. Fetzer, Bestselling Author of
The Irish Princess

HOW SWEET IT IS

"Ah, your aim is off," he teased. Mimicking the way she held her spoon, Garren flung a spoonful of dessert at her. The glob hit the side of her head and ran into her ear.

His crow of laughter filled the dining room.

"Yuck." Jocelyn said, trying to wipe the creamy mixture from her ear. This was not what she'd expected after dinner. She had assumed he would expect to consummate their marriage. Loading her spoon, she faked a shot. When he ducked, she lowered her aim, hitting him at his hairline.

"Yes!" She grinned.

She felt a cool splat on her chest and looked down as his second shot disappeared into her decolletage and between her breasts. Squirming, she looked at him, her eyes narrowing.

Loading her spoon, she started a rapid fire of her dessert, and Garren followed suit. By the time the bowls were empty, they both sported globs of the sticky substance in their hair and on their clothing; they were laughing like children.

Garren stood, offering his arm. Making sure her shoulders were straight and her spine stiff, Jocelyn placed her hand ever so slightly on his sleeve—but her regal bearing was lost when her slipper slid in one of the dessert puddles. Garren reached around her waist to steady her, and she slid to a halt in his arms. His warm brown eyes met hers and his warmth flowed into her body.

Her husband's lips came down, lightly brushing hers. "I love dessert."

SIXPENCE BRIDE

VIRGINIA FARMER

LOVE SPELL BOOKS NEW YORK CITY

To my parents, Pauline and Dick Moore.
Even a child with my imagination couldn't have conjured
up such perfect parents. Thanks for supporting and
sometimes feeding my love of stories. For this I sign over
the B-rights to you with my love.
And for my husband and our son—your love inspires me.

A LOVE SPELL BOOK®

June 2000

Published by

Dorchester Publishing Co., Inc.
276 Fifth Avenue
New York, NY 10001

ISBN 0-505-52385-X

The name "Love Spell" and its logo are trademarks of Dorchester Publishing Co., Inc.

Printed in the United States of America.

SIXPENCE BRIDE

Chapter One

Ramsgil, England, 1999

"Hot damn, I won!" The man jumped up, waving a paper in his hand, his bulbous nose slightly redder than the rest of his face.

Jocelyn Tanner groaned and stared at the pink foil star on her travel brochure. The pamphlet's words mocked her: *Step back in time. Experience a wife sale as it was in 1797.*

"So, who's the lucky lady? Where's my *wife*?" the balding, middle-aged man bellowed. He turned this way and that in the tour bus, searching through the twenty other occupants for his "prize."

"Congratulations, Mr. Owens." The guide placed a calming hand on the man's hairy forearm.

Jocelyn swallowed the lump of dread in her throat. Yeah, right, congratulations, she thought.

"If it weren't for bad luck, I wouldn't have any." The shuffling of the passengers muffled her whispered words.

Was this another one of life's cruel jokes? Wasn't it enough that she'd been left at the altar last year? Must she suffer the humiliation of an auction, too? And on what would have been her honeymoon trip! Was it some kind of sign?

Scanning the obnoxious man, Jocelyn considered trying to peel the star off the paper. Heck, she'd eat it if it would get her out of this!

Silence settled around her travel companions, none daring to look around.

Except, of course, for Mr. Owens. Jocelyn swore the man drooled as he looked the women passengers over.

His appearance and demeanor exemplified what every European associated with an American tourist. Uncouth—obviously. Unkempt—just look at the man. Impolite—without a doubt. And loud. She groaned, gripping the brochure to keep from covering her ears when he shouted again. Yes, he certainly was loud.

Jocelyn quickly lowered her eyes as his watery gaze passed over her.

She shook her head as she regarded him from beneath her lashes. He'd combed long strips of stringy hair from one side of his head to the other in a lousy attempt to cover his shiny pate. He sported a coffee stain and what looked like grape jelly on his short-sleeved cotton shirt. The buttons down the front strained to contain his over-large stomach.

Didn't Mr. Owens already have a wife?

Jocelyn glanced at his seatmate, only to find a man who shared a strong family resemblance.

If she sat quietly, maybe someone would take

her place. It wasn't just the man. The idea of even pretending to be auctioned off—it smacked of sexism. It had seemed cute when she planned the trip, but suddenly with no fiancé, things had been cast in a slightly different light.

Bending forward, she grabbed her purse from the floor and, at the same time, surreptitiously dropped her brochure. As she straightened, she pushed it under her seat with her foot, pasting an innocent look on her face. *Please let them find someone else.*

The tour guide's blue-eyed gaze scanned the bus's occupants. "Please, ladies, check your brochures. One of you will find the pink star," she chirped, her uneasy glance belying the cheerful ring of her young voice.

Papers rustled and the bus became quiet again. The guide pressed her hands together, anxiously waiting for the volunteer.

"Excuse me, miss."

Jocelyn glanced behind her at the sound of a masculine voice. The man flashed her an engaging smile and his attractiveness struck her.

Flustered, she returned his smile. "Yes?"

"I believe you dropped this." The devilish glint in his eyes clashed with his very proper British accent.

He handed her back her dreaded brochure with its pink star, and a grin replaced his smile. The change brought attention to the slight dimple in his chin.

Jocelyn frowned, exasperated.

Doesn't he understand how humiliating this will be? She wondered how such a handsome man could be so oblivious—or insensitive. *Scratch that*, she thought with some bitter humor. I've been engaged. Jocelyn's gaze traveled to the loud

9

tourist still standing in the aisle, then back to the infuriating Englishman waving her brochure in her face. With a cool glare, she snatched the paper from his grip.

Good looks don't equate to good deeds.

"Thank you," she said, insincerity dripping from each word.

"My pleasure." He chuckled, and she couldn't completely hold his humor against him.

"I'm sure," she mumbled, just loud enough for him to hear.

"Miss?" The guide walked toward her, hope lighting her gaze. "Have you the star?"

Jocelyn turned toward the girl, nodding mutely.

"I'm so sorry." The guide mouthed the words, and then cleared her throat. "Ah, thank you." Sympathy replaced the hope of seconds ago.

The urge to throw herself on the floor of the bus and cry nearly overwhelmed Jocelyn. *Grow up*, she told herself. *How bad could it be?* Resignation filled her and her shoulders slumped. *Bad enough.*

Another deep chuckle came from behind her.

The young guide returned to the front of the vehicle, edging around Jocelyn's co-star. "Miss . . ." The guide paused, waiting for Jocelyn to supply her name.

With all the enthusiasm of a woman heading to the gynecologist, Jocelyn raised her program.

"Tanner," she supplied with reluctance.

Leaning her head against the seatback, Jocelyn slumped. The notoriety of the wife sale had drawn her to this particular tour. She hadn't reckoned on being the center of attention.

"Well, looky there, I just got me a nice young wife. Stand up, gal, let me have a look at ya. Oooh, I'll get me a pretty penny for you I will." He gave Jocelyn a bawdy wink. "Gotta get in character, ya know."

Jocelyn rolled her eyes. "I believe you've accomplished that." She muttered the words with a grimace.

With an irritating snicker, Mr. Owens rubbed his hands together, grinned at her and took his seat. He obviously couldn't wait to sell her.

A separate chuckle came from the man behind her, and Jocelyn gritted her teeth, fighting the urge to whack him several times with her purse. His amusement at her situation had lasted far too long.

If she could just get off this infernal bus.

From the front of the vehicle, the guide lifted her voice above the occupants' conversations. The bus pulled into its final destination and parked.

"Please collect your costumes from the tour office next to the apothecary and be on the green at eleven thirty. And thank you for your participation."

With each compassionate glance from the departing tourists who passed, Jocelyn slouched further down in her miserably uncomfortable seat. Last came the man from behind her, but he just smiled and winked. It took all her willpower to sit and just glare at his retreating back.

Didn't he understand how horrible she found this?

For a moment she considered not showing up for the auction. But then, a picture of the chuckling stranger flooded her mind. A clear image of the townspeople lining the street, shaking their heads in disbelief as some self-righteous do-gooder dragged her kicking and screaming to the village green. What a spectacle that would be!

No, she decided, better just to put on a brave face and get it over with. After all, what woman in her right mind wouldn't beg to be sold if she were married to Mr. Owens?

She chided herself for her unkind thoughts.

Straightening her shoulders she told herself, if an eighteenth-century woman could survive this, so can I.

Leaving the bus, Jocelyn inhaled the fresh air as her sneakered feet hit the cobblestones of Ramsgil's main street. The scent of flowers and newly mowed grass swirled around her as a playful breeze ruffled her short hair. She crossed to the shops lining the street, squinting against the sunlight glinting off the display windows. She located the tour office and entered, the tinkle of a bell heralding her arrival.

Thirty minutes later Jocelyn stood before the mirror in the tiny dressing room of the tour office, admiring her reflection. A long blond wig covered her short brown hair, the color drawing attention to her lightly tanned skin. A dull yellow gown hung on her trim frame, the full bodice hiding her modest feminine curves, the gathered skirt barely reaching her ankles. She slipped on a vest-like garment, and pulled the laces tight, but it still fell loosely from her shoulders. With a huff, she adjusted the clothing. "A few years ago, this would have fit. Well, except for the length." She glanced at the scuffed, brown leather shoes she wore. "And these shoes could be more comfortable."

Raising her gaze from her feet, she frowned at the stranger looking back at her from the mirror. The fine hairs on her neck rose and an eerie feeling quickly skimmed over her senses. Shaking it off, Jocelyn turned from the mirror.

She left the office and wandered past the stores, beginning to enjoy the merchants and residents moving along in old-fashioned clothing like hers.

Seeing a group of tourists gathering on the green, Jocelyn headed for them. Because she had no choice but to participate in the reenactment, she made up her mind to enjoy herself. There was no point in allowing the situation to spoil her experience.

Feeling a bit queasy and weak, Jocelyn stopped, bracing her hand on the rough wall of a shop. She waited for the feeling to subside, mentally kicking herself for forgetting to eat something. Passing out from low blood sugar would put the icing on the cake.

Taking a breath, she let it out slowly, counting out the hours since breakfast. Surprisingly, it had been nearly four. She rummaged in her handbag for the crackers she stashed for emergencies. Her fingers scraped the bottom of her bag. *Shoot, I ate them last night.*

A dizzying lightness filled her head. She waited a moment for it to pass. Panic rippled through her. No, her mind shouted, I don't need this now. Clutching her bag, she stumbled to the green just as the grayness started to descend. Please don't let me pass out, she prayed. Reaching a block of wood she'd spied from the street, she sat. She closed her eyes, gripping the rough edge of the wood, ignoring the prick of splinters. A curtain of black followed, the ringing in her ears drowned out all other sounds.

The black turned to gray. Jocelyn took a deep breath, and her stomach rolled. The smell of food, unwashed bodies, animal droppings, and dust assailed her nostrils. A cacophony of noises

13

accosted her ears—a dog barked somewhere, chickens squawked, voices mingled amid shouts and laughter and the shuffle of feet.

Her head cleared slowly, and she opened her eyes, blinking away the last vestiges of gray clouding her vision.

Jocelyn's heart lurched.

The scene before her exactly matched the tour guide's description of market day in a typical English village.

Wow, these people work fast. Her blackouts seldom lasted more than a minute, and in that time, the changes to Ramsgil were nothing short of miraculous.

The costumed townsfolk had become a small crowd, all milling about. Animals scurried everywhere, bedraggled children chasing after them and each other. Vendors hawked their wares in loud voices. They really went for realism here, she thought, amazed at the detail.

Jerked by her arm to a standing position, a rough grip held her upright as a gruff whisper near her ear ordered, "Get up there now. I ain't goin' ta have ye under me roof another night. And keep yer trap shut if ye know what's good for ye."

Oh, Mr. Owens loves this, and playing his part with enthusiasm.

Jocelyn's gaze darted to the left and encountered the most grossly disgusting man she'd ever seen.

How had he done it?

Begrimed and ragged, the coarsely woven fabric of his shirt did a poor job of concealing his large meaty frame. Her nose wrinkled in disgust at the stench emanating from him. A rough stubble of beard accented the smudges of dirt on his face. His long, matted hair fell in greasy clumps about his face. Ham-like hands gripped her arms

14

as he shoved her atop the large block of wood, then joined her, shouldering her to the edge.

"Get yer arse in front where ye can be seen." Nudging her forward, he grimaced, exposing several missing teeth; those remaining were black with decay.

This wasn't Mr. Owens. Panic inched into Jocelyn's consciousness, crowding her thoughts, confusing her.

She tried to shake off his hold only to find he tightened his grip.

This was just a reenactment, wasn't it? And this man was playing the part of the husband, right? Something must have happened to Mr. Owens, and this man had taken his place. Yes, that made sense. But really, the man didn't have to be so zealous.

She felt something brush her legs and glanced down at the long, dirty skirt hanging from her waist and skimming the top of the well-worn brown boots on her feet.

How had it gotten so filthy? And why did the bodice feel so tight? Disoriented and scared, she took a deep breath, willing her heart to a slower beat. Jocelyn pulled the rough woolen material away from her body. She stilled, looking at her shaking hands. Why were her nails broken and ragged and her skin red and roughened?

Fingers of hysteria clawed at her mind.

What was going on? She felt different. The nausea and weakness had disappeared. And something else felt different. But what?

Frantically, she tried to assemble the confusion of details, but her mind spun in dizzying circles. Biting back the urge to scream, Jocelyn took a deep breath, fighting for calm.

The man next to her cleared his throat loudly, breaking into her jumbled thoughts.

"She don't eat much and she's a right fine worker. A bit free with her opinions, but she'll do fer a man who's strong enough to tame her," her captor touted.

" 'Tis plain you ain't strong enough fer her, Haslett," a jeering onlooker shouted back.

"Oh, aye, 'tis plain to all that she don't eat much, eh." Another man shouted with laughter as he turned to his cohorts for agreement.

"I'll give ye a ha'pence fer her," another hollered.

Jocelyn watched as an angry red stain began at Haslett's neck and traveled up his face. He cleared his throat before saying, "Now, gents, she's a fast worker and can do sums. Not many wives could boast the same. She's worth more than a ha'pence."

"Most of us ain't got nothin' fer her to count, Haslett."

A round of laughter rolled over Jocelyn.

Finding her voice at last, she spoke up, trying to shake off Haslett's hold on her arm. "Turn loose of me, you idiot . . ."

Jocelyn's mouth slammed shut. She couldn't believe her ears. That low raspy voice had come out of *her* mouth?

Haslett gripped her arm so hard she felt his fingers squeeze against bone.

"I said, not a word out of ye, Nelwina, or ye'll be gettin' a measure of the belt again."

Shock vibrated through her, followed by indignation. "You and whose army?" She muttered beneath her breath, frowning at the unfamiliar sound of her voice.

Feeling a tug on her skirt, Jocelyn looked down to find the gnarled hand of a brightly dressed old woman. A colorful scarf hid the woman's hair; a multitude of bangle bracelets jingled around her withered wrists, and a toothless smile lit her crinkled face.

"Don't fight it, luv. Ye can't change what's happened. Best accept it. It ain't goin' to be easy, but she that's took yer place will have a worse time of it than ye."

Jocelyn watched as the old woman gave a cackling laugh and turned away.

"Hey, wait a minute. What do you mean?" That voice again, Jocelyn thought, where did it come from? What had happened to her nice southern accent? The woman melted into the crowd.

An uproarious round of laughter and another jerk on her arm brought her confused attention to the situation in front of her.

"Ye best pray someone takes ye off me hands, or I'll be taking the strap to ye good when we get home."

Her husband's breath blew in her face, hot and fetid. His red, rheumy eyes glared at her. Spittle dribbled out the side of his mouth. Jocelyn's stomach pitched and rolled. She turned her head and lost its contents.

"Well, now, ye want to tell us she's healthy?" A burly man commented in a loud voice.

"Or maybe she's breedin', eh, Haslett? Ye trying to sell yer brats to someone else?"

Sweat broke out on her brow.

How could these people stand the stench of this village?

Gazing at the crowd gathered around, Jocelyn searched for a familiar face but found none. Where were the tourists from her group? Even that infuriating Brit who'd sat behind her would be a welcome sight.

The old woman's words made her even more

confused. She who had taken her place? What had that crone been talking about? This was all part of the reenactment, right?

Yes, that's it. If she just went along with it, everything would be over in a minute or so. She could get away from the foul-smelling man next to her and out of these filthy clothes.

Scanning the crowd once more, Jocelyn's gaze fell on a well-dressed man astride a large dark horse on the fringes of the crowd. A dark brown jacket encased his broad shoulders. Tan pants hugged the muscled contours of his thighs, disappearing into shiny black boots reaching to his knees. Squinting against the sun, Jocelyn tried to make out the features beneath his tricorn. The hat, pulled low, cast only his upper face in shadows, allowing her a glimpse of a familiar cleft chin and full lower lip.

It was the man from the bus. Of course, she thought, giving herself a mental thump on the head. Maybe that's why he'd been so enthusiastic at seeing her on the auction block. Maybe he'd been assigned to purchase her. Someone had to. Swallowing the whoop that threatened to erupt from her throat, Jocelyn shut out all the warning bells that clanged in her mind.

Sheer meanness hadn't been what had driven him to hand her brochure back. This handsome Englishman meant to play the knight in shining armor and save her from the dastardly husband. Jocelyn suddenly couldn't hold back her smile of relief and delight.

Chapter Two

You'll find a wife ... you'll find a wife ... you'll find a wife. ... The words pounded in Garren Warrick's head, keeping time with his horse's gait. The scene with his father, three weeks earlier, crystallized in his mind. It was the *only* thing clear in his brandy-soaked head. And it replayed for the hundredth time.

His father's blistering words had hit Garren the moment he'd entered the family library.

"You'll find a wife," he'd said. "And within the month or, so help me, I'll find one for you. And given your reputation, the only one I may find who'll take you is someone's wall-eyed, hag-faced, spinster daughter."

"Father—" he'd begun, but in long angry strides, his father had paced the length of the room.

"I cannot believe my son would be so crass as to wager on his ability to seduce a recently wid-

19

owed woman." Even now, Garren raised his eyebrows, experiencing his stunned disbelief at his father's displeasure.

"Oh, yes, you may look surprised," his father had continued, "but did you really think to keep it a secret?"

"What bet?" he'd asked, but his father had ignored him.

"That was no trollop you tossed, but a lady of quality. I would advise you to offer for Lady Melody without delay."

"What?" Garren had roared, his anger growing. Since when had his father been such a stickler for rules? "Have you any knowledge of the woman? You refer to someone who has squandered her husband's modest inheritance. She is a woman who flirted with and, I dare say slept with, any number of eligible and ineligible men."

His father had stopped pacing. "You impugn a lady, sirrah! And place yourself and the Warrick name in an untenable position. I'm deeply disappointed in you, Garren. I thought I'd instilled in you honor, respect, and loyalty, but I see now that I have failed. Even if all you say is true—even then it would be wrong of you to abuse her and to soil her reputation further. And that is exactly what you've done."

Riding now, Garren relived his shame. Through all his former misdeeds his father had simply shaken his head and patiently counseled him. Never had he expressed such profound disappointment before. It was a heavy burden, this newfound guilt.

With a morose sigh, Garren allowed his mount to plod along. Damn Tremaine and the others for wagering on the outcome of his evening with Lady Melody. And damn the lady for setting her lascivious eyes upon him. This whole farce could have gone by unnoticed had the debt not been paid within earshot of Garren's father.

How could his father even think Garren would truly be a party to something so sordid?

It was his past gaming and wenching, his conscience prodded. Well, yes, he conceded. I have been something of a rake. But really, he shook his head, why did his father refuse to believe that Garren had not truly been a part of this wager?

But his father had remained deaf to Garren's denials, and for the last three weeks Garren had attended every available musicale and soiree in search of a suitable wife. Yet the scandal surrounding him left the mamas cold and their daughters tittering behind their fans. He'd gotten heartily sick of being politely snubbed wherever he went. And where were his so-called friends, who'd made money off this whole affair? Hiding from his wrath, he thought with little satisfaction. Until another man became the center of gossip, Garren would find it deucedly impossible to find a wife.

So, with less than a week left, desperation had driven him from the London salons and ballrooms to the country, in hopes that he'd find a miss and her parents unaware of his so-called sins.

Parents—his mind wandered to the change in his father. For three years Richard had sunk into melancholia after Garren's mother's sudden death. He'd seen a gradual change in his father only in the last year—now, finally, at times Richard seemed his old self again. Never would Garren allow himself to be susceptible to the power of love. It was too painful.

Pressing his horse into a canter, Garren sent a plea heavenward that the solution to his problem would be found—and soon.

* * *

Garren slowed his horse to a walk as the village of Ramsgil appeared around the bend of the road. The effects of his past night of drinking were beginning to take their toll as a pounding began behind his eyes.

The rumble of laughter drew him from his thoughts as he came to a village green ringed with spectators. Halting behind them, Garren addressed a woman in mobcap.

"Excuse me, madame." She glanced up at him. "Why such a gathering?"

Her eyes rounded in surprise. "A wife sale, gov-'na." Nodding toward the center of the green she added, "That 'un there be selling 'is wife. She'll be a sight luckier to be rid of 'im too." The woman bobbed in a clumsy curtsy and threaded her way through the crowd.

Garren settled in his saddle to observe the spectacle. He'd heard of the "poor man's divorce," but had never witnessed one. From what he knew of them, the wife would probably be purchased by her lover—for a nominal fee—to the proposed satisfaction of all parties.

'Tis a shame I can't procure a wife as easily, Garren thought.

As he watched and listened to the man tout his wife's value, Garren's gaze moved from the man to the woman beside him. She stood atop the block, tendrils of blond hair flitting across her face. Beneath finely arched brows, her gray eyes were round with fear. Her narrow, straight nose tipped up slightly on the end, a perfect foil for her delicately bowed lips. Smudges of dirt couldn't hide her creamy complexion. If not for the circumstances, he might think her a lady, Garren realized.

Her gaze lifted to his, holding him immobile. A moment later a sparkle of happiness replaced her fear, and her lips lifted in a smile. Before Garren realized what he intended, he'd nudged his horse forward. The crowd quieted and parted to allow him to approach. His gaze still captured by hers, he reached into his vest pocket and pulled out a single coin. He spared it but a glance. "Sixpence."

The man just stood there, shock written plainly on his face. Blinking like an owl, he scanned the crowd, apparently looking for a better offer.

The blond woman tapped her toe impatiently. "Well, get on with it."

Her husband shot her a triumphant glare. "Done." Bobbing his head, he held out his hand.

Garren hesitated a moment as the headache from his hangover came roaring back. What had he done? *Gotten yourself a bride,* came the answer.

Who had said it couldn't be this easy for him? This seemed a perfect answer. If the truth be known, at this point he cared little who he took to wife, so long as she didn't interfere with his life. All he had to do was appease his father. The fact that she was a commoner could be his own little joke—on everyone. Yes, she'd do perfectly.

With a flick of his wrist, Garren sent the coin sailing through the air. It landed neatly in the man's palm, and the crowd shouted its approval.

"Well, then, we're done." Jocelyn heaved a sigh of relief as she stepped away from the auction block. The horse of the man who'd bought her moved, blocking her exit. The man's arm lowered and snaked around her waist, and he pulled her up before him on his mount. Her left hip nestled against his thighs, and his arms surrounded her.

Her shoulder pressed against the breadth of his chest, and the smell of liquor fanned her cheek when he exhaled.

" 'Tis a good thing ye didn't pay by the stone fer her, eh?" a man shouted from the crowd.

Laughter rumbled through the group that stood watching.

Jocelyn stiffened at the insult.

"The vicar be at the end of the lane there." Haslett pointed in that direction.

She let out a weary sigh. Surely they wouldn't carry this thing through to a marriage ceremony, would they? Well, as far as she was concerned the sale had taken place and that ended it. "You best put me down now."

She cleared her throat, her hand coming up to touch her throat. Her suddenly unfamiliar voice truly confused her. What had happened to her old southern drawl? Choking on confusion, Jocelyn searched her mind for a logical explanation and failed.

His arm flexed around her waist. "Quiet." His authoritative voice rang in her ear.

"Listen, your costume's great, but don't you think you're carrying this a bit too far?"

She felt him flinch. Wondering at that, she looked at him.

"Be quiet, I said." With a dismissive glance, his brows drew together, and he turned his gaze back to the busy lane before them.

Jocelyn fought for control. "You're an actor. You do this a lot, right?" She cocked her head to the side.

"Silence," he demanded, giving her a warning glare.

"Okay, we'll play it your way, then." Jocelyn shrugged. He seemed intent on carrying this performance to its completion. Once she got off this horse, she'd rush back to the bus and never again would she get involved in anything like this.

But the vicar never gave her the opportunity to escape. He awaited them at his front door, a large book in hand and a makeshift table before him.

The vicar was bald and spare of frame, but his voice made up for in volume what he lacked in height and hair.

The mercifully short ceremony passed in a blur for Jocelyn. Her attention was focused solely on the warmth of the hand encircling her arm, bringing an unreasonable fluttering to her stomach and wreaking havoc on her senses.

"If you'll just sign here, Lord Spenceworth." The fawning voice of the vicar grated on Jocelyn's nerves.

The clergyman gave her a condescending look, dipped the quill in the ink jar and held it out to her. "And if her *ladyship* would make her mark here."

Taking a moment, she studied the bold lines of her pretend husband's signature. Garren Warrick. *It has a nice ring to it at least*, she thought. And a lord no less! *Well la-di-da!*

"An X will do."

That was enough! Her patience and understanding exhausted, she snatched the pen from the balding cleric. Jocelyn wanted to grab the self-important idiot himself and engrave her name on his forehead, but she settled for a glare before she signed the documents, making her Js and Ts extra large and sweeping.

The startled look the vicar gave her from under his bushy eyebrows as he sanded the signatures and handed one of the copies to Garren only irritated her further.

Garren glanced over the document, his eyebrows rising as his eyes scanned the bottom. "Jocelyn." He murmured her name, sending an odd shiver through her.

As they turned to leave, she leaned over and confided to the vicar in a low voice, "As if I couldn't write . . ." Smirking, she tilted her chin a bit higher and twirled away from him, heading back to town—and the haven of the bus.

For the second time that day someone gripped her arm and jerked her around. Jocelyn found herself staring into Garren's shadowed gaze.

"I think I'd rather walk back to the green." She tugged her arm, trying to break Garren's grip as he pulled her back to his horse.

Without warning, he tossed her up on the saddle. Before she could catch her breath, he mounted behind her and the horse moved down the rutted road, leaving Ramsgil behind.

Pushing at his hand, Jocelyn tried to squirm off the saddle. "Let me down," she said through gritted teeth. She'd been manhandled enough for one day, especially by actors of some silly tourist outfit.

Her new "husband" tightened his hold on her waist, ignoring her struggles.

"Listen." Jocelyn tried for patience. "You can't leave town. We have to get back to the village." Why didn't he listen to her?

Jocelyn felt him tense with her words and wondered if he would stop and end this charade. She waited for his response, but none came.

Frustration sharpened her voice. "Okay, you've had your fun, but it's over, and we have to get back."

Still, he didn't respond.

Had the man suddenly gone deaf?

Her ire rose along with panic. "Listen, mister, I'm not someone you can simply ride off with. Just set me down off this horse so I can go back."

"Quiet." It came out more as a grunt than a word.

"Haven't you done enough?" Taking a deep, calming breath, Jocelyn moderated her tone. "If *you* don't want to go back, fine. Just put me down, and I'll walk back. You have no right taking me away."

"I've every right." He pushed his tricorn up and glared at her. "You belong to me now."

"What?" she shrieked, whipping around to see him cringe at her volume. His eyes narrowed. They were brown, like those of the man on the bus, and he had a similar chin, but there the similarities ended. This wasn't the same man. "Who are you?"

"Silence." He winced, his brow furrowing. "I've a blinding headache, and your constant wailing is not helping." The muscles in his lean jaw flexed as if willing the pain away.

His voice held her mesmerized. If a sound could take physical form, his voice would be warm whiskey and just as intoxicating. Then his words sank in.

"I don't care if you've got a headache. You're taking this mock sale a little too seriously."

"Mock sale? I think not." He focused his dark eyes on her, his eyebrows raised in disbelief. "I paid your husband sixpence."

"But the play is over."

"Play, madame?" Disgust laced his words and determination lit his gaze as he urged the horse into a gallop.

Jocelyn's angry retort died on her lips as she

27

concentrated on not falling beneath the pounding hooves of the animal.

At last she's quiet, Garren thought. Though the jarring ride was little better, at least it served to silence the gibberish she spouted. He frowned. He'd never heard a village woman speak so. She hadn't the heavy countrified accent of others of her class. He shook his head. And her strange use of words—well, it fair boggled his mind.

And this claptrap about a mock sale! He shook his head, again. Mayhap he got less for his sixpence than he had bargained for. Or more.

Her unbound golden-blond hair swirled in tangled strands about her head, pulling Garren's gaze to the woman he held in his arms. Her pale skin looked smooth beneath the patches of dirt smudging her face. His gaze flicked to her clothing. It hadn't seen wash water in some time.

Yet, she had a look of gentility. Light brown brows arched delicately over eyes that were large and soft gray. Her full, petal-pink mouth bowed perfectly beneath her small straight nose. He noticed her slightly pointed chin and struggled to recall if dimples complimented her smooth, plump cheeks when she smiled. Once cleaned up, she would be quite easy to look upon—the perfect showpiece to silence his father and society.

But, he reminded himself as he watched the road ahead, he'd not be around long enough to see. He would deposit her at Spenceworth and return to London. He would see his new wife placed and then neatly left behind.

His gaze strayed to Jocelyn's smudged face, and he chuckled. His father was in for quite a sur-

28

prise. *This would show the man for daring to give him an ultimatum.*

He threw his head back and laughed riotously, then winced as his headache returned.

Chapter Three

"Slow down!" Jocelyn shouted above the rhythmic thud of the horse's hooves. Her stomach lurched as she stared at the passing ground. Clutching the front of the saddle in a death grip, she shut her eyes. *Oh God, please get me down. The ground is too far away!*

Garren remained silent.

Jabbing her elbow up into his chest, she felt a small measure of satisfaction at his pained grunt. She turned her head and opened her eyes. He spared her but one furious glare before returning his gaze to the road ahead. Except for one disconcerting burst of laughter, he hadn't spoken a word since they'd left Ramsgil on the rutted track heading north.

Jocelyn's mouth dropped opened. She swiveled her gaze around, her fear of heights forgotten as she viewed the dusty lane. What had happened to the neatly paved road? What was going on? Was all this part of the stupid tour?

A chill stole up her spine, and she swallowed the panic threatening to explode in a scream. Clinging to one last thin thread of control, she blinked back burning tears.

Slowly, anger consumed her fear and she stiffened her spine.

"Stop!" She twisted and gave Garren a glaring look.

His eyes widened in surprise, but the man stubbornly remained silent, turning his attention back to the road. With a determined set of his jaw, he spurred the horse with his knees.

Jocelyn shrieked in alarm and tightened her grip. Her bottom bounced and rubbed against the hard leather saddle. She concentrated on the pain, shutting out her panic. Eventually, they had to stop, and she'd get some answers. Then she'd return to Ramsgil.

By late afternoon, Jocelyn doubted they'd ever stop—or that her companion would ever speak. One thing for sure, once off this horse, she'd never get on one again. Her entire body ached from the jarring ride. Her numb fingers clutched the front of the saddle and her spine felt like it'd been compressed at least two inches. She longed to get down and soak for three days in a hot tub.

A village appeared as they crested a hill, dappled sunlight lending a fairy tale-like quality to the ancient-looking structures that huddled together in the distance. She let out a shaky breath. At last, she thought, the end is near. They rode down and into the town.

Garren pulled at the reins, bringing the horse to a halt before a low wooden building. A weathered sign with a scraggly chicken, a sorry-looking crown perched on its head, proclaimed the place "The Royal Cock." Even through her misery Jocelyn couldn't help the grin that tweaked her lips. *"The Royal Cock," indeed.*

"My wife and I will be needing a clean room, hot food and a bath." The intoxicating warmth of Garren's whiskey-smooth voice infiltrated Jocelyn's tensed body. She flexed her hands, turning loose the front of the saddle. The blood flowed back into her numb fingers, bringing a painful tingle.

"Where are we?" Jocelyn scanned the village, noting the wattle and daub houses with their thatched roofs. Few people were about, but those she saw were all in period dress. This village had to depend on tourism, like Ramsgil. How sick the inhabitants must be of dressing like this, she thought to herself.

"Castleside." Garren answered her previous question. He dismounted and turned to her.

She slid off the horse, guided by his hands. Needles of pain shot up her legs, erasing her thoughts.

"Well, have you a room or not?" Garren growled behind her.

Jocelyn turned her head to find herself the object of a bewhiskered innkeeper's stare.

He glanced away. "Aye, m'lord," the man replied, bobbing his head. "Just follow me." His hand warm on her elbow, Garren propelled Jocelyn after him.

"Wait a minute." Jocelyn dug her heels into the dirt. "I'm not staying here with you." She jerked her arm out of Garren's grasp. The warm imprint of his hand remained. She stared at the area, surprised at the fluttering low in her stomach.

How could her body react to the mere touch of this man?

Turning her back on both the sensations and Garren, Jocelyn addressed the innkeeper. "Excuse me, sir, could you tell me where the train station is?"

The man's brow furrowed in confusion. He cast a sidelong glance at Garren.

Garren shook his head. "Come along, *dear*," he said through tight lips. "I'll explain everything in our room."

"When donkeys fly! I'm not staying with you. I'm taking the train back to Ramsgil." Jocelyn pulled away from Garren, her eyes traveling around the small village. There were no train tracks, just the rutted road they had come in on.

Garren's confused gaze scanned Jocelyn, ending at the bottom of the back of her skirt. "Train?" Grabbing her arm, he again steered her toward the door of the inn. "You've no train, and I've no more patience with your foolery."

"Let me go." Jocelyn twisted against his hold. His grip tightened, but not painfully.

He pulled her closer as he guided her to the inn. "Have a care, woman. I'll brook no more insolence from you." A shiver of fear raced through her veins at his chilling glare.

The door of the inn opened, and Garren nudged her into a low-ceilinged, smoky room with crude benches and tables scattered about.

"Yer room be this way m'lord." The innkeeper pointed to the left.

Jocelyn braced her hands on her waist and raised her chin. "I'll just stay down here." Her eyes slowly adjusted to the dim interior. She surveyed the room and its inhabitants—mostly male and all looking at her, lascivious grins stretched wide across their faces.

"Aye, mate, let 'er keep *me* company." A small wiry man held his hands out in welcome, a gap-toothed grin splitting his dirty face.

"She's too much woman fer ye, Jake, but I'm available." Another man stood, taller, heavier, and much dirtier than the first.

Jocelyn instinctively edged closer to Garren.

Her abductor spoke in a low voice. "Have you changed your mind, then?" A smug smile tilted his lips.

She moved nearer still, nodding mutely. Better to deal with one man than many.

"Sorry gents, the lady's with me." Garren flashed an engaging grin to the crowd.

"Ride 'er well and long, and once fer me."

Loud guffaws greeted the man's instructions. A furious blush heated Jocelyn's cheeks.

"Don't get cocky, buddy. You're simply the lesser of two evils," she muttered to Garren, following the innkeeper as he turned to show them their room. Lighting a stub of candle from a flickering taper on a nearby table, he mounted the narrow, rickety set of stairs.

Why didn't he just flip on a light, Jocelyn wondered, bewildered by the antiquity of her surroundings.

He opened the door at the end of the hall with a flourish, pride etched in every smiling line of his face. " 'Tis the finest room in all of Castleside, milord," he said. "And we've modern conveniences." He patted the washstand, where a chipped bowl and small pitcher sat. He ran his hand along the dingy linens draped over a small rod on one side.

He considers these *modern conveniences*? Jocelyn thought, scanning the room.

"I'll have yer bath up directly. We're used to having honored guests such as yerself, sir." He lit the candle resting on the stand. "If there's anything ye might need, ye have just to ask it. Milady." He pulled at the lock of hair on his forehead and bowed his way out the door.

Garren prowled around the room, running a finger over the few pieces of furniture. He flipped the bed coverings back to view gray sheets. "Umph. The finest room in Castleside. I'd hate to see the worst," he muttered.

Jocelyn chuckled.

What was wrong with her? Nothing about this was funny. She didn't know where she was or with whom. She didn't know how to get back to Ramsgil, the tour bus, or anything. Jocelyn glanced out the window, and through the grime, watched the last rays of sunlight fade.

She was stuck here for the night. Would they leave without her? Had her fellow tourists called the police?

"I've ordered a bath for you."

Turning away from the window, she regarded her kidnapper. With a lift of her chin and in an icy voice she responded, "So I heard, but I don't want a bath. I want to return to Ramsgil."

"Why would you want to return there? You'll be much better off at Spenceworth." His eyebrows drew together as he frowned.

A knock at the door interrupted Jocelyn's response.

Garren flashed her a warning look and called out, "Come."

The door opened and the innkeeper and a burly

young man entered, toting a large wooden tub between them. A girl followed, carrying two buckets of water.

After placing the tub on the floor, the innkeeper turned to Garren. "There be more water coming, milord. It won't take but a moment more." He hustled from the room, pushing his helpers ahead of him.

Jocelyn stood transfixed. Didn't they have indoor plumbing either?

Several more trips and the tub stood half-full of steaming water. A three-legged table held linens and a bowl of soap.

With a pointed look at the tub, Garren headed for the door, saying over his shoulder, "I'll see what is available in the way of clean clothing while you bathe. I assume it wasn't worth gathering up your old—" he paused, meaningfully glancing at her less than pristine outfit— "dresses." He closed the door quietly behind him.

Who does this man think he is? She glared at the closed door. *Well, there is no way I'm going to stick around here and find out. If I have to walk all the way back to Ramsgil in the dark, so be it.*

Jocelyn went to the door and opened it just enough to see down the empty hall. Edging out, she carefully closed the door behind her. At the top of the stairs, she paused and listened. She heard raised voices, the scrape of chairs, and shouts of laughter that drifted on the smoky air. She crept down the dark stairs. Light from the fire outlined the patrons of the inn. Staying close to the wall, she inched her way toward the front door. Just as she moved around the corner, the door in sight, a hand clamped on her shoulder from behind.

"Did you wash behind your ears, wife?" came

the familiar whiskey voice. He sniffed. "You don't seem any cleaner. Perhaps you need *my* assistance with your bath," he whispered in her ear.

Garren turned her around and pulled her up the stairs and back to the room.

"I've sixpence invested in you. Whether you're mad or not, you're still my property, and you'll do as I say. Do you understand? Now, remove those filthy clothes and bathe." He released her arm. "I'll send one of the serving girls up with clean clothes and something to eat. Stay in this room until I return."

He stood there in front of her, full of superiority. Oh, how she wanted to bring him down a peg. Property indeed! She smiled sweetly, waving her index finger. "First, you don't *own* me. You can't own anyone! And second"—she extended another finger— "if I don't want to bathe, I won't. And there isn't anything you can do about it!"

He took two menacing steps toward her. "You think I'm incapable of getting you into that tub?" He nodded to the steaming bath and took two more steps in her direction.

He raised his fist.

She swallowed.

Extending his index finger, his challenging gaze held hers. "You *will* bathe, Jocelyn, or"—he raised another finger in mocking imitation of her— "*I'll* do it *for* you!" Pausing, he seemed to invite her rebellion. When she remained silent, he continued, tilting his head. "Do I make myself clear?" He advanced another two steps and looked down at her.

Jocelyn stepped back, coming up against the foot of the bed.

"Now, shall *I* begin removing your clothes, or will you do it yourself?" His hand reached out toward her and she gulped, clenching the cloth at her neck. She leaned away from him, losing her balance and plopping down on the bed.

Batting at his hand, her voice trembled. "Listen. Don't you think this thing has gone far enough? I mean, this is kidnapping. I could have you arrested."

His unconcerned laugh further frayed Jocelyn's nerves. "Even if you could find a constable, how would you explain this 'kidnapping?' You're my *wife*, and I'm taking you home. How could that be kidnapping?" Garren arched an eyebrow.

"You're nuts. . . ."

"I beg your pardon?" Jocelyn watched as Garren reined in his impatience, inhaling deeply, then exhaling. "You *will* bathe. I'll hear no more argument from you." He gave her one more look—this time one more of resigned pity—and he left, closing the door with a thud. "Crazy, woman." She heard through the door.

Crazy? He's the crazy one, she thought. Tremors of fear started at Jocelyn's feet. What did he mean? Were there no police or constables here? And why was he still acting so . . . strange?

The shadows lengthened in the room. If she could just make it through the night, tomorrow she could find her way back to Ramsgil, take a train back to London, and catch the first flight home. She was fed up with this entire trip.

But until then . . . Jocelyn eyed the steaming tub.

Wrinkling her nose at her dirty, smelly clothing, she rapidly stripped down to a yellowed chemise, her thoughts still turning Garren's words over. Wiggling out of the chemise, she let it pool at her feet, and reached for the front clasp of her bra. Her fingers came in contact with bare skin. Her gaze dropped down . . . no bra . . . further down . . . no panties.

Her own scream startled her. Somewhere in her mind she registered the shriek as her own, but she felt powerless to stop it. Looking around frantically, Jocelyn reached down and snatched the discarded chemise from the floor, clutching it over her breast.

She ran to the door and fumbled with the latch. Hysteria edged in, giving her only a slight warning before it spread, blocking out everything.

The scream shook the rafters, echoing off the walls. The hair on Garren's neck stood up. Another scream, wilder now, followed in a higher pitch. Motioning to the innkeeper that he would handle the situation, fear pumping adrenaline into his veins.

Pushing open the door, he saw Jocelyn stumble back, an old chemise held over her chest. Her eyes wide, she advanced on him. Tangling her free hand in the front of his shirt, she yanked him closer. "Where's *my* body?" she shrieked. "What have you done with it?"

Tears welled in her eyes, turning them to liquid silver as Garren tried to pry her hand from his shirtfront. Fear and confusion marked every line of her pale face, and the sight softened his heart.

Taking her wrist in a firm grip, he spoke over her frantic cries. "Quiet woman. Lower your voice and calm down."

Jocelyn sniffed and clamped her mouth closed. Large silver-gray eyes looked up beseechingly at him. A little hiccup shook her shoulders.

"Now, what is all the fuss about?" Garren released her wrist. Bringing his hands up, he gently rubbed her shoulders, halting when he saw purple bruises marring the warm smoothness of her skin. No doubt he could be blamed for a few of them. Shifting, he dropped his hands to his sides, ashamed of his rough treatment of her. His gaze slid to the floor, then back up to her. His body tightened and he stepped away, all too conscious of the woman before him.

Her hands came forward in a pleading gesture, the chemise forgotten. It slid down, and with a gasp, she snatched it back up, shrugging the sleeves over her shoulder. But not before she had treated him to a glimpse of the full, creamy flesh of her breasts. He clenched his fists at his sides, resisting the urge to test the softness of her skin.

Taking a deep breath, he forced his body to relax. He raised his gaze from her shoulder to the hands covering her face and muffling her words.

"Something's wrong with my body."

Garren bent closer and moved her hands away. He must have misheard her. "What?"

Her head came up and she said, "Something's wrong with my body."

Leaning back, his gaze raked her form. He could find little fault with the curves beneath the thin material veiling her body. Warrick, he silently chided himself, this isn't where your mind should be wandering. Shaking his head, he returned his scrutiny to her face.

"Are you ill? Where do you hurt?" That's all he needed, a half-naked, sick female on his hands.

"No." She shook her tangled mane of hair. "I'm not ill, and I don't hurt."

"Well then, what's *wrong* with you?" Irritation sharpened his words. But whether it was with her and her peculiar behavior, or him and the

40

strong physical attraction he felt for her, he wasn't certain.

"This isn't my body."

He gave her an annoyed look. "So, whose body do you think it is?"

"I don't know . . . I don't know." Taking a quivering breath, she wrapped her arms around herself. "I just want to get back to Ramsgil and the tour group. I want to go back to my hotel, take a bath, and go to sleep."

She spoke with a genuineness that touched him. If she were pretending to be crazy to escape him, her eyes gave nothing away. Part of him admired that. She'd be a bloody good card player, he thought. He shook his head at his own musings, slanting a glance at her.

What was he to think of her? She did not sound like a commoner, and what of her strange use of words? Now she believed she wasn't even in her own body. Was she truly mad? Looking into her gaze, he saw no hint of it.

His patience, both with himself and her, expired with that thought.

"The bath is there." He pointed to it. "And after, you can sleep—but I won't be taking you back to Ramsgil. You'll have to live with that. Now, I'll leave you again. I'll return in an hour." With one last fierce glare, he left.

Jocelyn stood in the middle of the room looking at the closed door. "I sound crazy, and he doesn't even blink an eye."

She looked down at the chemise, seeing the deep cleavage above the neckline. Her knees quaked. They were still there, those large, full breasts. And with them came all the old anxieties.

41

She ran her hand down her side, noting the slight indentation of her waist and the full fleshiness of her hip. Her hand glided across her abdomen and she sickened. A rounded stomach matched the full breasts. The hysteria threatened again. She swallowed and then took a deep, calming breath.

Sitting down on the edge of the bed, she struggled to make some sense of her surroundings. Thoughts kept tumbling around in her mind.

This must be a dream. She'd had plenty of dreams that seemed real, even after she woke. Yeah, she thought, but Mel Gibson always appeared in them. Where was he now? Garren certainly wasn't Mel. Granted he was nice to look at—okay, he was great to look at, but gallantry definitely was not his strong suit. And he lacked communication skills, too.

Shaking her head to clear the image of Garren, she frowned. The picture was replaced by that of the old woman from the green.

"It ain't goin' to be easy, but she that's took yer place is having a worse time of it than ye." What had the woman meant?

She recalled the brochure. *Step back in time.* The words echoed in her mind. No, she thought, *that* couldn't happen, could it? Time travel? She shook her head in disbelief, dismissing the thought.

Unable to make sense of the whole situation, she put her head in her hands, threading her fingers through matted hair. She pulled the golden blond mess down in front of her face and stared at it. The hair wasn't hers. And neither was the body or the voice. She was in her right mind, but the wrong body.

Another thought rolled to a stop in her mind. Jocelyn pulled her hands from her hair and gripped the sheet from the bed. Had she switched bodies with someone? With Haslett's wife? What had he called her?

She snapped her fingers as it came to her. "Nelwina." Jocelyn shook her head. "Lord, what a horrible name."

It made sense that if she were in Nelwina's body, Nelwina would be in hers.

Panic and hysteria churned in her head, her fingers pleating the sheet in nervous jerks. What was happening in her time? To her life there? How would she get back? Her hands stilled as a more dreadful thought took hold.

Could she get back?

Smoothing the sheet, Jocelyn tried to calm her tumultuous thoughts.

Her hands went back to the matted hair on her head, and she tugged on it in frustration. "So what do I do now? I'm fat." Tears blurred her vision. "And I promised myself never to get this way again," she ranted to the ceiling.

Her mind went numb, coming back to life when she pulled her fingers from the snarls, leaving the hair to fall forward into her line of vision. Her practical nature took command. "It needs a good brushing and a healthy application of shampoo. Lice are probably running around in there," she said to herself. The tingle of imagined microscopic feet raced over every part of her scalp. Her fingers curled into claws, and with a low moan she scratched every square inch of her scalp, but the tingles persisted.

She bounded from the bed, scrambling into the tub of cooling water, chemise and all. She doused her head beneath the surface and, working the soap into a lather, scrubbed for all she was worth. Sinking below the water, she rinsed away the soap. She glanced down, groaning when she saw raised nipples push against the nearly transparent, wet fabric. Slouching down in the tub, she crossed her arms over her—no, Nelwina's—chest.

How could she . . . wash another woman's body?

She could just swish around in the water, but after examining her hands, feet and legs, she knew she'd have to scrub this body if it were to be clean.

And she desperately wanted to be clean.

Gritting her teeth, she grabbed a linen square from the table and lathered it with soap. She scrubbed at the unfamiliar arms and legs. Rinsing them off, she sighed, "That wasn't so bad." She took a deep breath. "Now, for the rest."

Biting her lip, she gingerly rubbed the washing linen over the chemise-covered body, forcing her mind away from the odd chore.

She finally emerged from the bath, skin scrubbed pink and clean, and the chemise a paler shade of yellow.

A timid knock startled her, freezing her in place. Was he back already? The rap came again and she edged to the door, damp linen held before her. Surely it hadn't been an hour yet. She opened it a crack.

With a sigh of relief, Jocelyn pulled the door wider. A young girl of about fifteen stared back, her arms piled with clothing. " 'Is lordship asked I should bring ye these things to wear, milady."

Jocelyn opened the door wider and, hiding behind it, allowed the girl to enter.

"Ain't what yer used to I'm sure, milady, but 'tis the only thing he could find." The girl smiled, revealing small, yellowed teeth, minus a front tooth. She moved to the bed, depositing the clothing, her red, chapped hands smoothing the fabric of the top item with loving care.

Jocelyn's eyes widened. "Those aren't your clothes, are they?"

"Oh no, milady." She plucked at the coarse brown material of her skirt. "I only got this and a church dress of dark blue. I'd love to have a gray dress like this one." Her hand moved from her skirt to the gray garment, stroking it gently.

"Will ye need help getting dressed? I could help if ye do." The eagerness in the maid's voice was transmitted to her face, lighting it with hope.

Jocelyn started to say no, but couldn't resist the girl's earnest smile. "Thank you." Offering her hand, Jocelyn continued, "I'm Jocelyn. And you are?"

"Bethany, milady," she said, staring in confusion at Jocelyn's extended hand. Turning to the clothing, she pulled a chemise from the pile. Shaking it out, she offered it to Jocelyn.

"You said these were the only clothes available?" Jocelyn stepped to the bed, fingering the garments there. At Bethany's nod Jocelyn asked, "Does everyone in this village wear period clothing *all* the time?" Clinging to the hope that Bethany's answer would explain the unexplainable, Jocelyn held her breath.

Squinting, Bethany considered the question a moment. She smiled brightly and shook her head. "One of the other girls said as how she'd seen one of the gentlemen without a stitch on in bed when she brung him his morning meal. So I guess some people don't wear clothes *all* the time."

Startled, Jocelyn pursed her lips, fighting back hysteria.

45

" 'Ere now, we should get ye dressed afore his lordship comes back." Bethany bit her lip, casting a worried look Jocelyn's way. "He don't seem like a very patient man, does he?" She extended the chemise to Jocelyn, again.

She stared blindly at the proffered garment, despair settling around her.

"Milady?"

Bethany's voice broke the spell and Jocelyn shook her head. "No, I'll wear this one." Uncomfortable with the thought of exposing this body she'd somehow inherited, she chose to wear the slightly damp article, earning a confused glance from Bethany.

A few minutes later, Jocelyn glanced down at her new clothing and gasped. Everything tied or hooked or buttoned. The girdle pushed the ample breasts up, displaying a good deal of cleavage.

"I can't walk out of here like this. It's indecent," she said to Bethany, a blush warming her face and exposed chest.

"But Lady Jocelyn, there be nothing wrong with it. If ye like, we'll pull a bit more of the chemise up in front." And Bethany put action to her words, bringing a little more fabric up with a gentle tug. It was better, but Jocelyn still felt exposed.

"Yer hair sure is in a tangle." Bethany hesitated before rushing on. "If ye like, I could comb the snarls out."

Tugging at the nearly dry hair, Jocelyn said, "I don't have a comb."

She didn't have anything. No identity, no friends, no job, no home. Not even a comb of her own.

A sudden depression descended upon her like a

black cloud. Adrift and feeling totally lost, Jocelyn reached out to the only sympathetic soul she'd met so far in this sordid nightmare.

From a pocket in her dress, Bethany produced a wooden comb. "I always keep me own comb with me. I only got the one, and around here things turn up missin' if ye don't keep yer eye on 'em. Sit down, and I'll start working on it."

Jocelyn sat down on a stool next to the table. Taking Bethany's hand, she looked into the maid's startled eyes. "Oh, thank you, Bethany. You don't know how much I appreciate this."

She gave the young girl a watery smile, squeezed her hand, and turning around, gritted her teeth for the torture to come. She normally kept her hair short for two reasons. First, she had no talent with arranging long hair. Curling irons and blow dryers were beyond her. And second, she was extremely tender-headed.

It took Jocelyn a few minutes to realize that Bethany's tugging and pulling on her hair didn't hurt as she had expected. She almost slapped her palm against her forehead. It wasn't *her* scalp, but Nelwina's, and apparently the woman had a tough one.

Twenty minutes later her hair was combed and plaited in a single braid down her back.

Heavy footsteps in the hall were punctuated with a knock on the door. A brief pause and Garren entered, another serving girl following him with a tray of food.

Edging around him, the girl placed the tray on the small table next to Jocelyn and bobbed her way out, never once raising her eyes.

Bethany's gaze dropped, she bent her knee in a swift curtsy, and scooted out the door. Jocelyn called out, "Thank you, Bethany." Her hand lifted in farewell.

As the door closed she felt the loss of the young girl. Garren eyed her closely; he looked from the scuffed toes of the brown shoes that peeped out from the hem of her dress, to the neatly braided hair. She watched his eyes travel back down to the top of her girdle, and a blush heated her face and chest. She sat there with her hands in her lap, nervously twisting her fingers.

"The tray is for you." He sat down on the bed.

Jocelyn, already self-conscious because of her clothes, became even more uncomfortable under his constant scrutiny.

Placing the dingy napkin from the tray in her lap, she picked at the dark bread also there, sipped the drink she couldn't identify, tasted the cheese, stared at the strange stew-like substance in the bowl, and blotted her lips.

"I've finished."

He cast her a look ripe with suspicion. "You hardly touched your meal. You aren't going to be sick again, are you?" He hesitated. "Are you with child?"

"No. . . ." She wasn't, was she? How would she know? No, she thought, shaking her head, it couldn't get *that* bad, could it? Surely Haslett wouldn't have done that . . . would he? What would make Garren even think such a thing?

Recalling the episode on the block in the green, her eyes shot to him. "The only reason I was sick was the stench of the man standing next to me." With a pointed glare at him, she added, "And I find it difficult to eat with you staring at me."

His eyebrow lifted and he stood up, glancing at the tray. "See that you eat and get some sleep. We leave early in the morning." At the door he turned. "I'll try not to disturb you when I come in." The door closed with a quiet thud.

"You . . . you . . ." Jocelyn choked on her words. Stumbling from the stool, she flung the door open, poking her head out in the hall. "And just where do *you* propose to sleep?" She shouted at his retreating back.

He stopped, turned slowly, and then in three strides stood nose-to-nose with her, pushing her back into the room and closing the door with a slam.

"Don't start." His dark brows collided. "I go where I please, when I please. I answer to no one." His voice underlined each word. He moved a step closer. "Do you understand? No one. I'll sleep where I like and with whom I like."

"Lord or no lord, it won't be with me." Jocelyn straightened her spine, bracing her hands on her hips.

His eyes widened and he advanced on her. "*You* are my wife," he poked a finger in her direction. "If I choose to sleep with you, I will." His eyes traveled with insulting purpose over her. "But you need have no fear of that, *Lady* Spenceworth."

Jocelyn had seen that look before from the boys in high school, and the hurt cut into her. She had never measured up in those days. There was simply too much to measure. She felt the sting of tears and turned away from him, blinking them back. Stiffening her spine she turned back to him. "Well I'm certainly relieved to hear that. We'll end up in a brawl if you try."

Footsteps and a quiet click of the door followed her words, and a heavy silence filled the room. The pain behind her eyes increased and Jocelyn sat heavily on the bed, fighting the tears, fears, and frustrations that clogged her throat.

Fatigue weighted her limbs and she lay down.

"I'll just rest for a while." Jocelyn's eyes closed and her tired mind gave in to slumber.

Chapter Four

Taking a deep breath, Garren gave a silent prayer that his new wife still slept as he quietly entered the room. He raised his candle high, its lone flame casting a halo over her still form. For a panicky moment, his wine-dulled mind thought the woman dead, so peacefully did she recline, fully clothed, with her hands crossed at her waist. A soft moan from her parted lips dispelled the image. He bit back a chuckle; apparently she trusted him no better than he trusted her.

The soft light flickering over her face pulled Garren's gaze back to her serene features. Scrubbed clean, her skin held a soft pink glow, her lips a dusky rose. Dark golden brows arched elegantly over delicate eyelids, obscuring the silver-gray eyes beneath. The gentle rise and fall of her chest drew his attention, reminding him of the earthy appeal of her full, feminine figure.

Stop right there, Garren old boy, remember your-self. Keep your distance.

He turned from the temptation Jocelyn unconsciously offered. Setting the candle down, he shrugged out of his coat and laid it across the table, ignoring the rustle of parchment from the inside pocket. Sitting on the stool, he removed his boots. His shirt followed, but his hands hesitated on the button of his breeches. No, he'd rather not start the morning out in conflict with this hellion. And finding a naked man in her bed would, no doubt, set her off.

He snuffed the candle, pulled back the coverlet, and carefully lay down, all too aware of the gentle breathing of the woman beside him.

Staring into the blackness, Garren saw the image of Jocelyn clutching her chemise before her. Her generous curves drew him like a lodestone.

She was a contradiction. Her speech was not that of a commoner—it was cultured and, except for the strange use of some words, even educated. But who had taught her? She couldn't have spent her entire life in Ramsgil. So where had she come from? And how could she be strong and independent one moment, then babble incoherently in the next?

He turned his head and felt the heaviness in his loins build as the clean smell of her skin rose above the mustiness of the bedding.

Yes, leaving her at Spenceworth would free him of this confusion. Especially since she was a little mad. She at least solved his immediate problem. And she would be happy to have a noble—if not attentive—husband.

His conscience pricked him. Damn it, he offered her a better life. She would not toil all the day long. Servants would look after her, and she'd have plenty of food, and fine clothes. What woman of her station didn't dream of becoming a lady?

She need only carry his name, mayhap even bear a child, and reside in Spenceworth.

His conscience grumbled.

It was not as if she were being sorely used. Surely it was not unreasonable for him to benefit as well. He had met his father's demand.

With a soft moan, Jocelyn shifted toward Garren, curling up on her side.

Justification forgotten, Garren groaned.

Why the bloody hell did he find her so alluring?

Frustrated at his lack of control, he rolled away from her. He buried his nose in the lumpy, stale pillow, blocking out her smell and her image, and settled down for an uncomfortable night's sleep.

" 'Tis time to rise, Jocelyn."

The smooth, intoxicating voice reached through the fog of her sleep. She smiled, burrowing deeper in bed.

"I'll send something up for you to eat, and we'll be on our way."

Jolting up, Jocelyn's confused mind refused to put a name to the voice. Squinting at the retreating figure, she caught a glimpse of broad shoulders and long, muscular legs. Garren, her sluggish brain supplied at last.

Jocelyn looked around the room and moaned as yesterday's events came flooding back to her.

A knock halted her thoughts. Rising, she opened the door and found Bethany holding a tray of food and smiling.

"Good morn, milady. Milord sent ye somethin' to eat." The little maid placed the tray on the table and turned her smiling countenance upon Jocelyn. "I'll just pop down and fetch some fresh water while ye eat." Taking the bowl and pitcher from the washstand, Bethany left, humming off-key as she closed the door.

Dazed, Jocelyn wandered to the window. Early morning sun revealed the rutted road from yesterday. People came and went, all in clothing similar to Bethany's. No sign of a tourist. Or buses. No quaint streetlights. Or sidewalks.

Just dirt.

She pressed her forehead against the cool glass and moaned, "Oh God, no." It hadn't been just a bad dream. This was real.

Closing her eyes, she moved her hands along the curves of her body, "No!" The plaintive wail echoed in the stillness.

Stumbling back to the stool, she braced her elbows on her knees, resting her head in her hands. She had been right. Somehow she'd traveled back in time.

But how far back? And why?

Searching for answers, Jocelyn's gaze flicked along the floor, spotting a rolled parchment. Picking it up, she unrolled and read the marriage certificate. "Married, this 23rd day of May, in the year of our Lord, 1797." She read the words aloud, a groan of despair punctuating the end of the sentence.

In the light of day, everything fell neatly into place. The old woman's words, Ramsgil and Castleside, the body that wasn't hers. And now, the written proof.

What should she do now?

"Milady?" Bethany entered. "Did ye not hear me knock?"

The girl's worried voice intruded on Jocelyn's tumultuous thoughts.

Shaking her head, Jocelyn rolled up the parchment and laid it on the table. Her stomach gurgled with agitation. Nervous and upset, she couldn't concentrate on anything. She reached for the bread and tore a hunk off; it was day-old and dry, matching her mouth. Curling her fingers around the cup, she took several gulps, only to have her stomach protest once the liquid hit bottom. She pushed her chair back and paced around the room before Bethany's concerned voice stopped her.

"Milady, are ye all right? Ye look a fright, all pale and shaky. Ye should sit down and let me comb yer hair." Leaving her post by the door, the maid stood in the middle of the room. "What has ye so upset?"

Numb, Jocelyn sat down on the bed. Bethany unbraided Jocelyn's hair and, bringing a comb out of her pocket, began to pull it through the long tresses, keeping up a low-voiced chatter as she formed it into a neat braid. Gradually, the fog of confusion and fright lifted under the relaxing ministrations.

"Tell me, Bethany—"

An abrupt knock sounded and the door opened, Garren's entrance effectively cutting off Jocelyn's question. He made a circuitous glance of the room. Spying the paper on the table, he picked it up and placed it inside his coat. "If you're ready, we'll be on our way now."

What should she do now? Her mind fumbled with possibilities. Should she stay here? Go back to Ramsgil? Go with Garren?

Recalling the leering men downstairs, Jocelyn knew staying in Castleside wasn't an option.

She could go back to Ramsgil. But what then? Face Haslett again? No, a shiver crawled over her, she couldn't do that.

So, again, Garren seemed the lesser of the evils before her. Somehow she'd find her way back to where she belonged. It would take time, no doubt, but she'd find it no matter what.

Shrugging her shoulders, she followed Garren out.

In the courtyard of the inn, Jocelyn confronted another problem. The horse. Her muscles still ached from yesterday, and Garren expected her to ride again today, and by herself. He waited next to the animal for her.

"Well, come on, we haven't all day." He threw her an impatient glance.

After a brief hesitation, Jocelyn closed the distance. The big animal shifted, its muscles rippling beneath a burnished coat.

Startled, she stepped back. "I can't ride this." Pointing a finger at the horse, Jocelyn moved back a bit more.

Grabbing her wrist, Garren pulled her closer. "I realize you may never have ridden a horse alone before, but it's too hard on my mount carrying the both of us."

That stung. Snatching her arm out of his grasp, she lashed out in a cold, cutting voice. "Don't worry. The last thing I want to do is ride with you or harm your horse."

After years of dieting and exercise, she had finally won the battle and her twentieth-century body was sleek and well conditioned. But the emotional scars from years of ridicule were still close to the surface.

" 'Tis something we agree upon then. Now, if

you'll allow us to be on our way?" Garren gave her a mocking bow.

"You expect me to just jump on this animal and ride into the sunset?" Jocelyn arched her eyebrows. "Just like that?" She snapped her fingers.

"It's a *horse*, it's sunrise, not sunset, and we're heading northeast not west. And you don't have to *jump* on the horse." Garren waved his hand to a hunk of wood. "There's a mounting block you may use. We'll go at a slow pace until you get accustomed to riding." Garren spoke in the slow, measured tones one used when dealing with a dimwit.

With a huff, Jocelyn marched to the block, eyeing it with trepidation, recalling the last time she'd utilized a block of wood. "I wonder whose body I'll end up in next," she muttered under her breath. "Well, it can't get much worse than this, I guess."

Closing her eyes, she stepped up and waited. One eye slitted open, then the other, only to find everything the same. "I'm not sure if I'm relieved or not," she said to the horse. He twitched his ears in response, and Jocelyn timidly patted his smooth neck.

Envisioning a cowboy getting on his horse, she stuffed her left foot in the stirrup and swung up.

Jocelyn squeaked in surprise as the cool smoothness of the saddle met her bare skin. Mortified at such intimate contact, her face heated and she struggled to adjust her skirts, placing a good deal of material between herself and the leather seat. A cool breeze whispered over her exposed knees. Leaning to her side, she frowned as her right leg rubbed, against the warm coat of the horse. Straightening up, she met Garren's shocked gaze.

She quirked her eyebrow. "I believe someone has misplaced the other stirrup."

Approaching the horse, Garren reached out a hand and yanked Jocelyn's hem down over her leg, flashing her a furious glare. The muscle in his cheek flexed. She could swear she heard his teeth grind as he informed her, "Sidesaddles have only *one* stirrup. Your right knee hooks around the horn."

Her face heated in embarrassment, again. "Oh." Taking in her position, she tried to figure out the best way to fix her mistake, short of climbing back down. Come to think of it, even if she did get down, she didn't know the proper way to gain her seat on a sidesaddle.

She glanced at Garren, hoping he would give her a hint. He just stared at her, his brow furrowed. Well fine, she thought, I'll manage.

She brought her right leg up and over the neck of the horse, hooking her knee around the horn. Adjusting her skirt to cover her left leg, Jocelyn gave Garren a smug look, quite proud of her accomplishment.

Garren stood there watching her efforts to mount. She was most definitely a strange woman. Not only did she talk to herself and the horse, but the inanimate mounting block had also seemed to inspire reservations in her. Added to the other things, he should believe her quite mad.

But something about her appealed to him, and for the life of him, he couldn't figure out what. She looked so triumphant atop the horse just now. And so enticing as she arranged her skirt.

He had slept poorly last night, awaking when Jocelyn's hand had dropped on his hip and slid perilously close to the bulge in his pants. He'd held his breath, perversely afraid to move, lest her hand brush his arousal or she remove her touch completely. Although what he would have done had she made contact, he dared not think on. It would be too easy to become truly involved with this woman. No, he thought, shaking his head, it simply wasn't in his plans. He had no time for a physical or emotional relationship. Best put it completely from his mind.

He mounted his horse, took the reins of Jocelyn's, and headed out of Castleside, battling his mounting desires. The less they said to one another the better.

This is what fairy tales are made of, Jocelyn thought as she rounded a curve in the drive and the manor came into view. The setting sun cast elongated shadows over the stone edifice, cradled amid tall trees. Lights winked in windows on each of the three floors, checkerboard style.

As they approached, the large front doors were thrown open, the interior light fanning out over the double set of stairs angling up to the entry and illuminating the man standing in the opening awaiting them.

"You live *here?*" Jocelyn couldn't help the amazement that stretched out the last word.

"No, you do." Garren looked back over his shoulder, pulled his horse to a stop, and dismounted.

"Me? You're kidding. I'll get lost." Jocelyn paused as the meaning of his words hit her. "Where do you live?"

"Evening, yer lordship," a young male voice chimed in. Behind them, a boy stood as straight and tall as his five-foot frame allowed. His shock of tousled red hair drooped over one eye, having escaped its queue in his dash to reach them.

"Good evening . . . Paddy, isn't it?"

"Aye, sir." His eyes brightened and a smile lit his face. "Ye remembered," he chirped.

"And how could I forget you, a fine figure of a man?" Garren smiled and rumpled Paddy's hair as he handed the reins to the boy.

Jocelyn sat mesmerized. Following behind Garren all day had given her plenty of time to observe the breadth of his shoulders, the leanness of his waist and the rippling muscles of his legs. She knew the rich, warm color of his hair, recalled the chocolate brown of his eyes, but she'd never seen his smile—until now. Her breath stuck in her chest as she gazed at his smile. Straight white teeth flashed from between his generous lips, and creases bracketed his mouth. Her stomach did a flip-flop.

He closed the distance between them and placed his hands at her waist. Her stomach did another somersault.

Heat blossomed in her cheeks and tingled at her neck as the warmth of his firm grip penetrated the layers of clothing. At his gentle tug, she slid from the saddle, and instinctively she braced her hands on his shoulders, aware of the flexing muscle beneath her touch. The tips of her breasts tightened in response, straining against the fabric.

The crunch of pebbles beneath her feet brought awareness of the dangerous direction of her thoughts. Her knees weakened, whether from too many hours in the saddle or the desire his touch elicited, Jocelyn couldn't tell. Her cheeks flamed anew and she stepped out of his grasp on shaky legs.

The sardonic lift of Garren's eyebrow told Jocelyn he had noted her response. Dismissively, he turned to Paddy, handing her reins over. "Paddy, say hello to your new mistress, Lady Spenceworth."

Paddy turned, his green eyes near to popping out. "Yer *wife?*" Unabashedly, he looked her over; then recalling himself, he lowered his gaze.

"Yes." Garren's shuttered gaze traveled the same path as Paddy's and Jocelyn shifted uncomfortably.

"Evening, yer ladyship," the boy said, tugging at his forelock, his eyes downcast.

"Good evening, Paddy," Jocelyn said, extending her hand.

Paddy looked at it and then at Garren.

"See to the horses, lad." Paddy turned, his confused gaze skimming over Jocelyn as he took the horses away.

A throat cleared, and the butler approached. "Your lordship, your valet arrived, and we've been expecting you. Cook has your meal awaiting you as soon as you've refreshed yourselves," he said, his eyes never leaving Garren.

Garren propelled Jocelyn up the stairs to the door and said, "Jocelyn, this is Spalding, the butler. Spalding, my wife, Lady Spenceworth."

"Good evening, your ladyship." He gave her a slight bow, his face a mask of propriety.

"Spalding, as in tennis balls?" she said in disbelief.

"Your pardon, my lady?"

Shaking her head, Jocelyn said, "Nothing. Nice to meet you," and stepped into the brightly lit manor.

Jocelyn's gaze swiveled around as she took in the hall. It was a high-ceilinged room, twin staircases curving gracefully up to the second floor. A large, ornate chandelier illuminated the hall, casting a warm glow on the wood beneath her feet. Two elaborately carved chairs stood sentinel at the door opposite the entrance. Dour faces stared grimly down at her from the portraits lining the walls.

Spalding, a taper in hand, led the way up the right-hand stairway and proceeded down the hall that opened to the right of the landing. He opened the third door and entered the room. Moving about, he lit several thick candles as Jocelyn stepped over the threshold.

In the hallway, Garren continued on. The bump of a door closing brought Jocelyn's head around to stare at Spalding.

"Warm water will be up directly," he said in a stiff voice and left, shutting the door quietly behind him.

Jocelyn ambled around the room. Running her hand along the smooth, worn washstand, her fingers traveled from the warmth of the wood to graze the cool edge of the porcelain bowl resting to one side. The large canopied bed, draped in green velvet, beckoned. She moved to it and sat down, sinking into the deep feather mattress. She plucked at the tassel holding the matching hangings, the fringe shimmering in the soft candlelight.

A small table with a matching green cloth sat next to the bed, a single candle in a crystal holder resting in the center. Candlelight flickered over a small box painted with smiling cherubs. Lifting the latch, she gazed at the ruby velvet lining, void of any trinkets. She closed the lid, glancing at the little cherubs' smiles. They appeared strained now, sad even, that she knew they guarded nothing more than an empty box.

Sighing at her fanciful thoughts, Jocelyn turned from the table.

She wandered over to the wardrobe and, upon opening it, found it empty. How forlorn both seemed. The wardrobe should be filled with clothes, the box with jewelry. Their emptiness matched Jocelyn's. Like them, she had nothing. No friends, no job, no clothing. Nothing of her own.

Shaking her head, she determined not to dwell upon that. It would only depress her, making it harder to concentrate on finding her way home.

A chaise of green and white brocade took up the space before the window, inviting her to recline and rest.

A knock at the door stopped her in mid-motion as the door swung open to admit a man of middle age carrying a pitcher of water, a bowl of soap and linen towels. Without a word he placed the items on the dressing table and left.

"Friendly bunch," Jocelyn said. She washed up as best she could, wishing for a Jacuzzi and sports cream for her aching muscles.

Reclining on the chaise, Jocelyn groaned at the pull of sore muscles. She never wanted to ride another horse in her life.

A few minutes later two loud thumps on the door brought her off the chair with a pained moan. "Come in." She plopped back down.

The door swung open. Garren stood there wearing dark pants and a clean white shirt, moisture still clinging to his slicked-back hair.

"I've come to take you down to dinner."

"Thank heavens." Jocelyn bit back a whimper as she stood up. "My stomach is having a conference with my backbone." He gave her an odd look she ignored. She'd been the recipient of those looks for the last two days. It's probably the way I speak, she thought, but was in too much pain to give it more thought.

With as much grace as she could muster, she preceded Garren out the door. At the bottom of the stairs she waited, glancing right and left in indecision. There were three doors to choose from. Garren put his hand at the small of her back. The gentle pressure startled her, and she took two stumbling steps. Garren's other hand gripped her waist, sending a frisson of heat along her spine as he righted her.

"Careful." The warning, spoken quietly, close to her ear, made the hairs on her neck stand, and a shiver followed the path of heat of a moment ago. Removing his hands, he stepped away, nodding to the door on the left.

The dining room held the rich, warmth of polished wood panels. An ornately carved sideboard took up the wall opposite the entrance; chairs lined the wall on the right and the table, at least twenty feet long, presided over all. A multi-branched, silver candelabra, tapers ablaze, separated the two settings placed at opposite ends of the table.

"My, how cozy." Raising her eyebrows, and with an affected air, Jocelyn drew out the last word. She struggled with the urge to break into peals of laughter at the absurdly formal setting. Garren dressed so carefully, and she in borrowed clothing a little worse for the wear.

"This is how the gentry dine," he informed her through stiff lips as he passed her on his way to the other end of the table.

Spalding pulled her chair out for her, and she felt obliged to sit as Garren took his own seat.

Jocelyn looked at the butler and said, "We're

gentry, you know." Tilting her chin toward the ceiling, she folded her hands primly in her lap, smiling sweetly down her nose at the servant.

He bowed and left. Did the man never smile, she asked herself? Another servant entered next with a large tureen of soup. He served Jocelyn and then Garren and, leaving the covered bowl on the sideboard, exited the room. No smile, no greeting. Nothing. Jocelyn glanced at Garren. Was he such an ogre that his staff feared showing any feelings? Except for Paddy. But then he was just a boy, his exuberance harder to subdue.

She pulled her mind from those thoughts to deal with more immediate problems.

"So what happens now?" She questioned Garren, raising her voice to be heard down the table.

He glanced up. "I prefer not to converse during dinner."

Jocelyn shrugged, turning her attention to her meal. So he still wasn't talking. What would it take to get some information out of him?

Drastic measures, to be sure!

She picked up her plate, carefully balancing the soup bowl, silverware, and glass and marched militantly toward Garren. He looked up from his plate and watched her approach, but said nothing. Plunking everything on the table, Jocelyn grabbed a chair from against the wall and plopped down.

"There, that's better." Settling against the cushioned back, she smiled sweetly at him.

He simply quirked an eyebrow and returned his attention to his food.

"You know you're going to have to talk to me sometime. Why not now?" She picked up her spoon, took a taste of the soup and continued. "We can start small if you like, just a few sen-

65

tences at first, until you build up your strength."
Sarcastic humor had always been her weapon in
times of stress. And she was definitely stressed.

Again, the maddening quirk of his eyebrow.
Oh, how she itched to pluck the blasted thing
from his forehead. She gripped her spoon, fighting the urge.

The servant returned, his glance swiveling
between the empty far end of the table and Jocelyn sitting beside Garren. Recalling himself, he
snapped his gaze back to the head of the table
and removed the soup bowls, placing full plates
before Jocelyn and Garren, then silently left.

Jocelyn played with her food until the servant
removed her plate and placed a creamy confection in front of her. She stared at it for a moment
before a smile lit her face. This proper gentleman
wanted to ignore her? Fine. She'd see if he could.

"So are you going to tell me what happens next
or not?"

"Jocelyn, I've said before that I don't converse
during my meals." He blinked. A dollop of dessert
hit his cheek and slid down his neck to his collar.
He stared at her in shock. His lips tightened as he
took his napkin and wiped at the spot, casting
Jocelyn a cold, narrow glare.

She gripped her spoon, waiting for his silence
to give way to fury. But she waited in vain. He'll
need another push, she thought. Any reaction
would be better than none.

Opening her eyes wide, she gave him an innocent look, and daintily ate a spoonful of the
dessert. But when he turned his head away from
her, she filled her spoon again, raised it, and cat-
apulted another glob at him. He chose that
moment to turn back to her. Her gooey projectile
landed squarely on the bridge of his nose, slither-

ing down until, for a split second, it hung suspended at the end of his nose, then plummeted to his shirt front. Jocelyn bit back a gurgle of hysterical laughter.

His dark eyes blazed with anger. She watched as he clenched his jaw, and a muscle ticked near his eye.

"Yes?" Jocelyn tried for an innocent tone, but her voice shook with suppressed glee. This wasn't much of a revenge for her kidnapping, and his present silence, but it was something.

Still, Garren didn't speak. Frustration with the entire situation blinded her to his warning look. Filling her spoon again, she brought it up, preparing another volley.

He couldn't believe it. No one had ever flung food at his head before. This woman was impossible. He watched as she raised her spoon again. Did she not know he neared the end of his patience? Reaching across, his long fingers wrapped around her wrist. Their gazes met and the merriment drained from her face.

"I would not repeat your folly, were I you."

Tears shimmered in her eyes. "Then *talk* to me. Tell me what's happening. Just talk to me." She blinked rapidly. From the corner of his eye he saw her clench her napkin in her hand. Her valiant effort to stem the tears and gain control of her emotions touched him.

And served to further confuse him.

Through the haze of his thoughts, he became aware of the slender wrist in his grasp, the warmth of the pulse beating frantically against his palm.

"Damn!" As though he gripped a searing poker, he released his hold.

He'd had enough. Throwing his napkin on the table, he stood, muttering, "Infernal woman." He left the room, the door closing firmly upon his retreat. Tomorrow couldn't come too soon for him.

In the library across the hall from the dining room, Garren addressed his butler and steward. "Spalding, hire a housekeeper to reside here. Perhaps you could check with my grandfather's; see if she will return."

"Aye sir, I'm sure she will. I'll make certain of it tomorrow."

"Good. Also, hire a lady's maid." Garren added as an afterthought, Lord knew his new wife needed one.

To Baskins, his steward, he said, "Lady Jocelyn shall receive . . . oh, say, fifty pounds per annum to spend as she wishes. And see that she's clothed properly."

Garren turned to Spalding, standing at attention beside Baskins. "Allow her whatever duties she seems capable of handling, as long as it does not interfere with the running of the estate." Garren picked up a quill and pulled a ledger book from the stack in front of him. "If you have any problems, you may find me at my London house."

"Very good, milord," Baskins nodded.

Garren continued, "I'll be leaving early in the morning and will be entrusting her safekeeping to you. Keep an eye on her." Opening the ledger, he mumbled, "And the silver, too."

Baskins and Spalding exchanged confused glances.

"My lord?" Baskins' brow furrowed.

"And no visitors. Understand?" Garren refused

68

to elaborate. To tell these men that he'd purchased a commoner and married her because of an ultimatum his father issued would be the height of stupidity. Admitting that he didn't entirely trust the woman, either, would be too humiliating for words. He employed these men and, as such, they would do his bidding without question. The fewer who knew of Jocelyn's origins, the better.

"I'll review the accounts tonight before I retire. If I have any questions, I'll speak with you in the morning. Good night." Garren dismissed the men, opened the first of the estate ledgers and started the tedious task of examination.

A sigh of relief whistled from his lips as he heard Jocelyn's bootheels clicking past in the hall a few minutes later. With any luck, he wouldn't encounter the bizarre woman again before he left. Silently cursing himself for a coward, he again focused on the neat entries penned by Baskins.

Jocelyn's impish smile invaded his thoughts, their dinner scene playing again in his mind. The way her chin had jutted out in defiance as she'd gathered up her place setting and, with purposeful strides, approached his end of the table. She had dared him, with that look, to challenge her actions, but he'd been more interested in what she would do next.

She wasn't a woman he could anticipate. That was an understatement, he thought and shook his head, a smile stretching across his lips. He had never expected her to fling her dessert at his head to get his attention, not once, but twice. And she would have done it again had he not stopped her.

His chuckle died on his lips as he recalled the fragile wrist he'd held captive and the wave of protectiveness that had swept him. A heated current of attraction rolled through Garren, racing along his nerves, leaving him stunned. She was a common woman. Nothing out of the ordinary. He'd been with much more beautiful and alluring women.

So why the fascination with Jocelyn?

He ran a hand through his hair. He couldn't spend his time wondering about the woman; he had other problems to face.

His father, for one.

His father. He could only imagine what the man would say when he met his daughter-in-law—a plump, half-mad commoner.

I'll just send a note around when I reach London . . . no, better yet, I'll just send the marriage certificate. That should satisfy the Duke.

There came a light knock at the door, and his valet entered.

"Yes, Ivan," Garren looked up from the open ledgers.

"Everything is ready for the morrow, milord."

"I'll be up in a while." His gaze traveled over the neat stack of the books of account.

"Very good, sir." Ivan stood stock-still and looked directly at Garren.

"What is it? You've something on your mind." Ivan had been Garren's valet for the past ten years. He knew Garren better than anyone, and because of that he frequently voiced his concerns and opinions to Garren—but he was always careful to await a request for those opinions.

"Well sir, it's about your *wife*."

"And what about her?" Garren pushed the ledger he'd been reviewing away from him and leaned back in his chair.

"The word below stairs is that she's a bit queer."

"You shouldn't listen to gossip." Garren shifted in his chair, uncomfortable with the thought that the servants had noted Jocelyn's odd behavior.

"I was wondering what you hoped to prove to the Duke with your choice of brides."

"That I'll not react in a prescribed way to an ultimatum."

"At any cost to yourself?" Ivan raised his brows.

"And what do you mean by that?" Garren shifted in his chair.

"Only that you're the one now married to her, and you'll have to live with that. Had you thought about anything beyond your father's reaction to your deed? What about a year from now?"

"She'll reside here in the country and I in London. She will have little effect on my life."

"The court will learn you're married," Ivan reminded Garren.

"That will suit me fine. I'll no longer have simpering young girls casting dewy eyes and their mamas glaring daggers at me. I'll be free to pursue my own entertainment."

Shaking his head Ivan said, "I believe you'll not have everything your way, sir."

"She is but a *wife*, nothing important, Ivan. You worry too much."

With a slight nod and a lift of a brow Ivan asked, "You'll be taking your seat in Parliament when we return?"

"Aye. That should make my father happy. He's been after me to take up my responsibilities since Grandfather died. Still, I have no patience with those nobs in Parliament. They prattle and preen and wield their power indiscriminately. I fear I'll not fit in." A small smile touched Garren's lips.

"You'll make do, sir. Mayhap you'll even be able to set a few things to rights."

71

"Ha, many have tried but—'tis politics, Ivan, need I say more."

"Nay, sir. I'll leave you to your accounts now and await you upstairs."

"No, you should retire. We'll be up early tomorrow and we'll have a long ride ahead of us. I want to make London by tomorrow evening. I can tend to myself."

"But, sir—"

Garren cut him off. "Go, go." He waved his valet out. "I'll be finished here shortly. Get to bed, man."

He turned his attention back to the ledgers and did not close them until the candle had burned low. Rubbing his eyes and carrying a flickering taper, he went to bed, hoping Jocelyn was still asleep.

Lord, deliver him from a barmy woman.

Chapter Five

"So, why has the Ton ostracized *me*?" Lady Paxton's mumbled words went unheard in the empty hall, the swishing of her skirts the only sound as she strode to the table. She glared at the empty salver there. "*I* had nothing to do with that wager."

Entering the library, she took her seat behind the desk and stared at the mounting stack of unpaid bills.

"So I set my cap for Garren." She shrugged. "Half the eligible women in London have done the same." She'd used the only advantage she had and lured him to her bed. It wasn't as if it had never been done before. She snorted. Yes, but usually it worked and the couple found its way to the altar.

Melody still couldn't understand how Garren had slipped through her fingers. He was a peer with a strict code of behavior. What had gone wrong?

"Lady Paxton?" Her maid stood on the threshold of the library, an envelope in her hand.

Oh, please be an invitation, she prayed. Please let this be over. Excitement thrummed through her veins. "Yes, yes. Bring it to me." She waved the maid in, taking the proffered envelope. Sparing the plain seal a quick glance, Melody opened the missive and scanned the paper. With a groan, she tossed yet another demand for payment on the desk.

"Bring me some tea, Mary." She sat back, anxiety gnawing at her composure.

Jocelyn gave a contented moan and stretched, feline style, slitting her eyes open. The sun was just starting to brighten the morning sky, its feeble light struggling to illumine the darkened chamber. Warm and comfortable, she snuggled down in the featherbed, listening to the sounds of morning: scraping heels, muted voices, a door closing, and a fading rhythmic thud.

Her lids descended over sleep-blurred eyes as the import of the sounds slammed into her. A horse? Her eyelids flew open and she threw back the covers, racing to the window to look down on the front drive. A cloud of dust dissipated in the mists of the early morning air as two riders vanished around the curve of the drive.

So, nothing had changed since last night. Her shoulders drooped. She stared at the empty drive, wondering who could be about at this hour. Shrugging, she turned from the window, dismissing the strangers.

Jocelyn's gaze traveled over the room, finding it

hard to accept the truth of her situation. But how could she not? Evidence surrounded her.

Rubbing her arms, she sat on the edge of the bed. How in the world had she gotten to this time period? Had it been the block in Ramsgil—or the clothing? Was there a ripple in time that she'd slipped through? She massaged her temples, trying to ease the building tension. What to do now?

Straightening her spine, she forced confidence into her voice. "Well, I certainly won't find out up here."

Jocelyn pushed up from the bed, automatically turning to smoothe the sheets and bedspread before she set to tidying herself.

Uncomfortable with the thought of exposing a body that wasn't hers, she'd slept fully clothed for two nights now, and her wrinkled skirt was now evidence of it. Giving the material several futile shakes, she shrugged in resignation. The wrinkles were a permanent addition to the gown.

Well, she might be wrinkled, but at least she'd be clean. With a cloth and a little soap, she scrubbed the sleep from her face, rinsing and patting herself dry. Using the edge of the linen towel, she rubbed her teeth, wishing for her toothbrush and paste.

As she sat on the chaise and bent to pull on her shoes, her braid fell across her shoulder. Hairs jutted out at all angles from the woven plait. She considered trying to comb it, but dismissed the idea. Even if she could get the braid undone, she doubted she'd be able to braid it again. It was best, she decided, to just leave it.

Taking a deep breath, she smoothed the hair at her forehead and marched out the door, intent on finding Garren and some answers.

Descending the stairs, she found the house strangely silent. She poked her head into the room to the right. The large library exuded masculine strength. A pair of leather chairs sat before a massive desk. Floor-to-ceiling bookshelves bracketed the window behind it. The vacant room smelled of tobacco and an oddly familiar scent Jocelyn couldn't identify. The atmosphere of the room sent a tingle through her veins and she left in haste.

"He must be having breakfast." She mumbled the words as she crossed the hall and opened the door to the dining room. It, too, stood empty. Her gaze traveled over the impossibly long table, recalling dinner the night before. She chuckled, picturing Garren's shocked and furious expression as that glob of creamy dessert had seemed to balance forever on the end of his nose before plopping onto his shirtfront. Her grin faltered as she remembered the tremor that had traveled up her arm as his hand had grasped her wrist, preventing her from repeating the attack. Fear should have coursed through her veins, not a heated rush of blood that left her heart thumping madly. And still the stubborn fool hadn't answered her question. What was to happen to her?

"Blast the man." Jocelyn quickened her steps. She'd get her answer today, or die trying.

As she passed by a narrow set of stairs set back in an alcove in the hall, a clatter echoed from the stairwell, followed by a murmur of voices. Drawn by the sounds, Jocelyn descended the stairs. Opening the green door at the bottom, she stepped through and found herself in the kitchen, and the obvious focus of the kitchen staff and Spalding. The door bumped closed, nudging her further into the room.

"So this is where everyone is." She searched for her husband. "Has Garren eaten already?"

"Yes, milady." Spalding's monotone answer sapped some of Jocelyn's patience.

"Where is he, then?"

"Milord left early this morning, milady."

Fighting the frustration eating at her control, Jocelyn closed her eyes briefly and swallowed. "And he left for? . . ."

"London." Opening her eyes, her gaze met Spalding's stony expression.

Clenching her hands at her side, Jocelyn resisted the urge to shake the stuffing out of the man. "And when will he be back?"

The butler's gaze swept the room. His eyes returning to Jocelyn, his lips thinned as he drew his bony frame straighter, reminding her of a puppet on a string. Stepping forward, he held the door open. "If milady would like to retire to the dining room, I'll see that your meal is served immediately."

"Spalding—"

"This way, milady."

He leveled a glare somewhere beyond Jocelyn's shoulder. The rustle of clothing and shuffle of feet reminded her of the others in the kitchen. And the butler was trying to move the conversation out of their earshot. Bless the little statue of a man.

She nodded. "The dining room it is." And she ascended the stairs, Spalding behind her.

Once in the dining room, she turned to him. "So when will he be back?"

"Milord did not say." The butler pulled out a chair, holding it for her.

"But what am I supposed to do?" She took the proffered seat.

"The housekeeper and your maid will arrive

later this morning and the seamstress this afternoon."

The side door of the dining room opened, and a servant bearing a tray entered, placing it before Jocelyn.

She stared at the array of food. Did they really expect her to eat all of this? Several plates contained an assortment of cold meat. She pointed to something that appeared to be a piece of animal flesh with little bumps all over it. "What's this?"

Spalding's eyes rounded, but he responded, "Tongue."

Jocelyn's stomach did a flip-flop, and she turned her head away from the plate.

"I think I'd rather just have some bread and juice, if it wouldn't be too much trouble." Jocelyn pressed her hand against her stomach while the servant removed the tray. Turning to Spalding, she continued. "I prefer to eat a light meal in the morning."

He gave Jocelyn a look she couldn't interpret. Rather like stunned disapproval, she thought. A servant came back and placed a platter of bread before her, its yeasty smell wafting up to her nose. A bowl of watery brown liquid sat to her left, and the servant stepped back and out of her line of vision.

The bread had been cut into large pieces, not quite slices exactly, but manageable chunks. She took a bite and rolled her eyes. Warm bread from the oven, it was heavenly. Jocelyn remembered the aroma of her mother's fresh bread, cut in generous slices, topped with homemade apple butter. It was strange how, in the six years since her parents had died, the simple taste of bread could trigger so many memories.

Blinking back the moisture in her eyes, Jocelyn

firmly pushed the sad thoughts from her mind and looked around for her glass of juice. Nothing.

"Well heavens, don't they have juice in these days?" she said aloud.

"Milady?" Spalding stepped forward.

"Juice?" Jocelyn questioned.

He pointed to the bowl of watery brown liquid. "Juice," he said as if talking to a two-year-old.

"Not au juice. *Fruit* juice," Jocelyn responded.

"Yes, milady." And he turned and left, returning a minute later with a wineglass filled with a light red liquid.

"Your juice, milady," he said as he placed it in front of her and backed away.

"Wine? Well,"—she shrugged—"I didn't specify *what* kind of juice." With a little shake of her head she mumbled, "At this rate I'll be drunk and disorderly before lunch."

"Milady?"

"Oh nothing. Just talking to myself."

"Yes, milady."

"This 'milady' stuff is getting on my nerves. Would it be possible to just call me Jocelyn?" she asked, turning her head in his direction.

The horrified look on Spalding's face was answer enough.

"No, huh? Sorry, I'm just not used to such formality," she said by way of explanation and turned back to her meal.

She further horrified the dear man by dipping her bread in the bowl of broth he had called "juice." Well heavens, she thought, I'm starving.

With a decided huff, Spalding left her to her meal.

Moments later, her breakfast was interrupted as Spalding came back into the room, a stern look of disapproval pasted on his face.

"Oh God, what have I done *now*," Jocelyn said.

"Milady, I regret the intrusion, but the house-keeper and your maid have arrived. Shall I have them await you in the morning room?"

"Huh?" It took a moment for Spalding's stilted words to register. She brightened when she realized he wasn't put out with her, but with the servants. "Of course."

Panicked, she wondered what she was supposed to do with the servants. She really needed an ally if she hoped to get through this. She watched Spalding's retreating back. "Oh, Spalding?"

Spalding's narrow frame came to a stop and did a near-perfect, military about-face. Observing him, Jocelyn noted that everything about the man seemed narrow. His thin, straight nose sat defiantly between two squinty eyes the color of mud. Below the point of his nose, his lips appeared as a mere slash. The chin, too, was long and pointed. His narrow shoulders held his coat out at a sharp angle. His hands were long and skinny with protruding joints in the fingers, reminding her of Ichabod Crane.

Narrow of body, narrow of mind, Jocelyn thought as she looked at him. Not a person one would be given to confide in, she concluded.

"Yes, milady?" His nose inched toward the ceiling, his voice a chilling vibration in the room.

"When you have them settled, please come back and show me to the morning room." It was the best she could do. She raised her nose to the same altitude as his and put a chill in her eyes. Their encounters were beginning to have all the makings of a war—one she planned on winning, one way or the other. Who knew how long she'd be here? She had to find a way to fit in. By observing and mimicking those around her, she might be able to survive.

A few minutes later, Jocelyn followed Spalding as he led the way to the morning room. Throwing open the door, Spalding announced in his cold voice, "Lady Spenceworth."

Jocelyn breezed past him into the room to find a plump elderly woman and a young, freckle-faced girl dipping quick curtsies to her. From behind her, she heard Spalding say, " 'Tis Mrs. Cowan, the housekeeper, and Dulcey, your maid." The door closed quietly behind him as he left her alone with the women.

"Hello, Mrs. Cowan and Dulcey, wasn't it?" Jocelyn's voice filled with warmth. She was so glad to have the company of women, she wanted to hug the strangers. She hadn't seen another woman at this estate since she had arrived, and relief spilled over her at the sight of these two.

Mrs. Cowan's mouth pursed as her eyes scanned Jocelyn's form. "Lady Spenceworth." The woman nodded to her. " 'Tis plain ye're in need of a maid. Ah, that is, if ye don't mind me saying, milady?"

"Oh heavens, no. I just can't seem to manage." Jocelyn fidgeted.

"Tsk, tsk. Well, how can a lady be expected to look her best without the aid of a maid? No one to take care of her clothing"—Mrs. Cowan's gaze moved from Jocelyn's dress to her head—"and hair. 'Tis no wonder. But what have ye been doin' to become so wrinkled?" With rapid steps that belied her size, she circled Jocelyn. The little maid hung back in shyness.

"Oh well," Jocelyn hedged, embarrassed. "I've been sleeping in them."

"Ye have no sleeping clothes?" Her eyes widened in surprise.

"No. Actually, these are the *only* clothes I have," Jocelyn looked down at the rough gray material of her skirt and tried in vain to shake some of the wrinkles out, yet again.

The kindly blue eyes of the housekeeper opened wider. "What happened to yer clothes? Will they be arriving soon?"

Jocelyn had been afraid of this. This woman was going to ask all sorts of questions—questions Jocelyn didn't have the answers to. Lying wasn't her strong suit. She had best stick as close to the truth as she could.

"No. They were lost on the trip." Well, she justified, they were lost—somewhere in the twentieth century.

Jocelyn's hands went self-consciously to her hair, trying to pat the loose hairs down. She fidgeted under Mrs. Cowan's close scrutiny.

" 'Tis no matter. Dulcey is here to help ye with yer hair and yer dressing. We'll have to set to finding ye something else to wear until the seamstress can get ye something made up."

Mrs. Cowan gave her a considering look. "Come Dulcey, we'll get milady looking proper in a thrice." Mrs. Cowan's boot heels clicked on the wooden floor as she left the room. Jocelyn and Dulcey straggled after her like ducklings following their mama.

In the hall, as they passed the same servant who had brought water and towels to Jocelyn the night before, Mrs. Cowan called over her shoulder. "Heat water and bring up the tub to her ladyship's room. And be quick about it."

The housekeeper marched past Jocelyn's door.

"Mrs. Cowan?" Jocelyn stood before her door. "This is my room."

The elderly woman turned back, a confused look on her plump face.

"This room? Yer not in the master's rooms?" Her eyes rounded in surprise when Jocelyn shook her head.

" 'Tis strange, indeed," she muttered as she followed Jocelyn and Dulcey into the room.

As Dulcey struggled with the tangle of Jocelyn's hair, Mrs. Cowan strode around the room, inspecting the wardrobe, the bedsheets, the bed hangings, and running her fingers along the top of the mantel. Her eyes took in the condition of the floors.

"I didn't get here a minute too soon. This is what happens when there's no housekeeper to tend to the cleanliness of the place. That Spalding can't see beyond his own nose," she muttered to herself, but Jocelyn heard and secretly agreed with her.

The tub and water arrived, along with towels and soap. The entire time Dulcey combed out her hair, Jocelyn's mind struggled with the idea of stripping off her clothes. It was indecent of her to expose someone else's body to strangers—herself included. There had to be a way around it. She hoped that Nelwina was showing the same respect for her own body, wherever it was.

Mrs. Cowan interrupted her musings. "Yer bath is ready, milady. Dulcey, help her ladyship to undress and tend to her while I go in search of some clothing. See that the clothes she has on get laundered, in case I can't find anything."

"Mrs. Cowan, I'm perfectly capable of bathing myself. Take Dulcey with you. I'll be fine." Jocelyn

83

crossed her fingers, hoping Mrs. Cowan would do as she asked.

"At least let Dulcey help you out of your clothes, milady." Mrs. Cowan glanced between Dulcey and Jocelyn, capitulation within Jocelyn's grasp.

"That will be fine." Jocelyn didn't have any qualms about being seen in her slip. No, she reminded herself, it was a chemise.

Dulcey helped her out of her dress, and Jocelyn shooed her out. She slipped off her shoes and stockings and, in her chemise, stepped into the tub. Dunking her head, she came up sputtering, lathered her hair, and rinsed. She washed her arms and legs and stood up and emptied the bucket of clean water over her in a final rinse. Grabbing the linen from the table nearby, she toweled off and stepped out of the tub. Without warning, the door opened and Mrs. Cowan came in. Jocelyn started. Clutching the towel to her chest, she stepped away from the tub, nearly tripping over the table.

"Ye bathed in yer chemise?" Mrs. Cowan's incredulous look spoke volumes.

Unnerved, Jocelyn's mind fumbled for an explanation, but she came up empty. Drawing as much dignity around her as she could muster, she straightened her spine. She had to take control of situations like these if she planned on surviving this nightmare. This was only the first of many, she was certain.

"Mrs. Cowan, I'm not accustomed to strangers attending me while I bathe. I find it most disconcerting." Lord, where had that come from, Jocelyn wondered. She was beginning to sound like an eighteenth-century lady. A spark of pride warmed her heart.

"Yer pardon, milady. I was but surprised." Mrs. Cowan looked away and Jocelyn breathed a little easier. This could really get sticky.

"From where do ye hail, milady . . . if I might ask?"

"South Carolina." Jocelyn responded before she could stop herself. She eyed the housekeeper, wondering what she thought.

"Where is that?"

Jocelyn pulled her gaze from the woman. "Ah, that's in the United . . . ah, the Colonies," Jocelyn stuttered.

"Ye're a Colonial, then?"

"Well, yes, I suppose I am. It's strange to be referred to as a Colonial."

"How so?" The housekeeper's perplexed expression alerted Jocelyn to what she'd just said.

"It's just that we don't call ourselves that." Changing the subject before Mrs. Cowan asked any more questions, Jocelyn said, "Were you able to find anything for me to wear?"

"Aye, Dulcey is brushing the clothes off and will bring them straight away." Glancing around the room, the housekeeper continued. "I don't see a mirror in this room. If you'll excuse me, milady, I'll see to it." She dipped her head and left.

Surprised, Jocelyn realized that she didn't have any idea what she looked like now. She also knew she'd have to stop treating the body she inhabited as if it belonged to someone else. For now, it was her body—she'd have to act like it or risk a trip to Bedlam.

The thought again reminded her of Nelwina. Would she be able to deal with Jocelyn's world? She could only imagine Nelwina's confusion and fear. After all, Jocelyn had the benefit of knowing some of the history of England. She could survive here. What did Nelwina have? Would there be anything left of Jocelyn's life when she returned? Nelwina would be better off when she regained her body.

Dulcey entered with an armload of clothing and Jocelyn turned from her thoughts.

"Milady, Mrs. Cowan found a daydress and underthings for ye." She stopped talking as she took in Jocelyn's damp chemise. A frown wrinkled her brow and she opened her mouth to speak. Appearing to think better of it, she pressed her lips together and looked away from her mistress.

Jocelyn took a deep breath and grabbed her wet covering and pulled it off. Dropping it to the floor, she grabbed up the towel and said, "I hope there's a dry chemise in amongst those clothes."

Dulcey peeked at Jocelyn and nodded her head, pulling a white garment from the pile. Jocelyn took it from her and quickly pulled it on. Sitting on the chaise, she pulled on the white knit stockings Dulcey handed her and slipped on a pair of backless slippers. She stood and, at the maid's direction, turned around. A short boned corset was fitted just beneath her breasts and tightened. Over this came a full petticoat of pink and white stripes. Then came a pink cotton, high-waisted gown with three-quarter sleeves trimmed in a darker pink braid. The dress, cut away in the front, revealed the striped petticoat beneath. The edges of the skirt front were trimmed with the same dark pink braid. A long, white muslin scarf with ruffled edges draped over her shoulders, crossing over her chest and held by a dark pink ribbon tied just below the breasts.

Mrs. Cowan came in, trailed by one of the servants carrying a large, framed mirror. She directed the placement of it and glanced at Jocelyn. "I see the gown is a bit long for ye. Well, no matter, we can bring the length up. Dulcey, tend to her ladyship's hair. The seamstress will be here soon."

The maid combed and braided Jocelyn's hair, pinning it up. She attached a little bit of muslin with a dark pink bow in front of the knot of hair atop her head.

Mrs. Cowan looked Jocelyn over from head to toe and directed her to the mirror. "Ah, ye look much better now, milady. Come see."

The mirror revealed a woman with golden blond hair pulled away from her face, tendrils escaping and curling here and there. Gray eyes stared back at Jocelyn. She moved her gaze down the rest of the reflection. The full bust matched the full hips. This body was shorter than her own by about six inches. With hesitation, Jocelyn placed her hands on her hips and felt the extra pounds. "This won't do." She shook her head. "This won't do at all," she said.

"Milady, you'll only have to wear this dress until we can have yer own made for ye," Mrs. Cowan said with concern.

"No, no. I have to lose some weight." Jocelyn recognized the panic in her voice. Flashbacks of earlier days invaded her mind. Tamping down the pain and panic, she said. "I did it once, I can do it again."

"Milady, ye have a fine figure. 'Tis a womanly one, not one of a girl." Mrs. Cowan defended Jocelyn's figure with the devotion of a mother.

Jocelyn looked at her. "Not yet it isn't. But I'll fix that, don't you worry."

Chapter Six

"Who the bloody hell is Jocelyn Tanner?" Richard Warrick stood in the middle of his library, clutching a parchment. "Who are her people?" he ranted to the empty room. "And just where is this woman? He sends no note of explanation, just the marriage certificate. Hobbs," he yelled, ignoring the bell rope that summoned his butler in a more dignified way. He was much too angry to worry about dignity now.

Hobbs quietly entered the library. "Yes, your Grace?"

"Send a note around to my son. Tell him to get over here immediately."

Hobbs turned to leave, but stopped when Richard shouted. "The hell. I'll beard the pup in his own den, I will. Send around for my horse and tell my valet I'll be riding out."

In his room, he changed into riding clothes and

strode out the door, mounted his horse and headed for his son's residence.

Before Garren's elegant London home, Richard dismounted, handing his reins to the stable boy who came out at the sound of his approach. At the door he lifted the knocker and waited for the butler to answer. The door cracked open and Richard pushed in past the servant.

"There's no need to announce me, Stevens. Is my son still abed?"

"Yes, your Grace, but—"

"Fine. I'll announce myself." He headed for the stairs, taking them two at time. As Richard neared the top the butler called out. "But your Grace . . ." Richard waved him off and disappeared down the hall.

The door to Garren's room slammed against the wall and he bolted upright in bed, the sheet falling to his waist. His father stood in the doorway, a furious flush on his face, his hands braced at his waist.

"Do come in, Father." Garren yawned, rubbing the hair on his chest. He mentally braced himself for the coming confrontation. He had expected one, but not at this hour. He should have told Stevens to send the certificate around in the afternoon. He was at a definite disadvantage this early in the morning.

"What is the meaning of *this*?" Richard roared, shaking the rolled parchment in his hand.

Garren squinted. "I believe you hold my marriage certificate. The one you required me to obtain within the month." Garren kept his voice nonchalant. "I believe I met *your* requirement, did I not?"

"Who is this Jocelyn Tanner? And where is

she?" He questioned, looking around the room as if to spy her amid the furnishings.

"*She* is my wife, and she's residing at Spenceworth."

The silence stretched out, making Garren uncomfortable. He smoothed the bedding. In the light of morning, he knew he'd chosen the wrong road. He should have delivered the news in person. It would have given him time to consider what he would say to his father. Well, what's done is done, he thought, shrugging his shoulders.

"So you'll be leaving her to languish at Spenceworth? To what purpose?" Richard's eyes narrowed with suspicion.

Garren settled himself against the pillows propped beneath his back and took a deep breath before starting his explanation.

"She's not *languishing*, Father. 'Tis where she preferred to stay. Being a dutiful husband, I felt bound to let her have her way."

With a snort, Richard took a seat in the chair opposite the bed. "Oh, dutiful husband are you now?"

Garren nodded.

"You're married what . . . four days, and I find you here and your new bride in the country? You would term that *dutiful*?" His father's considering gaze unnerved Garren. "Will you not make this a true marriage?"

"As you and Mother had?" A shadow of pain flickered in the depth of his father's eyes and Garren wished his words back.

"Yes, as your mother and I had." Richard's gaze left his son. "I would want the same for you."

Garren shook his head. What need did he have for the kind of pain his father suffered at the death of his wife. No, it served him better to keep a distance from Jocelyn.

Richard leaned back in the chair, his legs stretched out before him.

"Tell me, son, has the marriage been consummated?"

Shock nearly brought Garren out of bed. "What? Now you want to be privy to my bedroom activities with my wife?"

"I but wish to know that the marriage is done and legal."

Lord, Garren hadn't considered that. If he told his father the extreme measures he'd taken to find a wife, mayhap the man could rescind his ultimatum.

Then the memory of Jocelyn the morning he'd left her entered his mind. He'd silently entered her room for one last glimpse of her. How vulnerable she had looked, sleeping on her side, her hands tucked beneath her pillow, the delicate fringe of her lashes fanning her cheek. His fingers had itched to trace the curve of her jaw. Before he could act on his urges, he'd turned and left, cursing himself for his silliness.

Garren felt a brief wave of guilt wash over him. Jocelyn needed his protection. But she had it at Spenceworth, he amended. Besides, she'd shown no attraction to him. No doubt she was happier at his country estate and far away from him.

His father's abnormally calm voice worried Garren. "I can see I'll get no answer from you." Richard's gaze slid to the window and Garren squirmed. "When will I meet my daughter-in-law?"

His mind scrambled for an excuse. "She is painfully shy and has asked to be left alone until she adjusts. I'll bring her around a few weeks before the Season." Garren hoped that time would, in some measure, allay his father's curiosity and give the staff time to educate Jocelyn. He realized now that he must bring her to town sometime.

"Painfully shy you say? Since when did you show an interest in shy women? It seems to me you detest the shy, simpering maidens. You've certainly always fallen for the more worldly ones." His father's eyebrow inched up, and Garren knew his father was referring to the incident with Lady Paxton.

"They were not wife material."

"And this Jocelyn Tanner apparently is."

"Mayhap." Garren hedged.

"Mayhap? What in thunderation does that mean?" His father's eyes squinted and he cocked his head. "What goes on here, Garren? There's something you're not telling me."

Tiring of sidestepping the questions, Garren clamped down on the urge to blurt out the entire fiasco. "Look Father, I did as you demanded. I married—and within one month. One can't be too picky under those circumstances." He threw back the covers and pulled on a silk robe to cover his nakedness. Tying the robe's sash tight, he turned to his father. "What more do you want?"

"I want to know more of the woman my son has taken to bear him heirs."

Garren turned to the window, staring out upon the gardens below. "Be damned," he muttered. Glancing over his shoulder, he spoke. His plan to throw his wife in his father's face was not working out as he'd planned. He couldn't bring himself to do it. "She is not of the ton. She's a simple girl, not given to airs, but she speaks well." Well, some of the time she does, he added to himself, turning back to the serene view of perfectly clipped hedges and bright splashes of colorful flowers.

"A *simple* lass? What does that mean?"

With a deep sigh, Garren pivoted from the window. Striding to the washstand, he poured in water from a porcelain pitcher. "It means she's not used to a lot of finery, pomp and ceremony. You know, a simple lass, uncomplicated." A little mad, too, he thought as he splashed cold water on his face. Patting it dry, he spared his father a glance.

"Ah." Richard rubbed his chin, nodding. He brought his gaze up to Garren, disbelief cooling the look. "Somehow I never saw you with a woman like that, Garren."

With a muttered oath, Garren threw the linen down. His patience went with it. "Tell me, would you rather I had married some doxy off the streets? Would it be easier to see me with a woman like that?"

His father's jaw clenched. A narrowing of the duke's eyes and a lift of the corner of his mouth made Garren squirm a little more. The look of disapproval meant only one thing: trouble. Trying to divert those thoughts Garren said, "I've decided to take my seat in Parliament."

His father's eyes grew large with surprise. "I beg your pardon? Did I hear you right? You're taking your seat?"

"Yes." Garren gave an inward sigh. It worked. His father stood stunned for a long moment.

"And what brought this on?" Richard asked suspiciously.

Grabbing a pair of dark green breeches from the back of a chair, Garren pulled them on. Slipping off his robe, he said, "Napoleon is becoming more a threat every day. A vacant seat in Parliament will not serve the country."

His father raised a skeptical eyebrow.

Garren took a shirt from the drawer of a chest and pulled it on. "Contrary to your impression of me, Father, I do care about my country. I simply doubted my ability to do anything for it."

His ploy had worked. His father had warmed to this topic quickly. "Ah, but son—as I've told you before, a persuasive man can bring about change. And you're right about Bonaparte. He's climbed too far too fast to be stable, and he has great charisma. That is dangerous, especially with his ambitions."

"Just so." Garren stuffed the shirttails into his breeches, pleased with the turn of the conversation. "And I can't help but feel the Directory has set its sights on Britain next."

"I'm surprised and pleased, Garren." His father's look of pride disappeared for a brief moment, replaced by one of distrust. "Still, I wonder about this change of heart."

"I found, over the last month, the truth of your words. It is time I took life a little more seriously. Getting married, settling down and such . . . well, it seemed the next logical step was to take my seat in Parliament." He held his breath.

"I see. Well, it's none too soon, son." His father rose, a half-smile on his lips. "I'll leave you. I'm certain you have much to do. We'll have dinner soon, eh?"

"Of course, Father." Garren let his breath out.

"And we'll bring your wife down to London soon, hmm?" His father smiled over his shoulder as he left, a twinkle in his brown eyes.

His *wife*. With Richard's exit, a thick blanket of trepidation settled on Garren's shoulders.

Breathing hard, Jocelyn took the stairs rapidly for the ninth time. One more time and she'd call it quits. Then she'd go back to her room, close the door and go through her toning exercises.

Mrs. Cowan had nearly suffered heart failure when she saw Jocelyn pounding up the stairs for the first time last week. Heaven only knows what would happen if she were to happen along during a set of crunches. Jocelyn gave a breathless chuckle at the top of the stairs.

As she ran down the stairs, the full cotton skirt of her dress fluttered around her legs. It had taken some strong words to get the seamstress to make a loose-fitting, cotton gown that reached only to Jocelyn's ankles. But the woman adamantly refused to make the drawers Jocelyn had made a pattern for. So Jocelyn had purloined some cotton fabric and made them herself. They were nothing to write home about, but at least she felt dressed.

Instead of wearing a corset, she lightly bound her breasts and wore her new drawers beneath the loose shift. Barefoot, she climbed the stairs ten times everyday. With careful eating and all this exercise, the weight had just seemed to melt away.

At the bottom of the stairs, she turned and climbed to the top, pumping her arms in one final effort to increase her heart rate. At the landing, she stopped, pressing two fingers to her neck, pleased with the rapid thud of blood through her veins. Yup, she'd had a good workout so far.

"Forty-five . . . forty-six . . . forty-seven . . ." Jocelyn leveled a gaze on the door as it opened and Mrs. Cowan walked in. Too late to climb to her feet, Jocelyn lowered her upper body back to the floor.

Well, here we go, she thought, but refused to quit before she reached fifty.

"Lady Jocelyn? Oh my word . . . Dulcey, tell Spalding to fetch the doctor for milady. She's fallen ill."

Dulcey bolted out of the room, leaving the door open as her footsteps receded down the hall.

Jocelyn lay on her back, with her knees and elbows pointed toward the ceiling while her feet dangled lifelessly and her fingers interlocked behind her head. Mrs. Cowan could only liken the scene to a dying cockroach on the kitchen floor. But a cockroach didn't seem to suffer so.

"Forty-eight . . . forty-nine . . . ugh."

Mrs. Cowan dropped down on her knees next to Jocelyn and caught her by the shoulders as she came up for the last crunch of her set.

Pushing her down flat on the floor the housekeeper said, "Just lie still, milady. We'll have ye in bed in no time, and the doctor will be here straight away to tend ye."

Jocelyn took a deep breath and brushed Mrs. Cowan's fluttering hands away. While she might be a competent housekeeper, always in control of the household catastrophes, she became completely undone where Jocelyn and her exercises were concerned.

"Dulcey," Jocelyn shouted. She had no desire to explain what she was doing on the floor to the entire household and a doctor.

Mrs. Cowan's eyes rounded and her mouth opened. "Oh Lord, you're hysterical." The elderly woman tugged at Jocelyn's shoulders, trying to get her to lie back down. "Just lay quiet, Lady Jocelyn. We'll take good care of ye." The soothing words were colored with a hint of hysteria.

"Mrs. Cowan, there's nothing to take care of. I'm fine." She shrugged off the woman's hands. "Please, stop Dulcey before she gets to Spalding.

There'll be a host of servants at the door. Please," Jocelyn nearly begged, but the thunder of foot-steps told her it was too late. Heaving a sigh of annoyance, she got to her feet.

Grabbing the blanket Jocelyn had laid upon, Mrs. Cowan threw it over her mistress' shoulders, covering her just as Spalding and several servants descended on her opened door.

"What's happened?" Spalding demanded from the threshold.

"Nothing!" Jocelyn ground the word out, shoot-ing Spalding a quelling glare.

Mrs. Cowan wrung her hands. "Her ladyship has had a spell—"

"Blast it, I'm fine," Jocelyn shouted. Surprise silenced everyone and she shifted under the weight of their gazes. "Well. Now what?" she muttered to herself.

"Lady Jocelyn?" Spalding inquired.

Taking a deep breath, she said, "I'm fine. Please, everyone, go back to what you were doing."

With some hesitation the servants slowly left, all except for Spalding, of course. He had to be the nosiest person Jocelyn had ever met. She wasn't sure if she liked him or not. He was always so . . . so . . . sober. She wondered briefly if he would even loosen up after a few glasses of wine.

The butler cleared his throat, his tactful way of directing attention to himself.

"Yes, Spalding?" Her words came out on an exasperated sigh. "What is it?"

"Milady, since you are in good health, it is my pleasure to inform you that the seamstress has arrived."

"What? Again?" Jocelyn turned to Mrs. Cowan. "Was this your doing?"

The housekeeper straightened her shoulders and, pasting a prim look on her face, replied, "Yes, milady. I believe the gowns ye ordered will need to be altered and a new corset made."

"It's pointless to make clothes for me. I'm losing weight and it's just a waste."

The movement of Spalding's head caught Jocelyn's attention. It would be better to take this up in private, and maybe with the seamstress as well, she thought.

"Spalding, have her come up, please."

With a nod, he left, closing the door.

"Milady, surely ye don't plan on losing any more weight? Ye're thin as a reed now."

"Hardly a reed, Mrs. Cowan."

A light knock and the seamstress entered, a servant following, her arms filled with garments and fabric.

"Milady?" Anna, the seamstress, a small plump woman of middle age, smiled at Jocelyn as she bobbed a little curtsy.

Anna's quiet demeanor tugged at Jocelyn. Far from affluent, the clothing she made for Jocelyn would, no doubt, feed her for quite a while. It just seemed stupid to have clothes made, just to have them altered a week later.

With a huff of resignation, Jocelyn threw off the blanket and submitted herself to the measuring, poking and prodding of being fitted for a new corset and for the alteration of one of the gowns poor Anna had just finished.

After lunch, Jocelyn spent her day following behind Mrs. Cowan, learning about the running of Spenceworth.

Awed by the things the housekeeper told her, Jocelyn's respect for Mrs. Cowan and the staff grew. Everything took so much more time and effort. Jocelyn thought of all the modern conveniences she'd left behind and wished she knew more of how they worked so that she could pass along the information to the servants. But then, she thought, what would happen when some archeologist came along in two hundred years and found a microwave here? No, she decided, she had to adapt to things as they were.

Mrs. Cowan was determined that Jocelyn would know every inch of the manor. She took her down to the far reaches of the house, into the servants' wing, the kitchen and pantry. Out to the buttery, brewhouse, bakehouse, stillroom, and laundry rooms.

Their tour ended in the linen room. Shelves covered every wall, filled top to bottom with stacks of linen. Jocelyn stood in the middle of the room, her mouth agape. "Good Lord, would you look at this?"

Pointing to the shelves along the right wall, Mrs. Cowan said, "These are the working linen. These roller cloths are for the kitchen, stillroom, servants' hall, pantry and laundry. There are the special kitchen rubbers for scouring, the china cloths, glass cloths and the housekeeper's cloths."

Jocelyn's head spun. "How in the world do you tell them apart?"

"Each is marked." She pulled one from the shelf. "See the stitches of colored thread? These are duster cloths. Linens used by the servants have a blue thread. The family and guest linens are marked with a white thread."

"How do you remember all of them?" Jocelyn wandered around the room, running her fingers across the neatly stacked rows of linens. "There are so many."

"Aye. My mother was housekeeper here and I learned at her knee." Pride filled Mrs. Cowan's voice.

"So you've always worked here?"

"Aye, until the old Earl died. My sister took sick and I went to tend her and her family for a while."

"The old earl? You mean Garren's father?"

Mrs. Cowan shook her head. "Oh my, no. Milord's father is in fine health. 'Twas the grandfather who died. Milord's mother's father."

"Oh."

Mrs. Cowan gave Jocelyn an odd look. "Ye didn't know of Lord Spenceworth's passing?"

Uh oh, Jocelyn thought, there was so much she didn't know. This was like walking in quicksand. She longed to ask after Garren's mother, but knew that would bring more suspicion upon her. Why she worried about it, Jocelyn didn't know, but instinct prodded her to be cautious.

"Yes, of course, I just get a little confused. Is your sister doing better?"

The housekeeper slanted a glance at Jocelyn, then turned to the rows of neat linens, smoothing imaginary wrinkles from one. "Aye." She turned from the shelves and smiled. "Thank ye."

"Good," Jocelyn said as they left the linen room behind. She liked the elderly woman and the care she took of not only Jocelyn, but the entire staff. She was more a mother hen than a housekeeper.

As they emerged from the lower part of the house, a man Jocelyn had never seen walked briskly by them.

"Who's that?" Jocelyn whispered to Mrs. Cowan.

"Ye've not met the steward?"

"No."

"Baskin?" Mrs. Cowan called to the man.

He turned. "Yes, Mrs. Cowan?" He retraced his steps to stand before them.

The housekeeper nodded to Baskin. "Milady, this is Baskin, the steward. Baskin, Lady Spenceworth."

Jocelyn swallowed the giggle tickling her throat. First Spalding and tennis balls and now Baskin. . . . "Do you have a friend named Robbins?"

"Milady?" He gave her a baffled look.

Jocelyn realized she'd spoken her thought out loud. "Sorry. I'm pleased to meet you." He stood there in front of her a moment as if he waited for something. Jocelyn took a moment to study him. Of average height and middle age, he had nondescript brown hair and matching eyes. A long nose with a bump in the middle and thin lips added to the plainness of his face. He had an air of distraction, like his mind was working on something else. Recalling herself she said, "Please don't let me keep you. But if you have some time later, I'd love to know more about how the estate is run."

"Milady?" His eyes rounded and he shook his head. " 'Tis hardly the proper subject for a lady."

"What's so improper about it?" She watched suspicion appear in his eyes. So, he didn't trust her, was that it?

That distrust rankled her. Back home, she was responsible for million-dollar corporations, and valued people's faith above all else. Of course, he didn't know that. He'd probably crumple at her feet if she told him. Either that or have her committed. Smoothing her ruffled feathers, she told herself, I'm a stranger to him. He's only protecting Garren's interests, as he should.

Straightening, the steward composed his features into a mask of superiority that she felt sure was chauvinistic in origin. " 'Tis only that milord has myself and a receiver general to take care of these matters. I'm certain that you have little time for such things."

Well, Jocelyn thought, he went and rumpled my feathers again. He should have just bobbed his pointed little head and left. But no, he had to use that condescending tone. "How much time could reviewing a few debits and credits take? I assure you reading through a general ledger won't tax my limited intelligence. Still,"—she paused—"maybe you haven't kept them up as you should." She arched an eyebrow, meeting his gaze. "In which case, I wouldn't want to cause you any embarrassment." She pasted a smile on her face.

Baskin's incredulous look was comical. With a satisfied smile, Jocelyn turned to Mrs. Cowan. "Shall we proceed? I believe I've finished with Baskin." She nodded to the man. "For now."

Later that evening, Jocelyn lay in bed, her fingers itching to get at the estate's ledgers. She told herself it was merely curiosity about how accounts were maintained in this age, rather than outrage at having been forbidden to see them, but either way it didn't matter. She had plotted and planned since this afternoon and now, as the house quieted, she rose and pulled on the robe draped over the foot of the bed. Taking the candle from the table, she slipped from the room, making her way quietly into the library.

Silently closing the door behind her, she crossed the room. Settling herself in the leather chair behind the desk, she pulled a pin from her hair and jimmied the lock of the drawer. A few minutes later she pulled the ledgers from their place and stacked them before her. Taking the oldest one out, she opened it and began her education in eighteenth-century accounting.

It took her the better part of an hour to decipher the writing and the method used in the accounts. The cook and butler kept their own accounts, recording the income allotted them for the year and all expenses paid out. Detailed entries were recorded in the general ledger. Every pound and ha'penny was tracked. The detail amazed her. She became familiar with the people who lived or worked at Spenceworth. Entries for the removal of the cook's tooth and the purchase of an apron for a maid lent insight into the care given to the employees. The lord carried an awesome responsibility.

Jocelyn itched to reformat the ledger and arrange it as something she could analyze. But she recognized the futility of that wish. It would do her no good. And it would only raise Baskin's distrust further if he discovered she'd even read the records.

Her eyes ached from the strain of deciphering the handwriting of the stewards of Spenceworth. With a new respect for Baskin and those of his profession, Jocelyn returned the ledgers to the drawer and closed it, working the hairpin in the lock so that the steward wouldn't know she'd seen the records.

Chapter Seven

" 'Tis been nearly three weeks since Garren came back and not a word has he said about his wife." Richard adjusted the collar of his shirt. "I've a mind to go to Spenceworth and meet the girl myself, Hobbs." He turned to his butler. "What think you, man?"

Hobbs's head bobbed between stooped shoulders, a lock of pure white hair drooping over his brow. "As you will, your Grace. Shall I instruct your valet to begin packing?"

The duke rubbed his jaw thoughtfully, and a mischievous twinkle lit the depths of his brown eyes. Aye, he thought, I'll get the two of them together, just see if I don't. With a little coaching, she'll overcome her shyness.

"Yes, Hobbs. I've no notion how long this will take. Best have him pack for a lengthy stay."

Richard went to his library to pen a note to the

Duchess of Tinsbury. He chuckled as he gave the note to the butler. It would arrive at her country estate a day after he arrived at Spenceworth.

"Milady, *must* you persist in this exercise every day?" A scandalized Mrs. Cowan stood just within Jocelyn's room, the door closed.

From her position on the floor, Jocelyn glanced at the housekeeper. "It's healthy, Mrs. Cowan, and yes, I will persist in doing them every day."

Raising her leg up and down from her hip, Jocelyn counted to twenty. "Did you need something?"

"Aye, milady. The gowns have arrived from the seamstress."

"Gracious, that didn't take long. Poor Anna's fingers must be numb."

" 'Twill be good to see ye dressed as befits yer station, milady. Now, if I could only convince ye to let the servants make yer bed each morn." The housekeeper moved around the room, straightening things that didn't need straightening. Finishing her exercises, Jocelyn got up from the floor and put on the robe the woman held open for her.

"I'm sorry. It's habit. But I think I've done well in everything else, don't you?" Tying the belt at her waist, Jocelyn marveled at the change in her body. At some point she'd come to think of the body as hers. And this body metabolized food much faster than her twentieth-century body. Jocelyn smiled as her hands glided over smooth hips, maybe just a bit more round than she wanted, but firming up quite nicely.

"Aye, milady, ye've improved mightily." The woman's words pulled Jocelyn from her thoughts. "But enough of that. Let's get ye dressed and ready to break yer fast."

Opening the door, Mrs. Cowan nodded her head, and a servant entered, bearing several packages and boxes from the seamstress.

All in all, Jocelyn thought, later that day, things were getting better. Baskins still considered her suspect, Spalding watched her like a hawk, but the rest of the household staff treated her with respect colored with a bit of confusion.

Mrs. Cowan had been a dear, teaching her comportment, as she called it. Jocelyn could serve tea like a born lady now and sit perched on a chair, her back ramrod straight. But when Mrs. Cowan tried to get her to flutter a fan and simper like a schoolgirl, Jocelyn drew the line.

"For heaven's sake, I'm a full-grown woman, what do I need to do that for?" Jocelyn dropped the offending fan in her lap and stared at the housekeeper.

Mrs. Cowan's brow wrinkled in concentration. "Well now, ye may be right about the little giggle and such, but the fan comes in right handy if ye don't want to be seen well or ye become embarrassed. I even saw it used as a weapon once."

"What, this little thing?" Jocelyn said, looking at the ivory and silk fan in her lap. "What damage could this thing inflict on anyone?" She picked it up, examining it closely.

"Well, Lady Simone didn't appreciate Lord Langley's touching her arm, so she slapped her fan smartly on his hand. He pulled it away, much embarrassed at such a set-down."

"I would have just told him to remove his hand now, or he'd be pulling back a bloody stump later."

"Lady Spenceworth, ye can *never* say that in

polite company. Or *any* company for that matter. Remember, yer a lady."

She had thoroughly scandalized Mrs. Cowan with that remark, but the lessons continued. She could now embroider, which she hated. She could direct the servants, who didn't need any directing. She could prepare a menu, which the cook mostly ignored.

The bellrope gave her the most trouble. She hated to pull the stupid thing. To interrupt some-one else just because she wanted something she could get herself was absurd. But the look on Spalding's face when she'd knocked on the baize door to the servants' wing looking for Mrs. Cowan convinced her it would have been better to use the bellrope than encounter that sober, slightly contemptful look again.

Her musings were interrupted by the soft thud of horse's hooves and muted voices. The front door slammed and a robust voice shouted, "Where's this new daughter of mine?"

Jocelyn froze. The thought of meeting Garren's father had never entered her mind. She glanced in the mirror, and with trembling hands, smoothed the skirt of her soft blue high-waisted dress. Patting the coil of hair at the nape of her neck, she fluffed the little wisps of curls that framed her face and tickled the back of her neck. She breathed deeply to calm her racing heart and waited for Spalding to inform her of her father-in-law's arrival—not that it could have gone heard by anyone in the entire countryside.

"Yes," Jocelyn answered at the soft knock, her voice a bit shaky.

Mrs. Cowan entered, not Spalding, earning the housekeeper Jocelyn's gratitude. "The Duke of

Warrick has arrived, milady. Spalding has shown him to the salon and given him a glass of brandy."

"What'll I do now?" Jocelyn's voice sounded panicky even to herself.

"First, ye'll calm yerself." Mrs. Cowan came forward and grasped Jocelyn's hands, squeezing them gently. "Then ye'll go down and meet yer father-in-law. Remember yer manners and keep yer head up."

"What's he like? From the bellow he let out announcing his arrival, I suspect he's a bit of a brute."

"Nay, he's no such thing. His bark is much worse than his bite, milady." The housekeeper's encouraging smile and warm gaze helped Jocelyn to calm her fluttery nerves.

"So you know him well, then?"

"Oh, aye. He came to see the old earl at least twice a year. The two got on like best friends, they did. Always drinking and laughing and enjoying themselves."

Mrs. Cowan patted Jocelyn's hair, straightened a ribbon on her gown and said, "Don't keep him waiting, milady. Just remember, he's a big bear of a man with the heart of a puppy."

Jocelyn gave her an uncertain look and hurried into the hall.

Downstairs, Spalding stood before the door of the salon. As Jocelyn approached she felt his gaze travel from her head to her toes.

"Well, Spalding, old boy, will I do, do you think?" She turned full circle in front of the butler.

His lips thinned, and his face colored a delightful shade of red. He turned from her without a word and opened the door with a flourish.

"The Lady Spenceworth, your Grace."

Jocelyn took a deep breath and let it out slowly before she entered the room.

A man of about fifty stood before the hearth. His six-foot frame supported a well-muscled body; though not lean, it was nonetheless impressive. A sprinkling of gray hair gave him a distinguished look and served to call attention to his lively brown eyes.

Jocelyn watched his gaze travel over her from head to toe, and then it hone in on her face, daring her to drop her gaze first.

So it was a stare-down the man wanted, she thought. Keeping her face serene, she dropped into a deep, graceful curtsy, her head high, her eyes still locked with his. "Your Grace."

A smile broke over his face revealing twin dimples. "Come Lady Jocelyn, I'm not royalty. No need for such a curtsy to me."

Jocelyn blinked at last. She allowed a small smile to tilt the corners of her mouth. This man was one she could get to like. "Oh, I didn't mistake you for royalty. That's hard to do when you bellow like an enraged bull. No, it's just that I got my heel caught in my hem." Liar, liar, she thought to herself. *I just haven't gotten that half: curtsy thing down yet; so Duke, it's all or nothing.*

Richard's eyebrows rose and his eyes widened in surprise. He studied her a moment. No woman other than his late wife, Leona, had the brass this chit had. She'd likened his voice to the bellow of an enraged bull . . . and looked him straight in the eye while she said it.

Jocelyn interrupted his thoughts. "But then, maybe you don't have bellropes in your home and must shout at the top of your lungs to bring your servants." Inclining her head, her gray eyes questioned him, a teasing sparkle lighting them. "Or perhaps they're all hard of hearing?"

He chuckled. How could Garren have found this woman shy?

And simple? Anything but!

Her features were fine and delicate and she carried herself well, spine straight, shoulders square.

In a low voice Richard confided, "It's for Spalding. It does him good to get his blood pumping now and again."

"I believe I've taken care of that for you already." She smiled and whispered, "Didn't you notice his face when he announced me? Nicely mottled, I thought." Her infectious giggle tickled his ears.

Her speech hinted at a Colonial background. Her direct manner certainly also supported his suspicions.

"Ah, I see I have an accomplice now. We must put our heads together and see what mischief we can invent for my son's butler." Richard was pleased when he saw an answering gleam in Jocelyn's eye. "I think I shall stay for a bit, and get to know my new daughter."

Richard took her around the estate Garren had inherited from his maternal grandfather, showing her again how it was run—telling her everything. She, in turn, found him receptive to her questions and ideas. He listened to her views on auditing the accounts and explained to her the workings of the goldsmiths. She was delighted to learn that money left with them could earn as much as six percent. Richard pointed out that Garren's grandfather had never trusted the goldsmiths; instead, all transactions necessary for the running of

Spenceworth were conducted in cash, and the money was held in a chest in the library. After a heated debate, Jocelyn convinced Richard to see that the bulk of the money was transferred to a London goldsmith.

Several days later, as Jocelyn and Richard shared conversation over breakfast, Spalding entered, a folded piece of cream parchment resting on the salver he carried. Richard took the missive the butler offered.

His gaze scanned the paper. "Jocelyn, I've wonderful news. The Duchess of Tinsbury is giving a costume ball next week. I would be honored if you would attend with me."

"Where does the duchess live?" She dabbed at her lips, laying the napkin beside her plate.

"Her country estate is but a few hours' ride from Spenceworth."

"It sounds like fun." Jocelyn smiled. As a child, she'd always fantasized about attending an old-fashioned masked ball. And now was her chance.

"Wonderful. Now, you'll need a costume. Shall we send for the seamstress? You should have something spectacular. I want my daughter-in-law to outshine even Lady Tinsbury's chandeliers."

Her mind spun with the possibilities. She wanted to do this herself. "I don't think I'll need the help of a seamstress."

Richard glanced up at her in surprise.

"Don't worry." She patted his hand. "I'll take care of everything." She smiled again, arching an eyebrow and giving him a wink.

The evening of the ball found her new father-in-law pacing the hall waiting for Jocelyn. She'd been very secretive about her costume, and he

111

wondered, not for the first time, what she would be wearing. He hoped it would dazzle his son when he saw her, for he was ashamed that Garren seemed to have taken his marriage vows a little less than seriously.

A light step above him drew his eyes to her, and his breath caught in his chest. Mrs. Cowan stood behind her, twisting her hands; her eyes were large and round with fear. "I told her, yer Grace, that it just wasn't proper. She can't go dressed in such a . . . a *revealing* costume."

Richard's gaze left Jocelyn's mischievous smile and traveled down her unusual garb. The gown, made of material with a striped design resembling a tiger, revealed one shoulder. The upper part of the dress molded itself to her chest before it fell in a straight line to the floor. Jocelyn's toes peeped from beneath the jagged points of the dress's hem.

His eyes traveled back up to her face, and he noticed the light brown wig she wore. Her hair, styled into a knot atop her head, was held in place by, of all things, a *bone*. He blinked, hardly believing his eyes. But no, it *was* a bone. He smiled. If this didn't get his son's attention, the boy was blind, he thought. He chuckled. Yes, this was going to be a most interesting evening.

"It would seem your marital state has redeemed you in the eyes of the ton," Jamie said quietly in Garren's ear.

"So it would seem," he replied.

It had been quite a surprise to receive an invitation to the duchess' ball. Most of society had quietly excluded him from the social rounds since rumors of his affair with Lady Melody had circulated, and though he'd taken up the reins of his political responsibilities, society had been slow to take notice and open its doors to him.

But then, the Duchess of Tinsbury seldom followed the lead of her peers. And she was a family friend.

Now, at her masked ball, Garren was pleased to be returned to the glamor and hustle of society.

"Will you be going to Spenceworth before you return to London?" Jamie's question interrupted Garren's thoughts.

"Yes. I've some matters to look into there." Jocelyn's image came to mind. Of late, it happened more frequently than he liked. Resolutely he pushed her from his thoughts. He would stop by only to see to the business of his estate, not to see Jocelyn, he assured himself. The servants saw to her needs, he need not worry over her welfare. No, he simply needed to consult with Baskin.

"How long will you stay?"

"A day or two." Garren shrugged. "Maybe longer."

"Eager to get back to your bride, eh?" Jamie grinned, nudging Garren's shoulder.

Garren shrugged, silently cursing the memory of Jocelyn in his embrace, her blond hair flowing over his arms her soft, plump cheeks and curving lips, her gray eyes dancing with devilment as she prepared to launch a volley of syllabub at his head. He couldn't help but wonder what the indomitable Mrs. Cowan had thought of Jocelyn. Surely that good woman would turn his wife into a lady, *if* it were possible.

Jamie interrupted his musings with another nudge. "I say, 'tis an unusual costume that one's wearing. Who do you think she's portraying?"

Garren looked in the direction in which Jamie nodded. He watched the woman move into the room, the simplicity of her gown setting off her alluring figure and drawing the appreciative gazes of more than a few men. Her bare shoulder, exposed by the dress, gleamed pearlescent in the candlelight. The mask she wore hid her features from his gaze, allowing him only a glimpse of a full lower lip that promised strong passion. As she turned and walked away, Garren wondered who she was.

Chapter Eight

"How in the world did *Charles* manage an invitation to Lady Tinsbury's ball?" Jamie's tone intruded on Garren's contemplation of the tantalizing sway of the mystery woman's hips. He turned his gaze to his friend's much-affronted countenance.

Garren stiffened at the approach of Lady Paxton's brother. He hoped the boor hadn't come to harrass him—hadn't the scandal caused enough trouble for both Garren and Melody? "No doubt, he hasn't one." He lowered his voice. "Wonder what he's about." He didn't have to wonder long.

"You dare to come here after what you've done to my sister? I should call you out now and be done with it." Charles' white-blond hair fell in limp strands around a face contorted with rage.

"Charles, that would be foolish at best and

would solve nothing. I've sent around an apology to your sister, the Lady Melody—"

"Don't even speak her name. You befoul it." Charles' watery gaze swept over Garren.

"Just one moment." Garren straightened. "I made my apologies—and the whole thing was wholly exaggerated. I'll not stand here and suffer this kind of insult." How dare the little mouse roar at him, he thought. He curled his lip in disdain.

"This kind of insult?" Charles tilted his head, glaring at Garren. "You have the audacity to stand there and tell me *you* won't have *me* insulting *you*?" He snorted indignantly. "After what you've done to my sister?"

Garren raised an eyebrow. Looking down at the shorter man, he ground out, "May I point out that your sister is a woman who knows her own mind. She was a willing participant." Charles moved back as Garren stepped closer. "And may I also point out that she had set her cap for me. Think you that she would have breathed a word about that evening if I had offered marriage?" He shook his head in disgust. "No, she would not have— because that was her strategy. When I did not offer for her, she thought to force my hand. I'll grant you the fact that my friends wagered on the outcome didn't make things any better, but I had no part in that."

Charles sneered. "As if I would allow such a marriage." Garren smiled and spoke dryly. "Oh, no, of course not. I should have known you would refuse a marriage that might not only save your sister's reputation, but bring your family up in society."

Charles sputtered and fumed and looked about to commit murder. "I've offered my apologies," Garren continued, "and I will make them public.

More than that, I cannot do. You would be wise to accept that."

Garren turned to leave, but Charles' words brought him back around.

"There is the question of compensation." Charles rubbed his hands together, his sly gaze boldly meeting Garren's.

Garren's eyebrow rose. "Ah, now I see. You've gambled away you inheritance, have you?" Shaking his head, he chuckled. "Charles, you were never good at the tables. I thought you'd learned that by now. If you think I'll offer compensation to you, you'll be disappointed. Your sister's reputation would have been compromised, if not by me, then by the next earl or marquis who came along. She searches for a husband and financial security. It's apparent that you offer her neither. You'll take the public apology or nothing. That's my offer."

Garren turned, stepping away from a mottled-faced Charles. "This is not the end of this, Garren. I will avenge my sister's throwing over. That I promise you." Charles's low-voiced threat followed Garren as he headed for the library and a strong drink.

Later, calmed by the fiery heat of superb brandy, Garren joined the masked throngs in the ballroom and his gaze once again fastened on the tantalizing woman with the bone in her hair. Then as he watched, Charles appeared. At the man's slightly staggering approach to the object of Garren's attention, he swore under his breath. The man seemed determined to make a fool of himself.

Charles placed his hand on the woman's arm. Garren chuckled as she picked it off like an offensive bug, with the tips of her thumb and forefinger grasping the sleeve of his coat. Her lower lip curved in a chilling smile.

Again, there was a tug of familiarity. Had he met her before? No, certainly he would remember a woman with such a lush figure.

Garren moved his gaze from the woman to Charles strained face, reflecting his anger at her rejection. Didn't the man realize that society didn't consider him a matrimonial catch; he was only a mere baron, cash-poor, and not too pleasant to look upon.

Determined to relieve the lady of Charles's unwanted attention, Garren wove through the masked and costumed people toward the couple. As he approached, Charles spared him a frosty glare and bowed stiffly before leaving.

"Little toad." Her mumbled words reached Garren's ears, and he chuckled. She started in surprise and turned to him. "My Lord, you scared me." She raised her small, soft hand to her chest.

"I do beg your pardon, milady." Garren arched an eyebrow and smiled. "I only meant to compliment you on your costume." He glanced at Charles's retreating back and then back to the lady.

Her lower lip turned up in a rueful smile. "You weren't supposed to hear that remark."

"What remark, milady?" Garren arranged his face in an innocent expression.

With a smile she responded, "Oh, no remark. Nothing. Nothing at all."

Garren took a step back and bowed at the waist. "I'm Garren Warrick, Earl of Spenceworth. Might I know your name?"

With a low chuckle and a shake of her head she said, "Now, what is the point in dressing up in costume to hide your identity, only to run around telling everyone who you are?"

"Point well made, milady. Might I ask as to your unusual costume?"

"Yes?"

Garren tried to look into her eyes, but the mask cast a shadow over them, and he was unable even to discern their color. She cleared her throat, and he recalled himself, "Who are you portraying, milady?"

"You can't tell? Doesn't the bone give you a hint?"

"Alas, milady, I know of no one in history who wore a bone in her hair."

"Maybe you should look farther back in history."

His eyes widened. "And how far back should I look?"

She shifted and moved back a step and with a nervous laugh said, "Oh, to the beginning of fashion. Don't you think that this could well be the first fashion?" She cocked her head. "When there were no looms to make cloth, might not a woman clothe herself in animal skin? And before the discovery of gems, isn't it possible that a woman might wear a bone for adornment?"

He smiled, spreading his hands out. "Alas, I've not thought on the origins of fashion, milady, but it is apparent that you have. 'Tis a charming and most unusual costume."

She bobbed a quick curtsy. "Thank you, sir."

"But tell me, where is your escort?"

Suddenly a deep voice interrupted him. "Well, Garren, I didn't anticipate seeing you here this evening," his father said.

"Speak of the devil." The woman with the bone in her hair turned and placed her hand on Garren's father's arm.

Garren struggled with the shock. Surely she was too young for his father. And what of the

Lady Tinsbury? He'd thought that she and his father were . . .

"It's good to see you. Would you do me the honor of introducing your lovely companion?" Garren's tone was stern, in spite of his efforts to cover his dismay.

"Of course, of course. Lady Pebbles, may I present my son, Garren Warrick, Earl of Spenceworth. Garren, this remarkable woman is Lady Pebbles Flintstone." The duke's eyes nearly outshone the twinkling lights of the room.

"I don't believe I'm familiar with the Flintstones." Garren watched his parent's obvious glee and wondered at it.

"Well, if one is to choose a fictitious name, one should use one's imagination don't you think?" The lady tilted her head.

For a moment Garren was confused. Then he looked at both his father and the lady, noting the teasing smiles they both wore.

"Did you think I would give you my real name?" Her soft chuckle was joined by his father's.

"I could but hope." He suddenly felt he'd be in for a very long evening.

Garren's chocolate eyes lit with warmth and humor and Jocelyn found her heart softening toward her husband.

She had given an inward sigh of relief when Richard had come up and interrupted their conversation. She had almost blurted out Darwin's theory; and though she couldn't remember when his theory was first known, she didn't think it was 1797. Times like these were so stressful. She had to watch everything she said.

Richard hadn't warned her that Garren might

be here, and she had nearly fainted when she'd seen him in the crowd. Well, Richard would feel the rough side of her tongue at the first opportunity. They'd grown to be friends, of a sort, and this was not the sort of treatment she expected from friends. The duke's eyes were sparkling with good humor; he was thoroughly enjoying his son's ignorance, too. But he wouldn't be laughing long, Jocelyn vowed.

The music started up, and Richard turned to her. "Would you honor me with this dance, Lady Pebbles?"

"Sir, the honor would be mine."

Turning to Garren she said, "Please excuse me, Lord Spenceworth."

Once on the dance floor Jocelyn said, "You *knew* Garren would be here this evening, didn't you?"

The steps of the dance separated them, and when they came together again he said, "Are you angry with me?"

Again they were separated, and it was long moments before she could reply. "Yes. Well, no, I suppose not. In a way I think he deserves it, for just dropping me off at Spenceworth like so much luggage." After a moment's thought she shook her head. "No, I most definitely am not angry with you. Shall we continue the masquerade?"

"Oh, but of course. This could prove highly entertaining." Richard laughed.

"He looked rather suspicious. Do you think he recognized me?"

"Nay. But I can see he's taken with you, and he is trying to understand the strong attraction he feels. He has been known to be a bit of a rake. He is no doubt grappling with his honor about now." As they turned in the dance, Richard glanced in Garren's direction. "He has spoken vows, now, though. And while he has not always considered others' honor, he is always cognizant of his own. This will be an entertaining sight to behold."

"Your imagination has run away with you again. Garren is not attracted to me, or else why would he have dropped me off at Spenceworth and hightailed it back to London?"

"My dear, Mrs. Cowan described your appearance when she first met you. You were not yet polished enough for my son. If Garren had seen you as you are now, he would never have left you alone at Spenceworth."

"But this is only skin-deep."

"That is true, but offtimes it is the external beauty which draws a man to a woman and enables him to see with his heart the beauty within."

"Richard." She said somewhat bitterly, then laughed. "All men want a beautiful woman. She doesn't need to be beautiful inside, and you know it."

Richard's deep rumble of laughter reached Garren's ears, and he cast his gaze in his sire's direction. He's old enough to be her father, he thought. What did she see in him? Granted, the duke cut a fine figure, but what could they possibly have in common? Was this relationship serious?

He glanced around and found the Duchess of Tinsdale looking in his father's direction, a stunned look on her face. As he watched, the look changed to one of hurt. Rather than greet her guests, the hostess turned her back and headed toward the refreshment table.

The duchess and his father had been friends for quite a while. Richard and the Duke of Tinsbury had been cronies, and when the duke had passed away, it had been a natural thing for Richard to be of assistance to the newly widowed duchess. Over the past year, Garren had begun to expect his father to marry her, but it had never happened; and Garren wondered now if there was some obstacle that impeded their relationship. One could find his father at any event the duchess either sponsored or attended. It was plain there had always been great affection between the two. What was his father's interest in this new girl? Was he trying to make Lady Tinsbury jealous? Turning, Garren made his way to her side.

"Ah, milady, you look positively ravishing this eve," Garren said with a bow.

"Ah, now, Garren, you were not to recognize me."

"It would be impossible to conceal such beauty. It fairly lights the room."

"Ah, well, you young rascal, you've your father's blood coursing through your veins and that's a fact." She tapped his arm with a purple feather fan. "Such blatant flattery no doubt turns many a woman's head, but not mine. So tell me, did you not bring your new bride?" She craned her neck, looking around the room.

"Alas, no. She's recuperating from a slight indisposition."

"Ah, well, I see. 'Tis a normal thing for brides—it's nothing to worry your head about. She'll be up and about in no time," she said, patting his arm in a maternal way.

Seeking to divert her attention from his affairs to those of his father he said, "Who is the lady with my father? He introduced her as Lady Pebbles Flintstone, but I was informed that is a fictitious name."

"Well, I'm sure I don't know," the duchess responded somewhat peevishly. "She doesn't seem familiar, but then you know how these balls are. Invariably, someone brings along a visiting cousin or such. Whatever is she portraying?"

"I believe she said it was her version of the first fashions worn by women."

At her startled glance he hurried to say, "Before the invention of the loom and the discovery of gems, she implied a woman might dress in skins and adorn herself with bones."

The Duchess let out a small chuckle. "What a refreshing imagination. If anyone in this room could carry it off, she's the one." Her tone sharpened. "It would seem she and your father are well acquainted."

"Yes, it would. Father did not offer any details of their acquaintance. She seems a bit young, don't you think?" Garren arched his brows.

"You are absolutely correct. It wouldn't do for him to make a laughingstock of himself now, would it? Mayhap we can be of aid to the duke, Garren. If you'll take care of Lady Pebbles, I'll have a word with your father," she said, a calculating look in her eye.

Garren followed the duchess with some satisfaction as her short militant strides took her to his father and Lady Pebbles. He was pleased by her suggestion. Though claiming the next dance would clear the path for the duchess, he refused to examine his real reason for wanting to dance with the mystery woman.

Waltzing with Lady Pebbles was a sacrifice he would make. Gladly.

"Richard, I don't believe I've met your companion." Garren marveled at Lady Tinsbury's smooth, solicitous voice.

"Lady Tinsbury, may I present Lady Pebbles

Flintstone. Lady Pebbles, Lady Elizabeth Tinsbury, the Duchess of Tinsbury."

Both ladies nodded. The duchess took the punch cup from Richard's hand, placing it on a nearby table. "Richard, I believe this is your dance."

Richard's brow rose in surprise, and a smile turned up the corners of his mouth. "Well, so it is. Excuse me, Lady Pebbles. Garren, please watch over this lady in my absence, won't you?"

"Richard, who *is* that woman?" the duchess hissed as the dance began.

His eyes twinkling in merriment he whispered, "Why Elizabeth, are you jealous?"

"And what have I to be jealous about?"

"Lady Pebbles?"

"Humph. You'll make a cake of yourself if you pursue her, you know."

"Well, now, that would cause some problems, I guess."

"You guess? You're a fool, Richard. A plain fool," she said, shaking her head.

"Now, now calm down, Elizabeth. 'Tis not as it seems. Can you keep a secret?"

"Of course I can."

He bent his head to whisper, "Lady Pebbles is Garren's wife."

A small gasp emitted from the duchess as they parted in the dance. Once together again she said, "His wife? Are you sure?"

"Of course I am." He chuckled. "I would know my own daughter-in-law, would I not?"

"Aye, but would not your son know his own wife?"

"Not dressed as she is." He smiled, hugely proud of himself.

"Richard, what are you up to?" Elizabeth pursed her lips, her eyes narrowing.

" 'Tis a longish story, Elizabeth. Shall we retire to the gardens, and I'll tell it?"

Garren watched as his father and the duchess left the dance floor. What was his father up to now, he wondered, arriving with one woman and taking a turn in the gardens with another?

He turned to Lady Pebbles to gauge her reaction to his father's departure, and was surprised to see her nod of approval.

"You seem not to mind my father's desertion."

"Any why should I mind?" She shrugged elegantly, drawing his gaze to the smooth skin of her bare shoulder.

"Well, he is your escort for the evening." Garren swallowed, tearing his gaze away.

"Yes, but there is no reason for him to forego Lady Elizabeth's company. Besides, I'm a big girl and fully capable of taking care of myself."

"Would you do me the honor of this dance, milady?" He bowed to her.

"Of course, milord," she said, her smile suspiciously sweet.

He'd found his eyes following her movements as she danced with his father and felt heat course through his veins. Now, he was painfully aware of the warmth and slight pressure of her hand resting on his arm as he guided her to the dance floor. Inhaling the soft floral fragrance that swirled around her, Garren struggled with the urge to pull her close in his arms. It seemed he was aware of every minute movement about this lady. She was confident and graceful, from the turn of her head to the sway of her hips.

He was immediately contrite. He was a married man and had no business letting his mind wander in this direction—but he couldn't think of anything else.

The music began, and his hand touched her waist as the dance prescribed. Did she feel the warmth pass between them? Was she aware of his response? He looked to her for a reaction and found her nibbling on her lower lip in concentration.

"Do you have difficulty with the steps, milady?"

"A little. I've not danced this one much."

"Have no fear; I'll not be stepping on those dainty toes of yours." He smiled as her pink tongue moistened her lower lip nervously.

"I fear that if you do, there'll be a howl fit to bring the rafters down on your head."

He chuckled, releasing a little of the tension between them. Glancing down he inquired, "Are you without shoes, then?"

"Oh, no. I'm wearing sandals, but my toes are still vulnerable."

"I shall endeavor to avoid trampling them."

The last musical note ended and Garren bowed over her hand. Tucking it into his elbow, he escorted her away from the other dancers, who were preparing for another set. "Would you care for another glass of punch?"

"Oh yes. It's terribly warm, isn't it?"

He walked her over, near the doors that opened onto the gardens. "You should be able to catch a breeze while I fetch our drinks."

Jocelyn watched as he threaded his way through the crowd of people, stopping now and then to greet a friend. It wasn't the heat of the room that caused the warmth to fill her body. No, it was the look on Garren's face; it could melt lead. A small thrill raced along her spine. Even though she wasn't thin as a rail, he still found her attractive. A bit of anger colored her mood. He didn't know she was his wife. Would he still have the same reaction to her? Or was it just the rush of the forbidden?

She felt a tap on her arm and turned to find the thin, pointed face of Charles Martin. He'd introduced himself earlier, and she'd found him repulsive. His red-rimmed gaze stared back at her. She moved a step away from him, uneasy. "Yes?" The chill in her voice did not deter the man's advance.

"I was wondering, milady, would you care to take a turn in the gardens? 'Tis unbearably warm in here this eve." His brandied breath surrounded her and made her wince.

Jocelyn moved back a step more. *I'd rather take a turn with a snake.* "No, thank you, Lord Martin," she scoffed and turned to walk to the crowd and Garren.

His hand gripped her arm, stopping her retreat. She jerked away, any pretense of politeness gone. "You've had too much to drink. Go somewhere and sleep it off." The words came out a rough whisper.

His pointed face mottled with rage, he growled. "I'll have my revenge on Garren first." He wrapped a thin arm around her waist. "Now, come quietly."

Not wanting to make a ruckus—she didn't know exactly what would happen in this time period—Jocelyn kicked her foot out, trying to make contact with his shins. When that didn't work, she wiggled her body, attempting to loosen his hold. For a tall, thin man he sure was strong, she thought. She caught a glimpse of Garren as Charles turned her toward the door. He hadn't seen her. With one last effort to free herself, she threw her body back against Charles, dislodging her wig and mask.

To hell with propriety. She took a deep breath, intent on screaming for Garren, but Charles's hand clamped over her mouth. The arm around her waist tightened, forcing out her indrawn breath. He pulled her roughly through the door and out into the night.

Hands encumbered by two glasses of punch, Garren cautiously threaded his way back through the crowd. Glancing at the window where Lady Pebbles awaited him, he swore under his breath. Damn! Charles again. A fat nobleman in a blue outfit jostled him, and punch slopped onto his hand. Garren swore.

When next he looked up, the spot where Lady Pebbles had stood was empty. He caught a glimpse of long, golden blond hair as the woman disappeared through the garden doors.

"And I thought she had more sense than to take up with *him*." He frowned. "Damn fickle woman."

Chapter Nine

Jocelyn's breath came out in forced whooshes with each jarring motion of the horse. As she dangled over the side of the animal, the blood rushed to her head and started a pounding equal to the worst migraine she'd ever had. Her legs had lost all feeling and flopped limply against its heaving side. The pressure of Charles's hand against the small of her back was the only thing, she was sure, that kept her from falling head-first to the ground.

"You're a dead man when I get off this beast," she gasped, each word punctuated with a whoosh of breath. She knew he couldn't hear her voice over the sound of his mount's hooves, and a perverse part of her wished that he could. He obviously didn't realize with whom he was dealing; but he would soon, and he would rue the day.

The horse careered off the road. Jocelyn felt her

body shift and slide, her hips moving to the right of center. She could find nothing but Charles's leg to grab for purchase, so she dug her fingers into the flesh just above the top of his boot.

"Damn, woman! Don't pinch my leg off!" He pried her fingers from his person, easing back on the reins, slowing his steed to a bone-jarring trot.

Finally, Charles brought the horse to a stop. The smell of pines and damp earthen decay told Jocelyn that she was in a densely wooded area. Here and there, moonbeams penetrated the darkness.

Charles dismounted and pulled Jocelyn from the saddle. The minute her feet touched the ground, needles of pain shot up her legs, and without his support she crumpled to the ground.

"Come on, get up." He led the horse to a small bush and tied the reins to it.

"Jerk." Squinting, she followed his shadowy outline through the darkness.

He came back over and yanked her up by the arm. "Come on." He released her arm, moving back to the horse.

"Ow!" And again, she found herself sitting on the forest floor. "You idiot. My legs are asleep."

He scowled at her, untied a satchel from the horse and came back and pulled her up. Keeping hold of her, he dragged her toward a cottage set back in the shadows. He kicked the wooden door open and shoved her inside. Jocelyn tripped over the threshold and careened into something on the floor, landing on her backside in a cloud of dust raised by her undignified entrance.

In the brief silence, the scurrying of tiny feet was followed by Charles's staggering footstep. Revulsion clutched at her throat and she bit back the urge to scream. Great, she thought, a four-legged rodent and a two-legged one. For what more could a girl ask?

Charles's muttered curse accompanied the scraping of flint, and light flared as he lit a candle. The lone flame cast eerie shadows in the one-room cottage.

Jocelyn scanned the room as she untangled her legs from her long skirt. The hard-packed dirt floor beneath her could use a good sweeping, she thought, dusting off her hands.

She eyed the rickety cot in the darkened corner. The rat had, no doubt, taken refuge somewhere under it. A shudder shook her shoulders and she inched a little farther away.

The only other furnishings gracing the cottage were two stools. One lay turned over in the middle of the room, the other, rather worm-eaten, sat next to the cold, ash-filled hearth. An unpleasant mustiness clung to the shabby walls and tainted the air, making Jocelyn long for the freshness of the outdoors.

She turned her gaze on Charles and could tell by the red rimming his eyes that he was heartily drunk. So far, it seemed that every male in this century had a drinking problem. Everyone she saw was either holding his head, careful to avoid loud noises, or his eyes were bloodshot and watery. Boy, Alcoholics Anonymous would have a real challenge here, she thought.

She waited, wondering what he was up to and why. The silence stretched out before them. He placed the satchel on the floor, near his feet, and looked at her, saying nothing.

"Well, cowboy, what do you do now?" she muttered to herself.

His eyes narrowed. "What did you say?"

"Nothing." Jocelyn shifted on the floor, tucking her feet to the side. This guy was pathetic.

He reached into the satchel and brought out a length of rope, advancing on Jocelyn.

"Just what do you think you're going to do with that?" She scooted away from him.

Reaching out, he grabbed her wrist. Jocelyn lowered her head, sinking her teeth into the top of his hand.

He howled in pain. Digging his fingers into her hair, he pulled her head back, dislodging her teeth from his hand.

Drawing back her free arm, Jocelyn struck out, using her shoulder to power the punch that landed just below his left eye. She felt a numbing pain ricochet up her arm at the contact. Her head was jerked back with more force, and she felt the sting of his slap, her head snapping to the side.

Charles took advantage of the moment and tied her wrists in front of her, then hauled her to the rickety cot in the corner. Shoving her down on it, he pulled the stool up and sat down.

"What in the blue blazes are you doing?" Jocelyn demanded, bringing her tied hands up to rub the sting from her cheek.

"Retribution," Charles sneered.

"Retribution? I've never done anything to you. Heavens, I just met you this evening." She let her hands drop to her lap.

"It's not what *you've* done, but your husband, Garren."

He has me mistaken for someone else, Jocelyn thought with relief. No one besides Richard knew she was Garren's wife. "I hate to tell you this, but you've got me confused with someone else. I'm not married."

"Why is it everyone thinks me so stupid?"

"Possibly your actions," Jocelyn muttered, fighting the insane urge to giggle at the picture Charles presented on the stool. His bony knees rose a few inches above the cot, his collar was limp, and his eye had begun to turn a delightful shade of blue.

His gaze narrowed. Reaching into a satchel, he pulled out a bottle, opened it, took a long drink, and replaced the stopper.

"I overheard Lord Warrick tell Lady Tinsbury in the garden that you're Garren's new bride." He replaced the bottle in the bag. "So, you see, I know who you are. It's useless to play those games with me."

Why was Charles set on retribution? For what?

"So you know we're married. What's that got to do with anything?" She adjusted her weight, and a tingling of blood circulated down to the numb fingers of her left hand.

"You truly don't know what kind of man you've married?" Charles said in disbelief. "He seduced my sister. Took advantage of her vulnerability. And then he refused to offer for her." He paused. When Jocelyn just stared back at him, he rushed on. "Her reputation is ruined. No man of any station will wed her. She won't leave the house because she's snubbed wherever she goes. And your husband is responsible."

"Wait a minute. You're seeking retribution because of a fling Garren had with your sister?" Disbelief wrinkled her brow.

He reached for the bottle again, removed the stopper, and took another drink.

"Your husband is a rake and a deflowerer of women."

"And that's so unusual?" Weren't all men the same, no matter the century?

He gave her a quizzical look. "We'll find out if you say the same thing when it's you whose reputation is ruined."

This sorry excuse for a man was whining over his sister's bedroom activities. This was unreal, she thought.

"And you think this will ruin me?" She shook her head.

Charles nodded. "It will appear that you left the ball with me. The whispering will start and then you'll know what my sister Melody has suffered."

"Buddy, I think you're a sandwich short of a picnic."

Charles gave her a confused look and drank again from the bottle. "Sometimes, I don't understand what you say. You're a strange one." He eyed her as he stopped the bottle.

"You're not the first to notice that," she mumbled.

"What?" He rose to his feet unsteadily, moving nearer.

"Never mind. I still don't understand what you're so upset about."

"You don't understand?" he asked in honor. "What kind of woman are you?" He ran a thin hand through his hair. "Your husband seduced my sister. She was still in mourning over the loss of her husband. He took advantage of her vulnerable state."

"Whoa! You called Garren a deflowerer. If your sister is a widow, the flower was picked before Garren came along." Jocelyn shook her head in disgust.

"Shut up."

"You, sir, are in need of a padded cell with an 'I love me' jacket to go along with it," she muttered.

"And stop that muttering. You're driving me mad."

"Ha, driving you mad? That's a short putt; you're rimming the cup now."

"No more!" He took another swig from the bottle, and eyed her with obvious annoyance.

"We'll see how your husband feels when *his* name is whispered around drawing rooms. Melody can't go anywhere without those whispers. She never receives visitors, none come calling. Invitations to balls or musicales have stopped. And me," he snorted. "Why, I can't even get into my club. They've closed the doors to me. And all because of Garren."

She rolled her eyes heavenward. *Lord, he's pathetic.* She couldn't feel sorry for him; she had little respect for men who were so weak that they used alcohol to bolster their sagging courage and blamed others for their own shortcomings.

Charles fell silent as he sat on the stool, gazing at the bottle in his hand. "It's not fair. If you have money, you get more. If you have none, you get none. Luck is only for the rich. And Garren is rich. Every time he sits down to play cards, I watch my winnings travel to his side of the table. Then he humiliates me more by telling me I haven't the knack for cards. Always says in that condescending voice of his, 'Charles, mayhap you should sit out this hand.' Acts like he's trying to do me a favor."

Jocelyn listened to this and found herself wondering exactly what kind of man Garren was. She had felt a strong physical pull when they first met at the ball. And when his hand had rested at her waist, her stomach had done a flip-flop. *No, don't*

136

*fall into that trap again, Jocelyn. You always think
the best of everyone and get burned for it. He's just
as his actions indicate, an inconsiderate jerk, and
the sooner you're back where you belong the better.*

Charles took another long drink from the bottle, stoppered it, and carefully placed it back in his satchel, then moved the bag aside. As he stood up, his legs wobbled beneath him and he fell. Jocelyn scooted over as he tumbled onto the cot. The decrepit bed gave way under the sudden weight. She started to rise, but he grabbed her wrists. "You're not going anywhere."

Off-balance, she toppled onto him. She brought her knee up, trying to brace herself. But her knee instead glanced off his groin and, with a howl, he shoved her away. She landed near the hearth, overturning the stool.

"Are you trying to unman me?" Charles moaned.

"You'd have to be a man first," Jocelyn spat as she struggled to stand up.

With an animal roar he rose and staggered toward her. She grabbed the stool in her bound hands and, when he came within range, swung it as hard as she could at his head. His arm came up, but not in time to deflect the blow. As the stool made contact with his forehead it broke, sending its shattered pieces flying across the room. He threw himself at her, and they landed hard on the floor. She struggled beneath him, but he was too heavy.

Then a gentle snore blew into her ear, and Jocelyn nearly laughed aloud. The silly fool had passed out.

It didn't take long to untie the rope, using her teeth. Being careful not to awaken Charles, she carefully rolled him over on his stomach and tied his hands, using the length of rope that had been around her wrists.

The snores became deeper. He's out like a light, she thought.

She crouched at his feet and pulled off one of his boots, waiting after she got it off to see if he roused. The snoring continued. She removed the other boot. Looking around the room, she spotted the satchel sitting on the floor and, finding another length of rope in it, she bound his ankles.

Hiking her dress up to her knees, Jocelyn sat down on the stool Charles had occupied earlier, quickly slipping off her sandals and pulling on his boots. Cursing under her breath when the shoes proved too big, she pulled them off. Snatching Charles's necktie from his neck, she used her teeth to rip it in half. Stuffing the toe of each boot with the material, she donned them again. They made a clumping sound as she left the cottage.

Locating Charles's horse, she grabbed the reins, stuffed her foot into the stirrup and swung up into the saddle. She still wasn't completely comfortable with horseback riding, but right now she didn't have any choice. Nudging the animal, she set out in what she hoped was the direction from which they had come.

"What the bloody hell do you mean, Charles has likely kidnapped my wife? Jocelyn is at Spenceworth."

Richard cast him a sheepish look.

"Isn't she?" Garren hissed.

His father took him by the elbow, edging into an alcove. "No, I brought her with me."

"What? To what end?" Garren struggled to keep his voice low.

"Garren, there's no time for this. You must go

after them. If word of this gets out . . . your wife alone with another man . . . Charles especially."

"Why did you bring her here?"

"I only thought to bring the two of you together. Something you seem reluctant to do. Listen Garren, there's not much time." His father's grip tightened on Garren's arm. "Charles has been drinking. There's no way to judge what he'll do. You must go after them, now."

"Aye. I'm going, but I'm not finished with you yet." With rapid strides, Garren left the ball behind, passing through the gardens to the stable.

How could he not have recognized her swaying hips? And her voice, now that he thought on it. Why had she played this game? No doubt, his father was at the root of it all. Anger bubbled within him as another thought struck home. They were playing him for a fool.

Had his father let everyone in on the fact that he didn't know his own wife? Or was this a private joke shared with Jocelyn? When he found her, his wife could be assured of finding herself over his knee and receiving the sting of the palm of his hand.

But the thought of that rounded derriere draped over his lap cooled his anger and heated his loins. He hadn't recognized her because the woman had changed much in the short time of their marriage. She was now a bit slimmer, but she still had very womanly curves. He recalled the heat of her body and the heady attraction he'd felt.

"Bloody hell," he mumbled to his horse. "And Charles has laid hands on her."

The danger of her situation pressed in on Garren and he increased the pace of his mount.

He was thankful for the bright moon and clear

night. Leaving the estate behind, he turned his horse into the lane. He had no idea where to look for the missing pair. He knew that Charles had no property in the surrounding area. So where would he go to be alone? He looked down at the ground, but it was useless. Moonlight cast shadows over the uneven road, making it impossible to decipher fresh prints from those of the earlier traffic to the ball.

Worry for Jocelyn ate at him. Charles was not given to physical confrontations. He was a weak, sad man. The alcohol must have given him the false courage to kidnap her. But had it also made him violent? Garren put his terrified imaginings from his mind. He needed to concentrate on locating his wife and do so quickly, before the fool could do her harm.

The blush of the rising sun was just lightening the sky when Garren noted a set of prints leaving the main road for a trail off to the left.

He followed the tracks through the dense growth of the forest. A small, rundown cottage sat at the end of the track, deep in the woods.

Getting off his horse, he tethered it to a bush, keeping his gaze trained on the cottage. The place boasted no windows, only a door that hung crookedly from its leather hinges. Fighting the urge to rush in, Garren picked his way carefully to the door. With a gentle nudge, the door swung open, revealing the gloomy interior and a bootless Charles, bound hand and foot, snoring loudly on the floor.

Rage coursed through Garren's veins. With a final shove, the floor fell into the room with a loud crash.

"Where the hell is my wife?" he boomed at the

man trussed up on the floor. He nudged him none too gently with the hard toe of his boot.

"What . . . what do you want?" Charles mumbled, trying to roll over.

"Where's Jocelyn?" Garren braced his hands on his hips, his feet planted on either side of Charles's head.

Charles struggled a moment before he realized his hands and feet were tied. "Oh Lord, I don't know, nor do I care. Can you not untie me?" The whine in Charles' voice grated on Garren's nerves.

"What happened here? Who tied you up?" Garren demanded in a loud voice.

"Please," Charles begged, squinting his eyes against the pain, "Please, don't yell."

"Then tell me what's happened. How did you become tied up?"

"It must have been your wife," Charles said, his forehead creasing in confusion.

"My *wife*?"

"If you'll just untie me I'll be able to think better," Charles moaned.

Garren reached down and untied the rope at Charles's feet and pulled him to a standing position.

"Ow! Damn, that hurts." Charles gingerly stepped from one foot to another. "Where the hell are my boots?" He turned an accusing glare on Garren.

"How the bloody hell should I know? Why don't you tell me what happened here. Then, you can worry about your blasted boots." Garren gripped Charles' arm.

Charles jerked back from Garren's hold and gave him a one-eyed, angry glare. Garren arched his eyebrows in question and looked him up and down. Charles was dirty, his clothes wrinkled

141

from sleeping on the floor, and his hair was jutting out at strange angles around his head. A jagged scratch in his forehead was surrounded by smaller scratches with bits of wood splinters. Garren noted an eye that was blackened and puffed up, so much so that Charles couldn't open it.

"Who took Jocelyn from you?" That was the only solution that Garren could think of. Someone had taken Jocelyn from Charles, inflicting a great deal of damage in the process. And right now, he had to find out who, and where they went.

"No one took her."

"What?" Garren's mind fumbled with Charles' words. "Then what the hell happened to you?"

"Your crazed wife. That's what happened to me. She's as mad as a hatter, that one is, and you can have her. Now, will you untie my hands?" Charles had the temerity to glare at Garren.

Pondering Charles's words, Garren reached around and untied the ropes, then watched as Charles rubbed the feeling back into his hands. Charles put his fingers to his obviously pained head. The red outline of a full set of teeth marks stood out against the pale skin of his hand.

"She bit you?" Garren was more than a little surprised. His wife apparently was a kitten with claws.

"She did more than bite me." Charles rubbed at his hand. "She nearly unmanned me, hit me in the eye with her fist, cracked a chair against my head, tied me up, and stole my boots. I can tell you truly, Garren, any revenge I might have wanted to inflict on you, she'll do a better job of it than I. You've finally gotten what you deserve." He snorted as he attempted to tidy his clothes. "That woman's a hellcat."

Amused and shocked by his wife's ferocity, Garren forgot his rage at Charles. "Aye, you're right in that. She's just what I deserve," he said, a broad smile lighting his face. He turned to leave.

"Wait a minute. What's to happen to me? I've no boots, and she no doubt took my horse. How am I to get back to London?"

"That, Charles, is *your* problem," Garren called as he exited the cottage. "I've a wife you kidnapped to find. I haven't the time to deal with you now. And were I you, Charles, I'd pray I find her hale and hearty or what my wife did to you will feel like nothing."

Chapter Ten

Jocelyn went in circles for the first hour or so after she left the cottage and Charles. She had no idea where she was or which way to go, so she let the horse take the lead. He, at least, was not directionally challenged. They wandered through the forest, finally coming upon a track.

Jocelyn thought she would find herself close to civilization; but after a few hours along the trail, she realized that she was getting well and truly lost. Finally, exhaustion weighed down her eyelids.

The jingle of bells caught her attention, suddenly causing her eyelids to snap open. She guided the horse in the direction of the sound. Through the trees, she saw a glimmer of light and hoped, silently, that she hadn't come upon thieves or highwaymen. Some things never changed, and criminals scared her in any time.

Leaving the horse tethered, she made her way

toward the light. Then, stationing herself behind a large pine, she looked carefully at the camp.

A fire was burning and an old wagon sat beyond it. A swaybacked horse, with bells woven into its mane, stood off to the side, munching on grass. A bent silhouette shuffled in front of the fire.

"Ah, we meet again, do we, missy?" The voice crackled like old parchment.

Where had she heard it before?

"Come, join me at me fire, won't ye?" The woman's voice sparked a memory only half-forgotten.

"It's you!" she cried out, moving from behind the tree and walking toward the campfire.

"Of course," the woman replied. She gave Jocelyn a simple shrug.

"What are you doing here?" Jocelyn wasn't sure if she should feel relief or more fear. This woman was a little spooky.

"Came to help ye." The crone reached into the front of her wagon, pulling out a multicolored quilt.

"How did you know I needed help?" She was *definitely* spooky, Jocelyn amended.

"Have ye not been going in circles?" The woman shook out the quilt, laying it on the ground.

"Well yes, but how could you know that?" Jocelyn reached down, straightening a corner of the blanket. The withered woman gave her a speculative look.

"Ah, there's lots I know, missy."

"Like what?" Jocelyn braced her hands on her hips and waited as the strange woman paused to look at her.

"Like ye're here." She pointed to the ground. "And the other woman's there." She pointed vaguely into the air.

145

"But why?" Jocelyn implored her.

She shrugged. "Some things I know, though I don't know why. Some things I don't. I've learned to accept that." Crossing back to the wagon, she pulled two more blankets from the front. She handed one to Jocelyn, the other she laid on top of the quilt. "My name is Hilda." She proferred her hand to Jocelyn, who shook it limply.

"But I can't just accept this. I don't belong here. I need to get back."

Unconsciously, Jocelyn wrapped the blanket around her shoulders, suddenly aware that she'd been shivering.

"Well, come tomorrow, I might be able to tell ye the way back." Moving to the back of the wagon, the old woman pulled a cloth bag out and rummaged around before bringing out some cheese and bread.

"You know the way back?" Jocelyn couldn't help the eagerness in her voice. Her heart thumped rapidly in her chest.

Hilda bristled. "Not offhand, but maybe if I sleep on it—things just come to me in dreams, sometimes. Now, why don't ye have a little something to eat and sleep a spell, yerself, eh?" She placed the food on the blanket on the ground.

At the suggestion of sleep, fatigue swept over Jocelyn, and the thought of food and rest drew her like a magnet.

She ate, feeling her exhaustion overtaking her. She felt comfortable here, strangely protected. The night's horrors faded. Before she closed her eyes she asked, "You'll still be here in the morning, won't you? No disappearing, right?"

The old woman just gave a cackle. "Old Hilda'll

146

be right here when ye wake, missy, and no mistake about that."

She folded her arms and smiled at her, showing several broken yellow teeth. Still, the smile was quite motherly.

"Do you know why I'm here?" Jocelyn asked sleepily.

"Tomorrow. We'll talk about it tomorrow."

"Why did you rush off in Ramsgil?"

"I got other things to see to, too. I can't always be staying around in one place," Hilda said. She covered the remaining food and put it back in the wagon.

Jocelyn just nodded. She settled on the quilt, pulling the blanket over her shoulders. Sleep claimed her the moment her eyes closed.

"Time to wake up missy."

Jocelyn's shoulder was shaken until she opened her eyes. She was stiff from sleeping on the ground, and she stretched and rose slowly. Ah yes, the joys of camping, she remembered. She'd done a bit of it in her youth. She stepped outside the little camp to find a bit of privacy. Answering the call of nature in the great outdoors was embarrassing enough, but add a long skirt and well, it became an exercise in humility. Thank heavens she only planned to do it this once.

She returned to the campsite to find that Hilda had hitched her swaybacked old mare to the wagon and tied Charles's horse to the back. Chunks of bread and cheese lay on the blanket Jocelyn had slept on. A tin with water was set next to the food. Jocelyn's stomach growled, and she ate the meager breakfast as she watched Hilda affectionately stroke the mare.

It was evident that the withered crone was getting on in years. Jocelyn wondered how she managed living like this, in such reduced circumstances. "Thank you for breakfast."

"Aye." Hilda looked up from the horse. "Don't eat much, do ye?"

"No." Jocelyn gathered up the leftovers, placing them in the bag. "I wish there was something I could do for you. I mean, in return for your help."

" 'Tis what I was called to do."

Despite her grandmotherly nature, Jocelyn was afraid that Hilda was definitely a bit odd. "What do you mean 'called to do?' " She handed the bag of food to the other woman.

"Ye ain't never heard of people getting called to do something?" Hilda cackled.

"Well, yes, of course, but usually it has to do with religious life." Jocelyn folded the blanket she'd used, giving it to Hilda before picking up the quilt. She gave it a vigorous shaking, folded it, and gave it back to the woman. Hilda had stopped laughing.

"Humph. And ye're supposed to be so smart. People get callings to do all sorts of things." She packed the last of her things in the wagon.

"So, what's your calling?" Jocelyn watched Hilda shuffle around to her own horse and rub its neck.

She looked to Jocelyn. "To help lost souls when they get found."

Jocelyn rolled her eyes. "That doesn't make any sense."

"Ye were lost, weren't ye?" Hilda grinned.

Patience, Jocelyn reminded herself. "Well, yes, in a way." She nodded.

"And ye was found, weren't ye?" The old

woman's gaze locked with Jocelyn's, her grin disappearing.

"What do you mean 'found?' "

"Well, ye know where ye are, don't ye?" Hilda's thin eyebrow raised in challenge at her enigmatic question.

"Yes." Jocelyn hedged, not liking the direction this conversation was taking.

"So, ye were a lost soul that's now found." Hilda shrugged. "Simple."

"Sure." Just humor her, Jocelyn thought. Maybe she'll have something useful to impart. "So, how do you help us?"

"I tells ye what ye need to know, of course." Hilda shuffled to the side of the wagon and pulled herself up on the seat. With a glance at Jocelyn, she nodded to the empty space next to her. "Come along. I'll get you home."

"Well, how do you know what we need to know?" Jocelyn walked around the front of the mare. Pulling her skirt up, she climbed aboard.

"Most usually why ye were lost." Hilda shook the reins and the mare started plodding along, jerking the wagon along, heading out of the forested area.

"This is ridiculous." Jocelyn gripped the edge of the vehicle as it bounced along the bumpy terrain. "I don't want to know *why* I was lost, I want to know how to get back to where I belong."

"Mayhap, *this* is where ye belong. Ye thought of that?" Hilda raised an eyebrow, leveling a stern look at Jocelyn.

"No. I don't belong here." Jocelyn bit her lip and stared straight ahead. She couldn't belong here. She had . . . well, what *did* she have at home?

Hilda looked over at her. "Ye seem pretty sure, but ye're here, ain't ye?"

"Yeah. Whatever. The question is, how do I get back?" Jocelyn gritted her teeth. What right did this woman have to tell her where she belonged?

"Easy."

"Easy?" Jocelyn was shocked. "Then, tell me how. Tell me how to get back!" A sudden elation filled her. Hope finally blossomed in her heart. She could get back to where she belonged. She had been afraid it would be as impossible as her trip here had seemed.

"All ye have to do is sit again on the block on the green in Ramsgil—"

"That's all?" Jocelyn interrupted.

"—at the same time as the other woman does." A small grin teased the corners of Hilda's lips. "Ye both have been set on roads to happiness. So ye both must sit at the same time—and both of ye must want to go back."

Her euphoria evaporated. "The same time? How will I know when she sits there? And how will I know if she wants to return?"

"I don't know that." Hilda's apparent unconcern snapped Jocelyn's patience.

"Excuse me, oh wise one. You don't know? What good will that do me? Am I supposed to sit there forever?"

Hilda gave her a peevish look. "Could be. Could be she'll never sit there again. Could be she's not even in Ramsgil anymore, that she's already happy where she is. Who knows?"

"Who knows, indeed!" Jocelyn struck her leg in helpless frustration. "You mean to tell me that going home is easy. All I have to do is sit on that piece of wood at the same time as this Nelwina does, but there's no way to tell when this Nelwina person is going to sit on the block?"

"Right."

Jocelyn's shoulders slumped as despair flooded her. She'd gotten her hopes up only to have them dashed. All so quickly that it was almost unbearable.

Hilda added, almost absently, "Could be that a good lightning storm might be a sign. Don't know, but that's a magical time. Lots happens then."

Jocelyn moaned. "So, I just have to sit on the block during a lightning storm? And pray Nelwina does the same?"

"Aye." Hilda's eyes brightened and she grinned. Jocelyn got the feeling the old woman was enjoying this.

"With the kind of luck I've had, I'll probably get struck by lightning."

Hilda's extensive knowledge of herbal medicine, which she said had been passed down from her mother, helped pass the time as they traveled. She pointed out different vegetation, explaining its uses.

They had been making their way for about two hours when Hilda stopped the wagon.

"Untie yer horse."

"Why?" Jocelyn glanced around in confusion.

"Ye want to get back to Spenceworth, don't ye?"

"Yes. I suppose so." Where else could she go?

"Well, get on yer horse and follow that trail. It leads right where ye want to be." She pointed to a track that Jocelyn hadn't noticed.

"But what about you? You're all alone."

Hilda gave a cackle. "Nay, missy. I'm not alone. I'll be meetin' up with me friends. I'll stay with them till I'm needed again."

"Don't they worry about you when you're gone?"

Hilda squinted at the trees ahead of her. "Nay. They know I've a calling."

"Other souls to find?" Jocelyn raised her eyebrows.

Hilda smiled enigmatically.

"I don't feel right just leaving you like this."

"Be gone with ye now." The old woman nudged her. "I've places to go."

Jocelyn jumped down from the wagon. Untying Charles's horse, she brought it around to the front of the wagon and looked up at her withered benefactress.

"Are you sure you wouldn't like some food, or more blankets?" Well, she should try one last time to give this woman something. She *had* provided Jocelyn with at least the hope of one day returning to her own time.

The old woman shook her head. "I've enough. But remember this, though, missy. Ye may not want to return to where ye were. Things change, and usually for a reason. Perhaps ye might consider that ye're better suited where you are now."

Jocelyn nodded. It was wonderful of the old woman to think that the world worked in such mysterious ways, but all she'd seen in this time was a husband who'd ignored her, a man who'd tried to ruin her, and many conventions that seemed confining and silly. Still . . . she thought of her husband's eyes.

Hilda smiled over at her and snapped the reins, sending her horse into a trot. "Ye'll see, my dear. Ye'll see."

"A little more hot water please, Dulcey," Jocelyn rested her head against the side of the bathing tub. She had arrived home almost two hours before. All she had wanted was a nice hot bath and clean clothes.

Dulcey poured a bucket of hot water into the

tub. "Will ye be needing anything else, milady?"

"No. I think I'll just soak here for a while." Jocelyn smiled at the maid. "Go ahead and run downstairs. I'm fine."

"Yes, milady." The girl bobbed in a curtsy and quickly left the room.

Adjusting the folded towel beneath her neck, Jocelyn smiled as she recalled her homecoming. The stableboy's eyes had nearly popped out of his head when he saw her enter the stables wearing her prehistoric ballgown, Charles's boots, and leading a horse that was not her own. The lad had cast furtive looks her way as he'd taken the reins.

"I'll take him now, milady," he'd said quietly, his gaze darting everywhere but to her face.

She had then clumped across the drive to the front door and rung the bell. Spalding had opened the door, and with a totally straight face, had said, "Milady. How nice to have you home."

Now sluicing warm water over her arms, Jocelyn chuckled, recalling how she'd swept past him—as much as Charles's cumbersome boots would allow—and entered the hall. And when she glanced over her shoulder, she saw Spalding's lips lift in the first small grin she'd ever seen on him.

The racket of her entry had alerted Mrs. Cowan, and that woman had nearly run down the stairs to her.

"My, oh, my. What's happened to ye, Lady Jocelyn? Where have ye been? And why are ye wearing men's boots? Is Lord Garren with ye?" she asked, straining her neck to look behind Jocelyn for her husband.

It was then that Jocelyn had taken control. "Mrs. Cowan," she'd said, "Would you see that a bath is brought up to my room immediately? All I want is to get clean and find fresh clothing."

Jocelyn had climbed the stairs, then, with Mrs. Cowan firing questions at her from behind. Once in Jocelyn's room, the woman had taken a determined stand. "I'll get yer bath for ye, after ye tell me what's happened. Lord Warrick sent a message from Tinsbury that he'd be staying indefinitely, and we should send word when ye and Lord Spenceworth returned."

Knowing she would have no peace before she did, Jocelyn acceded. She had told the housekeeper of her encounter with Charles, leaving out only her time with Hilda. She didn't think Mrs. Cowan was ready for stories of time-travel and strange old women.

Straightening in the tub, Jocelyn raised a leg, running a soapy rag along it, wondering where her husband was now. Was he angry with his father and her because of their prank? Had he gone out in search of her—or had he thought himself better rid of her? And if he had gone in search of her, had he found the cottage Charles had taken her to? She paused in her thoughts. She didn't know her husband at all. What would he have done to Charles if he did stumble upon him? She had no way of knowing the answers.

She should at least send word to Richard at Tinsbury and let him know she was safe at home. *He* would surely be worried. If only she could get word to Garren, but who knew where he was?

Thinking of Garren, she remembered how he had looked the night before in his black formal attire. She wouldn't consider him classically handsome, not like the male models in the New York magazines. No, he was ruggedly handsome. He likely spent a great deal of time out of doors. His skin carried a golden hue, and his dark blond hair had streaks highlighting it where the sun had bleached the color away.

And those eyes! Oh, they could do a number on a girl in a minute. His hands had intrigued her, too. They were large, capable hands with nicely tapered fingers and smooth, clean nails. They hadn't looked soft, simply gentle. And when he had touched her waist in the dance, she wanted to melt from their heat.

At first she had mistaken the purpose of his gallantry, but then she realized that it was simply eighteenth-century charm. He had been careful to stay within what seemed the bounds of correct society etiquette.

She wondered which Garren she would meet next, the cold, uncommunicative kidnapper, or the warm, charming aristocrat.

Mrs. Cowan entered, "Milady, are ye finished? I've had Cook fix ye a bit to eat." The woman bustled around the room, picking up Jocelyn's discarded clothing. "And after ye eat, I'll see ye settled in bed. Ye've been through so much, ye'll need yer rest."

The housekeeper's words pulled Jocelyn from her musings.

"I don't need to rest, Mrs. Cowan." She poured a bucket of cool, clean water over herself and stepped from the tub. "Would you have Spalding send a message to Tinsbury Hall, informing Lord Warrick that I am home safe and sound?"

"Yes, milady. But are ye sure ye shouldn't take a nap, at least? Any lady would be exhausted after such an ordeal."

Mrs. Cowan's concerned gaze touched Jocelyn and she smiled. "I'm sure. And thank you for having Cook prepare something for me."

"After we get ye dressed, I'll pop down and get it. And I'll have Spalding send yer message."

An hour later, Jocelyn entered the library, leaving the doors open as she took a ledger from the desk. Baskins had finally allowed her access to one of the older ledgers, but even that had taken Richard's intervention. Now that she had returned, it seemed silly to put off business. Maybe she could do some good while she was here.

She glanced up as one of the servants walked by the door. She liked being able to look out into the entry hall and see the people moving back and forth. It made her feel less isolated.

She itched to get at Baskins' other ledgers, to prepare a financial statement, but had to content herself with working with these old entries. It was amazing the detail and history that could be found in them. Over the last few weeks she felt that she had gotten to know Garren's grandfather—all through the purchases entered in his ledger. It was apparent that the staff members here were treated more as family than as employees.

It was nearing the dinner hour when a banging on the front door brought Spalding hustling from the back of the house and past the room where Jocelyn worked.

The smash of wood against wood vibrated in the hall as the front door flew open and against the wall. Jocelyn glanced up and saw the shadow of a man cast across the hall outside. Spalding backed past the door, and from where she sat, Jocelyn could swear the servant's eyes were wide with surprise. He was apparently not used to people barging into the manor.

"Spalding, I need a bath, food and a fresh horse. Quickly, man!" It was Garren's familiar voice that rang through the house, and Jocelyn's pulse quickened. Quickly, she folded the paper she'd been working on, put it in the ledger and replaced the book in the drawer.

"Certainly, milord," Spalding's voice came in reply. The butler had regained his composure.

Garren walked by the open door to the library. She heard three footfalls as he passed, a long silence, and then the rapid tattoo of his heels as he retraced his steps.

He stepped through the opened doors. "Just where the bloody hell have you *been?* I've been scouring the countryside for you since last night."

Well, this certainly wasn't the welcome Jocelyn had expected, and it hurt. She'd convinced herself that her reunion with this man would be different. "I'm surprised you bothered."

"You're my wife. Of course I'd bother."

Jocelyn looked him over. A dark shadow of an incoming beard lent him a rather dangerous air, matching his apparent mood. His rumpled dirty clothes added to the overall effect. She disregarded it. "Funny, you didn't appear to feel that way when you left me here."

She watched as anger bubbled to the surface, tinging his face red and firing his eyes.

"I had my reasons." Garren folded his arms across his chest and glared at her.

"Not very good ones, I'm sure." Turning away from him, Jocelyn tried to rein in her own temper.

"It's not for you to question me." His chin tilted as he gave her a look of challenge.

"Oh, so I'm just the little wife?" Moving from behind the desk, she planted her hands on her hips, tipping her chin a little higher in defiance.

"'Do as you're told,'" she mimicked. "Is that what you expect when you buy a wife? Well think again, buddy." She advanced on him. "I don't need a condescending, overblown male in my life. I can manage quite well without one." Jocelyn spat each word and stood within inches of him when she finished. She was slightly disconcerted when she had to tilt her head back to glare into his eyes. Her old body had been taller. She was used to seeing more than the buttons on a man's shirt when she looked straight at him. Being short definitely had its disadvantages.

"Ah yes, you *don't need* a man. So why did you run off with Charles?" He glared down his nose at her.

"Oh, please. If you'd been able to find the cottage Charles took me to, you'd know I didn't go voluntarily." She backed away, suddenly unhappy that he'd suspect she wanted another man.

"I found the cottage," he said, his voice lowering to a more normal level. He dropped his arms to his sides.

"And what did you find? Was Charles sitting there having tea and crumpets?" She couldn't help the sarcasm that dripped from her words. "Did it appear that he had gotten what he wanted?"

"No, it didn't," Garren said. "When I found him he was still bound hand and foot. He looked like he'd tangled with a tiger and lost. Miserably." The beginnings of a smile lifted the corners of his lips.

Jocelyn watched in fascination as the anger left his face; it was replaced by amusement. Good Lord, but he was handsome. "He was still tied up?" She sat in one of the two chairs before the hearth. "So what did you do to him?" She couldn't wait to hear what vengeance her husband had exacted.

His amusement bubbled up. "I untied him

and let him go." Garren sat down in the chair beside her.

"You what?" Jocelyn felt completely let down. "That idiot kidnapped me, and all you did was untie him?" Chivalry was definitely dead.

"Jocelyn, I didn't know what happened. And you punished him enough. He'll never tangle with you again—I can vouch for that. He was humiliated." He looked over at her. "Also, he was thoroughly convinced I deserved such a terror. I left him at the cottage in his stockinged feet, without a horse. He'll have to walk to the nearest village bootless. I think that humiliation is an excellent punishment."

"Well, he deserved it. And more." Jocelyn folded her arms, fighting the smile that threatened her anger.

"It was clever of you to take his boots." Garren's brown eyes lit with warmth and admiration.

"I couldn't very well ride in my sandals. Besides, I didn't want him coming after me." Dropping her hands in her lap, she looked down at them before gazing back at Garren.

"He was well and truly trussed up like a Christmas goose." Garren's lips stretched into a smile.

"I doubt he'd fit in the oven."

Jocelyn looked deep into Garren's eyes, and warmth stole over her. His eyes twinkled, his lips lifted in a smile, and a rumble of laughter worked its way out. She smiled, and the next minute they were both chuckling. It escalated to hearty laughter, bringing tears to both their eyes.

"Oven or no, I think Charles got a serious roasting with your treatment, love." Garren wiped his eyes.

His mild English accent made the endearment sound sweeter, and Jocelyn's heart did a flip-flop.

Garren sobered, concern filling his voice. "But

tell me, are *you* fine? Charles did not harm you? I was worried." He reached a hand to her face, lightly skimming his finger along her jaw, sending bolts of desire through Jocelyn.

She gave a nervous laugh, moving out of range of his finger. "No, the silly fool. And he was an inept kidnapper." She was amazed at how quickly his anger had evaporated, replaced with laughter and then concern. This was a man who was ruled by his passion.

"Aye. And not a very good judge of victims, I think." Garren smiled again and Jocelyn felt like butter in the hot sun.

Needing to put distance between them to gather her composure, she jumped to her feet. "Shall I see if your bath is ready?"

"Spalding is seeing to it." he said and she saw that he was staring at her. There was something in his eyes that made her shiver. This was not the same man who had bought her in Ramsgil and deposited her with nary a word. There had been attraction before, she had sensed a hint of it, but now there was more.

Was it respect? She couldn't tell.

All she could tell was, if the way he was looking at her was any indication, he was thinking the same things about her that she'd dreamed about him. But she was inexperienced, and without a doubt she knew that he was not.

Suddenly, she felt shy and helpless.

Chapter Eleven

Garren climbed the stairs to his room, humming under his breath. Yes, he looked forward to the evening before him. For now, though, he needed a bath.

As he passed by the open door to Jocelyn's room, he heard the splash of water. Stopping, he pushed back the door and found Spalding overseeing the filling of his bath tub.

"Spalding, what goes on here?" Garren stared at the large basin, surprised. "Why is my tub here? It should be in the master's room."

Spalding turned from placing several towels on a small table and met Garren's gaze. "It was moved in here upon your departure, milord. I didn't think you would object. If you would prefer, I'll have it moved back."

"No." With a dismissive wave of his hand, Garren stepped farther into the room. "It's fine here."

The faint scent of jasmine permeated the room. As he inhaled the delicate fragrance, one he now associated with Jocelyn after smelling it on her in the library, Garren's gaze fell on the bath. Did the tub retain the warmth of her body? He moved to it, running his hand along its high back, searching for some sensuous warmth. Just the thought of his body sharing the same space as hers heated his blood and brought a heaviness to his loins.

"Very good, milord." Spalding moved around Garren. "I'll see that your robe is brought from your room."

The butler's words reached Garren, but his thoughts weren't on his clothing. No, they were on his wife—and her clothes were not involved.

The butler closed the door quietly. The click of the latch dissolved Garren's fevered imagining.

Shaking his head, he chuckled. As a young boy, he had never understood why his grandfather had commissioned such a large tub. As a man full grown, he now appreciated his relative's foresight. With a smile, he recalled the muffled laughter and splashing that had come from the master's room when his mother's father had been alive. As a child, he'd always wondered what was going on. Now, he had some idea.

Stripping off his dirty clothing, Garren slid into the tub. Steam rose from the water, surrounding him as he rested his head on the metal rim. His eyes closed and images of his wife played beneath his lids.

He saw her again—plump, dirty, unkempt and ferocious in Ramsgil. Then he saw her as Lady Pebbles, the first lady of fashion, slim and alluring. Yet, today when he'd returned, she had been shy and nervous, too. Her eyes were the windows to her emotions, flashing in anger, sparkling with laughter, and shimmering with intelligence. And beneath all those emotions lay an enticing innocence, and that he pondered. In buying a bride, this was not what he had expected.

Opening his eyes, he straightened in the tub. She was a woman, married twice now, and therefore experienced in the ways of men. But he saw no hint of that experience. He had not asked why Haslett had sold her. He couldn't see himself asking her now, though he wondered more than ever.

Had Jocelyn taken a lover? He couldn't see her having been happy with Haslett, and he hadn't exactly been attentive to her needs after he'd bought her. Damn, he hadn't expected to care. But if she had taken a lover, would she seem so shy and innocent? He shook his head in consternation. He had no answers for the questions plaguing him.

Lathering a rag, he scrubbed his arms and chest with brisk motions. Sluicing water upon himself to remove the soap, he thought of his plans for the evening. This would not be her first time, he knew, but with a shrug, he decided that there was little joy in initiating a virgin. Like as not her husband had been inept at the niceties of the bedroom, and in that sense, he would be her first. Perhaps that explained her innocence, he decided. Settling back against the tub, he closed his eyes and relaxed.

Placing the ledger she'd been working on back in the top drawer, Jocelyn left the library to change for dinner, grateful Garren hadn't caught on to what she was working at.

She'd felt so smug when she'd first come here, thinking that these eighteenth-century people couldn't possibly be as intelligent as she. Upon examining the records, her smugness had fled.

Yes, after time with the old accounts, Jocelyn had been put in her place and humbled. Her knowledge might be more advanced, but it didn't necessarily apply in the eighteenth century. They managed here without benefit of computers or calculators, copy machines or fax machines. It was mind-boggling and even a little intimidating; she had developed a healthy respect for these people.

She had also become familiar with many names: those who had served and passed on, *and* those who had *been* served and passed on. A sad shiver ran up her spine thinking about the long dead past residents of this, knowing this was the only thing that marked their lives. An eerie feeling stole over her at the thought of her name appearing in one of the books.

Would it also be the only record that remained of her in her own time?

No. She shook off the idea and climbed the stairs.

The thought of sitting on the block in the middle of the green in Ramsgil for an indeterminate length of time was silly. But she believed Hilda. When the correct time came, she would know. She only hoped that the time would come when Nelwina shared Jocelyn's desire to return home. Jocelyn knew she herself would make the effort to return to her own era. No matter what. It was, after all, where she belonged.

Entering her room, she closed the door. She heard movement and she addressed her maid. "I think I'll wear the royal blue dress with the ecru lace."

"A good color, that," a deep voice answered her.

Gasping in alarm, Jocelyn spun around. She found herself face-to-face with Garren, her eyes rounding in surprise, color flooding her cheeks with embarrassment. "What're you doing in my room?"

"I'm bathing . . . if it's escaped your notice." His calm, masculine voice shimmied along her nerve endings, the boyish smile he threw her over his shoulder casting her into oblivion.

"Yes, well, I can see that." *And more*, she thought. Her gaze glided over his water-slicked skin, snagging on the breadth of his shoulders and the play of muscles of his back. She took a step forward, the need to feel the warmth and texture of his skin taking control.

"Come, wash my back as a good wife."

"As a *good* wife?" His allure of a moment ago evaporated. The chauvinist. "You're a big boy. Bathe yourself."

She turned to leave, but his next words stopped her.

" 'Tis not necessary to turn from me, Jocelyn."

Dare she turn and confront him? She shook her head. It was one thing to see a movie star's naked behind on the screen, but quite another to be within an arm's length of a flesh-and-blood man. One she'd already felt more than a little attraction to.

Nope. She'd best get while the getting was good.

"Jocelyn, the water grows cold."

"I'll just come back later to change."

"Nonsense. Just wash my back and then you can change. Or would you care to bathe with me?"

Reaching a shaking hand toward the door handle, intent on escape, Jocelyn froze at Garren's firm voice. "Jocelyn, come here and wash my back. You need not play the virgin with me."

"I'm not playing," she whispered to the door, but she remained in place.

Lapping water and the quiet tread of wet feet was all the warning she got before she felt his lips rain whisper-soft kisses onto her exposed neck. Every fiber in her being ached to lean into his embrace, to turn and feel his lips against her own. She started to, but fear stayed her action.

She closed her eyes, willing away the old feelings of inadequacy. It hadn't been just hope of a white wedding that had kept her from her fiancé's bed. It didn't seem to matter how thin she got, her self-consciousness about her body always remained. To expose herself to the ridicule of a man required more courage than she'd had.

"Please. Just get back into the tub." Her whisper quavered with emotion. The thought of him without clothes, his skin slick with water, made her stomach drop like an express elevator.

"Then you'll come wash my back?"

Hearing the smug tone in his voice, she bristled. "Just get back in the tub."

She heard the slap of his bare feet against the wooden floor and the sloshing of water, followed by a splash. Turning around, she allowed her gaze to dwell on the perfection of the man kneeling in the tub. Why couldn't he have love handles? Just small ones, at least. If she could find some imperfection in him, maybe she could overcome her inhibitions.

Anger with his perfection and her lack of courage sent her marching to the tub.

So he wants a bath, does he? Well, I'll just see that he gets one.

Retrieving the rag from the floor beside the basin, she snatched the soap from his outstretched hand, avoiding all but the briefest of contact. Lathering up the cloth, she applied it

166

with angry force to his shoulders, glancing down long enough to be sure what she was washing.

"Damn me, leave a little skin, love. I can't be that dirty!" Garren caught her hand, stilling her. With his thumb, he traced lazy circles over the soap-slicked skin of her wrist sending a sensuous heat racing up her arm.

Her anger melted into trepidation, and with a tug, her hand slithered out of his grasp. Her heart slowed its wild beating as she gulped in a breath of air. She glanced around uncertainly, her gaze colliding with his and bouncing away like a rubber ball.

Her body wanted what he offered, but was she ready for this kind of commitment? For her it would definitely be a commitment. Once done, would she be able to leave Garren and return to her time?

A light knock brought both their heads around to stare at the door. Spalding's muffled voice reached them. "When shall I serve dinner, milord?"

Scrambling to her feet, the cloth falling with a plop into the bathwater, Jocelyn fled the room.

"Will you not rinse my back before you leave, wife?" Garren called to his wife as she escaped, his deep chuckle rumbling after her.

She slammed the door shut behind her, and she heard his frustrated bellow through it. "Haven't you ever seen a man bathe before?" *No*, she thought, in annoyance. *No, I haven't.*

"And you shouldn't be surprised. The man you bought me from," she continued, "looked as if he hadn't bathed in his entire life." She heard a splash as her husband flopped about in the tub.

Leaning against the door, her eyes closed, a

167

trembling hand placed over her chest, Jocelyn tried to still her heart's pounding. When someone cleared his throat, she jumped, stifling a gasp as she opened her eyes in alarm.

"Oh, it's just you." Her voice came out a wheeze.

A disgruntled look appeared for a brief second on Spalding's face before his stoic mask fell back into place.

"My husband will need a few more minutes, I believe." Taking to the stairs in rapid strides, Jocelyn hurried past the servant to the library, away from both her suggestive husband and the unwanted feelings he'd caused to well up in her.

Pacing in the library, she laughed. "I acted like an idiot." But Garren did things to her insides she'd never experienced before. Jocelyn clenched her hands, stopping before the window and looking out on the back gardens.

"Lord, he's handsome." She shook her head, trying to dislodge the image of Garren in the tub. No doubt the memory of his powerful torso, and gleaming muscles would haunt her dreams tonight.

Garren entered the library a scant fifteen minutes later, his hair still damp, and dressed in clean clothing. Jocelyn spared him a quick glance and turned to stare out the window.

She knew what he expected to happen tonight. To be honest, her body wanted it to happen—but how could she overcome her fears of ridicule? She already knew she was being somewhat silly—he'd shown he wanted her. Still, even if that wasn't an obstacle, the lack of love certainly was. No way could she be intimate with a man she didn't love or who didn't love her. She simply couldn't. She had to return to her time. She couldn't complicate things by making love. But how would she get out of it?

"Dinner is served." At the sound of Spalding's monotone voice, Jocelyn turned and found Garren less than three feet from her. A spasm of angst jerked through her body, and she tamped it down. *I can deal with this*.

Garren offered her his arm. "Shall we?"

Careful not to make eye contact with him, Jocelyn placed her hand ever so lightly on his arm, and they followed the butler into the dining room.

The table was set as it had been before, the first time she'd eaten here. Garren at one end and Jocelyn at the other. Jocelyn was thrilled with the arrangement. Distance was what she needed right now, and twenty feet of table would do nicely.

She glanced up at Garren. Frowning, he scanned the table. "Please see that milady's place is set next to mine . . . as she prefers."

Spalding quickly moved her place setting down the table and brought over a chair from against the wall. With slow dragging steps, Jocelyn approached her chair as one condemned, her hand still lightly holding Garren's sleeve. He covered her fingers with his, the warmth of his large, square hand sending shivers along her spine. Sliding onto her seat she remained silent, looking longingly at the opposite end of the table. "No reprieve," she mouthed sadly to herself.

He was watching her as the meal began, and Garren examined her strained mien in silence. She wasn't sure what to say.

"Jocelyn?"

Her spoon clattered against her soup bowl. "Yes?"

"Are you well?"

"Fine."

Her hand shook as she picked up her spoon again. Why did he have to watch her? He was making her nervous. *Please God, don't let him say anything about the bath.* She reached for her wine and took a long gulp, grimacing at the tart aftertaste. Lifting her gaze, she looked in Garren's direction, only to find his interminable regard.

"What is it?" she hissed. He simply smiled, making her more nervous. He was a cat playing with a mouse. The thought tumbled through her mind. She ran the tip of her tongue around her lips, dampening them in a nervous gesture.

Garren's eyes followed the path of her tongue as it traveled around her lips. He envied that rosy flesh for the treatment it received, wishing it was his mouth she laved instead. Her eyes were enormous pools of winter silver, unsure and frightened. His heart thumped painfully in his chest. He wanted her; of that there was no doubt, but at the same time he wanted to protect her, to hold her until her fears and nervousness subsided.

These were feelings unknown to him. The women he had known had been as eager to tumble as he. They had not suffered from fears or fits or nerves.

He didn't understand her reactions any more than he did his own. Mayhap she'd had a bad experience with Haslett. Or could it be that the first marriage was never consummated? He tilted his head, pondering the idea. Was that the reason for the sale? That would explain both her embarrassment and the innocent glow in her eyes. He wanted to ask her, but as he looked at her, he knew he could not.

Wanting to see her smile and hear her laugh, he searched his mind for something to say. Finally, when dessert was served, he smiled. He'd found the perfect topic.

"I wonder, will you be enjoying your dessert this eve, or will I be wearing it?" he asked with a chuckle.

He saw her shoulders relax a little and he continued. "I don't believe I'd ever experienced syllabub quite that way before. Had you?" His voice dripped of innocence.

Her head came up and she eyed him warily. Well, it was a start. At least she was looking at him, and if he had to fling his dessert at her to break her silence, then so be it.

He picked up his spoon and eyed it critically. "Now, how was it that you held the spoon?" He grinned wickedly.

Jocelyn appeared to relax a bit more. She was likely thankful that he hadn't brought up the bath. Why was she so nervous. She heaved a heavy sigh, and he saw humor light her eyes.

With a somber look, which for a moment threw him off her purpose, she picked up her spoon, scooped some of the creamy mixture up, and with a flick of her wrist, sent the mixture sailing from her spoon in his direction.

He had been watching her carefully, though, and he ducked. The sweet missile landed with a light slap on the floor just behind his chair.

"Ah, your aim is off this evening," he teased. Mimicking the way she held her spoon, he flung his own spoonful of dessert at her. She wasn't as quick, and the glob hit the side of her head and ran into her ear.

His crow of laughter filled the dining room.

* * *

"Yuck. You call that a good aim?" Jocelyn said, trying to wipe the creamy mixture from her ear. This was not what she'd expected tonight. Loading her spoon again, she faked a shot and when he ducked, she lowered her aim, hitting him at his hairline.

"Yes!" She grinned.

She felt a cool splat on her chest and looked down as his second shot disappeared into her décolletage and between her breasts, Squirming, she looked at him, her eyes narrowing.

"Two for two. I believe you're one for two, milady," he prodded.

Loading her spoon, she started a rapid fire of her dessert, and Garren followed suit. By the time the bowls were empty, they both sported globs of the sticky substance in their hair and on their clothing; they were laughing like children.

When Spalding came in, he stopped dead in his tracks. Gone was his stoic resolve. Shock oozed from every pore of the old man's face. Both Garren and Jocelyn turned in his direction and, at his expression, looked at each other and exploded into great gales of laughter.

To his credit, "I'll see that water is heated for another bath," was all the servant said. Gathering his dignity, he left, their chuckles chasing after him.

"I'll have to wash my hair, I think," Jocelyn commented with a rueful smile as she dabbed her napkin at the gooey confection clumped in her hair.

"Aye. You should run along. I fear I'm a better shot than you are." Looking at the floor around his chair splattered with the creamy mixture, he gave her a condescending look.

"I had a few good hits on you, too, mister. And if you'll notice, not all of your volleys hit their mark." She pointed smugly to a few pools of goo near her feet.

"Are you sure those are mine and not yours?"

"Why, you! Are you trying to tell me you never missed?"

He held up his hands in surrender. "I only asked." His eyes crinkled, a boyish grin twisting his lips.

She scraped back her chair. "Those are *your* misses, mister, not mine." With a pointed look at the puddles on the floor behind her, she continued. "And now, if you'll excuse me . . ."

Garren stood, offering his arm. Making sure her shoulders were straight and her spine stiff, Jocelyn placed her hand ever so lightly on his sleeve—but her regal exit was marred as her slipper slid in one of the dessert puddles. Garren reached around her waist to steady her, though, and she slid to a halt in his arms. His chocolate eyes met hers as Garren's warmth flowed into her body.

Her husband's lips came down, lightly brushing by hers. "Hmm. I love syllabub." His tongue darted out, leaving a molten trail as he tasted the corner of her mouth.

Jocelyn gasped. Her knees quaked and her insides melted.

"Your bath should be ready soon." Garren turned her around, sending her on her way with a gentle touch to her waist.

Jocelyn sailed into her room, bucket-ladened servants following her. Resolutely putting the encounter with Garren's enticing lips from her mind, she watched poor Dulcey mopping up the remains of her husband's first bath. *She must think we're nuts.*

The maid glanced up. Scrambling to her feet, her eyes rounded in surprise. "Oh, milady. What's happened?"

Water splashed into the tub and the procession of bucket-bearing servants left.

"Fat-free dessert!" Jocelyn smiled at the confusion filling Dulcey's face. "Never mind. Come, help me with this dress. I'm beginning to itch all over."

Jocelyn turned as Dulcey began unlacing her dress. She wiggled out of her petticoat and chemise, adding them to the pile of soiled clothing. Her stockings came off next, and as she stepped into the tub Dulcey said, "I best be taking these down and wash them now, or they will never come clean, milady. Do ye need anything else afore I leave?"

Kneeling, Jocelyn leaned forward. "No, Dulcey. Thank you," she said, then dunked her head into the water. Taking the soap, she lathered herself vigorously.

Garren stood at the door taking in the scene before him.

Jocelyn was bent forward in the tub, rinsing her hair, the candlelight glistening off her water-slicken back. His gaze followed its tapering line to the narrowness of her waist and beyond to the flare of her hips at the waterline. As her hands came up to squeeze the water from her hair, she turned slightly, affording him the sight of a breast. He watched as an iridescent bubble glided slowly over the milky white sheen of its fullness and came to rest against its pale pink crest.

Drawing in a shaky breath, blood throbbing through his veins, he struggled for control of his passions.

Arms still over her head, Jocelyn peered from beneath her elbow and gasped. Crouching down in the tub, she turned loose her hair and flung it out of her face, crossing her arms over her chest.

"Garren! What are you doing?" The question rushed out on a breathless gasp.

"Enjoying the view." He growled, and he grinned shamelessly.

"Garren, please." His new bride's gaze darted frantically around the room.

"But of course," he said. Pushing himself away from the door and sauntering to the side of the tub, he gazed down at her hunched form. Kneeling down, he took the soap and cloth, dipped them in the bath and reached for her. She scooted to the end of the tub, out of his reach.

"Garren, please. I can bathe myself." The plea in her voice was almost persuasive, until he saw the swell of breast above her crossed arms. He arched one eyebrow, the heat of desire pulsing harder through his veins.

"Ah, but why should you when you have a willing husband to wash you?" Moving to the side of the tub, he gathered her hair in one hand and twisted it, lifting it up and away from her neck, then he gently rubbed the soapy rag over her exposed back.

He watched in fascination as the soapy bubbles glided over her pale flesh. Letting the rag fall silently from his hand, he traced the path of the bubbles with the pads of his fingers. Beneath his touch, her smooth, cool, velvet skin trembled, and that ignited a slow-burning fire in him. He flattened his palm against her, craving yet more contact. His arms fairly ached to enfold her in a tender embrace, to feel her skin glide over his. But he wasn't ready to end this delectable torment just yet.

175

* * *

Holding herself rigid, Jocelyn flushed with the tingling path his fingertips traveled. His breath grazed her exposed neck just before the warm firmness of his mouth trailed soft, gentle kisses across it. His tongue left a trail of moist heat behind, enflaming her blood and liquefying her spine. Goose bumps rose on her skin and she shook beneath his touch. His low, tortured groan rasped near her ear, and he released the heavy wet strands of her hair. It fell back against her, both ticklish and delightful on her aroused flesh.

Taking a deep breath, thankful and yet disappointed that he was at last leaving her, she turned.

"What do you think you're doing?" Jocelyn's voice rose an octave, her eyes stretched wide as he shed his shirt, giving her a full view of his chest. She stifled the urge to reach up and run her hands over the bulging muscles, her fingers itching to test the softness of the whorls of dark hair that clung to the contours of his chest. Her gaze traveled from his chest to his broad shoulders— not sloping shoulders, but strong and square— and for a brief moment she pictured herself resting her head there, snuggled close to him.

She snapped her head around, shocked at the ease with which she'd slipped into such licentious thoughts.

"I thought to share your bath." There came the thump of first one boot and then the other, and a moment later she sensed his nearness.

"Like hell," she grasped, turning her head to glare at him. With a gasp she closed her eyes and looked away. "You're naked."

" 'Tis the best way to bathe, don't you think?"

176

"Oh, my God," she gasped as he slid into the tub, his hair-roughened legs tickling her hips.

Modesty be damned, she thought, I've got to get out of here. Hands that she'd held crossed over her chest gripped the sides of the tub, but before she could lever herself out, Garren wrapped a muscled arm about her waist and pulled her back down and against his chest.

"Oh my God, oh my God," she whispered. She knew she should fight her way free, but she couldn't make her body respond to her bidding. Instead it was responding to his, recalling the near-kiss in the dining room.

Pressed against his body like this, she could feel every square inch of him from chest to . . . oh, Lord. She tried to scoot forward, but his arm was anchored around her waist, giving her no leeway to move.

Her hair still hung over one shoulder and he took advantage of her exposed neck, planting warm, soft kisses just below her ear, nipping at her earlobe and then drawing it into the warmth of his mouth to lave it with his tongue. She tried to remain rigid, but the heat from his kisses was melting her spine.

A part of her mind said, *Relax. Enjoy. You know you want this*, but another part was appalled at what was happening. The indecision effectively froze her in place, and she was unable—and a little unwilling—to move.

Garren sucked in a breath as Jocelyn's bottom moved against him. His mind grappled with the apparent innocence of her expression. This was no untried virgin, but how was it that she acted as one? Gritting his teeth, he struggled to control his mounting desire. She was skittish as a colt, and he knew he must move carefully and slowly, allowing her time to adjust to the situation. But it went against everything in his body, and he fought to maintain control.

He brought his hands up to her shoulders and pulled her back against him, bracing himself for the intimate contact he knew would come. He felt her entire body tremble, and a concerned frown marred his passion-filled face. He didn't want her to be fearful.

His lips brushing her ear, he whispered, "Just relax, 'tis alright, love. Trust me." He stroked her arms as he spoke and felt a little of the tension leave her.

The knuckles of his hands brushed the sides of Jocelyn's breast. The intimate contact jolted her forward, but before she gained her feet, Garren grasped her waist and pulled her toward him. Off balance, she slid backward. Water sloshed over the rim of the tub as he reflexively brought his legs together. She landed in his lap, her legs on either side of his, his arms anchored around her.

Feeling his hard shaft beneath her, she gasped at this previously unknown touch of their bodies. Squirming about, she felt a warmth suddenly fill and stretch her. She focused on the fullness and heat that invaded her.

Though she was completely still, she felt a movement, deep within her, as her body heated. What was she to do? Her mind instructed her to bolt out of the tub, but the sweet warmth that seemed to gush from the center of her being over-rode her mind's instructions to flee.

"For the love of God, Jocelyn, don't move," Garren moaned in her ear as he pulled her back against his chest, his hands cupping the fullness of her breast, his fingers lightly brushing their aroused crests, sending frissons of tingling sensation to join those in the center of her being. One hand disappeared below the water. Jocelyn's breath caught in her throat at the sensual touch, and her body stiffened until the warmth grew into a heat and her breathing became a series of short gasps.

Though they were perfectly still, but for Garren's hands, she felt herself being rocked by the sensations he evoked. He lowered his mouth, pressing fevered kisses against her neck. Turning her head toward the heat brought his lips to her cheek and then to her mouth, his tongue teasing her bottom lip with light, warm flicks.

Her hands clenched the sides of the tub as she felt a wonderful passion rising inside. Her breath stuck as her pulse rose with that passion, and her body stiffened as she approached its peak. As if her body had been subsumed wholly by this core of intensity, these muscles straining to attain release, she plummeted over the apex, her body convulsing over and over.

When the last tremor had faded, she pulled much needed air into her lungs, realizing that she'd forgotten to breathe. She became aware of Garren's labored breathing, and then her passion-drugged mind cleared somewhat. In embarrassed panic, she started to rise. Garren's arms now held her tightly about the waist.

"Don't move." His gravelly voice stilled Jocelyn. She tried to turn to see him better, wondering if he was hurt; but at her movement he groaned, and her eyes widened when she felt him expanding within her. Then a pulsing rush of liquid heat burst forth.

179

* * *

His heart thumped painfully in his chest, and when his vision focused, Garren found himself gazing into Jocelyn's amazed gray eyes. He gave her a small smile and grunted as she turned away from him, the action causing their bodies to slide down into the tub.

His amazement matched hers. He'd never experienced anything like this before. This had been no pounding of bodies, no thrashing of lust. What he and Jocelyn had just done was beautiful, something so special he never wanted to repeat it with another . . . even if he *could*.

A shiver wracked Jocelyn's body, pulling Garren from his surprising thoughts. Shifting her from his lap, he stood up. He wrapped a towel about his waist and stepped out of the tub. Taking another linen from the table, he shook it out and offered it to his wife. She blushed becomingly as she reached to take it from him, managing to leave the tub without giving him so much as a glimpse of her naked body. She disappeared behind a screen, reappearing wearing a long, white nightgown.

She settled herself in bed, pulling the covers up to her chin, carefully avoiding eye contact with him.

Garren eased in alongside her, trying to gauge the mood of his bride. Her silence gave him no clue. She stared up at the canopy, her eyes seemingly huge in her flushed face. Had he shocked her? She truly seemed so very innocent, as if she were surprised and confused by what had transpired in the bath. He gazed at the smoothness of her cheek and wondered himself at what had just happened. Never before had he made love in such a way. Never before had there been so little movement and so much sensation. The potency of the experience started his blood to pumping, pooling in his loins, radiating heat upwards.

Snuffing out the candles, he moved closer to Jocelyn. She made no protest, so he moved closer still, until their shoulders touched. He heard the catch in her breathing.

Trying to think of something comforting to say to her, he suddenly felt clumsy and tongue-tied. Never having bedded a virgin, he suspected this must be how a man felt afterward.

But she *wasn't* a virgin, he reminded himself. No barrier had been breached. He would have known.

There came a rustle of material, and her breath fanned his cheek. He felt his arousal beginning to stir.

"Oh, Jocelyn," he whispered, and he turned on his side toward her, draping his arm about her waist. His lips traced a path from her ear to her collarbone and back, her womanly scent filling his head as he lifted her leg to rest atop his hip.

He filled his palm with the weight of her breast, grazing the tip with his thumb. He nuzzled her neck.

"You've a magnificent body, so soft, so smooth, so feminine."

He pulled back. Staring into her eyes he saw . . . tears? They were gone in a moment, whether they had been there or it had been a trick of the light, as she blinked. She smiled then, and all thoughts disappeared as he looked into her lovely face. He drew her close and savored her warmth, holding her long into the night.

Chapter Twelve

"What, govna, ye think ye're royalty or such?" The farmer's glance traveled insultingly over Charles Martin. "No shoes and dirty as a beggar." The farmer shook his head. "Ye can ride in the back or not at all." The old man smirked.

Charles gingerly walked to the back of the cart, biting the inside of his lip to control the angry retort welling inside of him. It wouldn't do to alienate the only ride that had come along. His tender feet could take no more of the rocky track he'd traversed.

He climbed aboard, falling face first into the mildewed straw as the cart lurched into motion. Settling himself as comfortably as the thin hay allowed, Charles rubbed his bruised feet.

Before long, his feet weren't the only tender area. The cart seemed to hit every hole and rock in the road, bouncing him around on the hard wooden surface of the wagon. The straw was little padding for his bruised posterior.

After what seemed like hours, but was no doubt less, the old man pulled up before a tavern. Glancing back at Charles, he growled, "Well, get yer arse down." He raised a bushy brow. "Or do ye expect me to help ye?"

The farmer's following guffaw grated on Charles's frayed nerves. Casting a supercilious glare at the lout, Charles stumbled out of the wagon, grimacing as he landed on his sensitive feet.

The old boor laughed a little louder.

Charles straightened, dusting off the bits of straw that clung to his rumpled clothes. Without a word, he turned and scanned the hovels that made up the village, ignoring his benefactor. The fool didn't deserve his attention, and certainly not a thank-you. His body felt bruised all over.

It had taken some time and a bit of coin to procure the ill-fitting boots Charles now wore, but at least his feet were covered, protected from the bite of rocks and the gouge of sticks and thorns.

Pushing open the door to the Weasel and Woodcock, Charles entered the smoke-filled inn. He wrinkled his nose at the smell emanating from the men sitting at a table in the center of the room. He took a seat in the corner, as far away as he could get. Still, their odor reached him.

A blowzy girl of indeterminate age appeared on his left. "What'll ye 'ave, govna?"

"A meal, and something to wash it down with."

The girl leaned closer, offering Charles a glimpse of prodigious breasts. "Will ye have anything else?" She smiled, exposing dirty teeth.

He shivered. "No, just the food and drink, and be quick about it."

She jiggled her shoulders, setting her breasts to bouncing. "Name's Maisy, if ye change yer mind." With a turn, the woman was gone and Charles was much relieved.

He paid scant attention to the men conversing at the table. His food and drink arrived and he ate, wondering how he would find his way back to London. After purchasing the boots and paying for his meal, he would have few funds left. He longed for a bath, clean clothes and sleep. Worse, he'd have to travel by public coach. Still it was better than walking, he thought.

A stab of light brightened the dingy interior as the inn's door opened. Charles turned from his food and watched as a grimy man entered.

"Hey, Haslett," one of the men from the table called to the newcomer.

The man joined his friends, his loud voice blending in with those of the others.

Charles sipped his ale, washing down his day-old bread.

"Ye buying a round, Haslett?"

"With what?" the new comer sneered.

"The auction money, o' course." His friend looked peevish.

"We spent that money the same day, ye idiot." Raising a meaty fist, Haslett swiped at the other man.

"Aye, but ye should have more coin now. One less mouth to feed, ye know."

"Did ye ever find out who that was what bought yer wife?" Another man asked. "He was a nobleman, I'd say."

Charles held his mug to his lips, this conversation seemed like it might get interesting.

"Nay, I didn't find him. But then I didn't try too hard." The man called Haslett chuckled as he took a seat. "I keep an eye out fer him, though. I'm surprised he ain't brung her back by now, demanding his coin back."

Loud laughter greeted his pronouncement.

Charles put his drink down, giving the men his complete attention. What would a lord be doing purchasing a wife from a common villager?

"Sat a fine piece of horseflesh," he did. Maisy placed a mug of ale before the man. As she turned away, the man swatted at her voluptuous backside.

"Aye, but why would a nobleman buy yer wife?"

My question exactly, Charles thought, leaning forward to better hear the response to the question.

"Don't know. Don't care. Just as long as he don't bring her back." Haslett quaffed his ale. "Though I do miss that honey-colored hair of hers."

The others nodded their heads in agreement.

"She was a looker, all right. Her hair fair sparkled like gold in the sun."

Haslett cuffed his friend. " 'Tis my wife ye speak of."

"Not no more, Haslett." Guffaws rolled around the room.

Golden blond hair? Charles shook his head. *It couldn't be . . .*

"Ye don't suppose she'll be coming back when the lord gets tired of her, do ye?"

"Well, if she does, I'll just sell her to another."

"Wonder who he was."

"He was a right handsome gent, he was. Blond hair and big. Ye could tell he was a strong'un." Maisy chimed in.

"Ah, Maisy, any bloke in britches is handsome to ye." There was a chorus of laughter.

Slapping the mugs of ale down on the table, the

185

serving girl left with a harumph and came over to Charles.

"Can I get ye anything else?" She leaned forward, again, swinging her vast cleavage under his nose.

"I couldn't help but overhear, those men talking about a wife sale." Charles ignored the gleam in the girl's eyes.

"Aye. Haslett there—"she nodded to the newcomer—"sold his wife. She were a real kicker. Drove him near-crazy, what with her learning and such."

"When was the sale?" Charles tamped down a surge of excitement, schooling his features into only mild curiosity.

"A few weeks ago, I guess. Why?" Her eyes widened.

Charles disregarded her question. "And you saw the man who bought her?"

"Oh aye." She brightened. "He were a right good-looking one. Not as good-lookin' as ye, though." She moved so that her breast rubbed against Charles's shoulder. "Clean, with shiny boots and a deep voice that fair melted me bones. He was strong, too, picked up Haslett's wife and only groaned a little." Maisy chuckled. "She were a curvy woman, sure."

"Did he not tell anyone his name?" Charles's fingers curled into fists, and he fought his impatience.

"Nay. Just rode up, bid on her, tossed the money to Haslett and rode off with her."

Warrick! The description fit and the timing was about right. According to rumor, Garren had just married a few weeks ago.

"What did the woman look like?"

186

"Why, be ye interested in buying her from him?" Maisy tittered.

"Just describe her." He ground the words out.

Casting Charles a wounded look, she answered. " 'Bout my height, gray eyes and long blond hair—kind of golden it was. A nasty temper, though. She don't take direction well, at all."

That was Jocelyn, all right. And Warrick had bought her. Oh, this was priceless. Charles resisted the urge to whoop with delight. Revenge was within his grasp. He had but to await the right time.

A short time later, the public coach carried Charles off to London, a gleeful smile stretched wide on his lips.

"Melody, I've the most wonderful news." Charles fairly crowed the words as he strode into his sister Melody's salon.

"The only wonderful news you could give me is that everyone at the duchess's ball has suddenly developed amnesia and can't remember your stupidity." She gave him a sharp look and rose from her seat to confront him.

Charles grinned hugely at Melody. "Ah, sister dear, 'tis much better than even that."

"What?" She stared at him dangerously. "Exactly what have you done this time?"

" 'Tis not what *I've* done, but what Lord Spenceworth has done."

Jocelyn shifted in her warm cocoon of sleep. Her foot slid across the mattress, bumping against something cold. Half-awakening, she ran her foot along the cold object. It went from cold and smooth to warm and . . . hairy?

187

She blinked.

Hearing the gentle breathing beside her, she turned her head cautiously toward the sound. Heat suffused her face as she gazed at Garren's sleeping form, remembering the night they'd just shared.

It was not yet fully light, but the rising sun had dispelled the darkest shadows, and glancing around the room, she wondered where she was. She put her hand out to awaken Garren, but stopped as she gazed at his relaxed face. Love welled up. Her heart lurched at the emotion. How could she love this man? He was still a stranger to her. Well, not completely, she admitted with a little embarrassment. But still, did she know him well enough to *love* him? She felt like she could gaze at his face for the rest of her life and it wouldn't be enough time. Was that love?

Remembering the evening before, she pondered the gentleness of his lovemaking. Could he feel the same about her?

No, she thought, shaking her head. That was stupid. For men it was just a physical need, nothing more. And if a woman denied a man, he left. She'd experienced that firsthand when she'd denied her fiancé. No, she shook her head, it didn't require love to have sex with someone—at least for some people.

Was she like that now? Was that why she was trying to convince herself that she loved Garren? So that she wouldn't be one of *those* women?

Jocelyn scooted to the edge of the bed. Sitting up, she gasped as the linens fell away, exposing her bare flesh to the cool morning air.

Garren's warm arm curled around her waist, pulling her back down.

"Oh, no you don't." His deep, sleepy voice near

188

her ear sent her pulse racing. "The sun isn't even up yet. We're going to loll around in bed until full sunrise."

Jocelyn found herself tucked beside Garren's warm body, the covers replaced, his arousal probing her hip.

Putting a little distance between them, she peered at him. "Where are we?"

He pulled her close again. "Our room." He yawned. "I couldn't get comfortable in that little bed you sleep in. So I picked you up and moved you here." His deep masculine chuckle tickled her ear. "You were so exhausted, you didn't even stir."

Jocelyn's cheeks warmed and she glanced around the room. Inhaling the smells of soap, tobacco and some scent inherently Garren's. She settled against him, content to be held.

"Hm." He nuzzled her neck. "How can you smell so good this early?" He rained tantalizing kisses from her neck to her shoulder, his arm draped across her waist, holding her still for his ministrations.

Her muscles were like jelly. A fever of desire pooled like molten lava at the junction of her legs.

"Garren?" Jocelyn's breathless voice brought his head up.

"Yes, love?" His hand moved, enveloping the fullness of her breast.

Jocelyn's thoughts scattered as Garren's lips teased the corner of her mouth. She started to protest, but he swallowed her words as he brought his mouth fully against hers. His tongue darted along the seam of her lips, coaxing them apart.

The kiss began as a gentle foraging, but soon turned into a fiery possession. Jocelyn pushed into his embrace, freeing her passions, giving up to her desire.

Later, they lay in silence, their limbs entwined.

Garren turned on his side to her. Taking a lock of her hair, he rubbed it between his fingers before turning the ends and trailing them along her collarbone and down the valley between her breasts, watching her nipples harden and swell.

He loved the way her body responded to his touch. He raised his gaze to her eyes. Their gray depths held a warm, satisfied glow. Gone was the peasant accent and the dirt, replaced by cultured speech and cleanliness. She was slimmer, as well. It was difficult to believe that this was the same woman he'd bought in Ramsgil.

Guilt tugged at his conscience. This was no woman to simply buy. She should have been courted and wooed. She was a treasure . . . his treasure.

"What shall we do today, love?"

A long moment passed before Jocelyn answered. She trembled as his voice flowed over her in warm waves. She couldn't remember a time when a man had such an effect on her. She wanted to please him, but didn't know how. She grasped at practicality to cover her ignorance. "No doubt we should get up."

He kissed her forehead. "And why is that?"

"The sun's up."

He kissed her eyelids. "Ah, I see."

"And Dulcey could walk in any minute now."

"Just one kiss and we'll rise."

But as Garren whispered the words and captured her lips, there was a knock at their door. He groaned and rolled away from Jocelyn, flinging back the sheets.

As Garren padded to the door, Jocelyn watched the play of muscles in his back, trailing her gaze down to follow the movement of his tight, smooth form. Closing her eyes, she took a deep, steadying breath.

Lord, he is beautiful, she thought. She gazed at him from beneath lowered lids. *Hmm, I could look at him all day.*

The thoughts so startled her that her eyes opened wide and she flopped over on her side, turning her back to the sight of her naked husband.

What was she doing ogling Garren? Burying her face in the pillow, she thought. I'm easy, that's all there is to it. A woman of easy virtue. For twenty-five years she'd guarded her virginity like Fort Knox. And it was a darned good thing she had, too. Look what emotional havoc it wreaked on her after her first experience. She drove her fist into the hapless pillow in frustration.

An unfamiliar masculine voice brought her head out of the pillow to stare in shock as a little man entered the room. He carried a steaming pitcher of water.

"Good morning, Ivan." Garren greeted the man. "Have you met my wife?"

Ivan poured the water into the porcelain bowl, arranging a mug and brush on the small table in the alcove next to the fireplace.

"A pleasure, milady." With a little bow, Ivan withdrew a cloth from his pocket, and buffed the mirror on the wall above the table.

Jocelyn screeched, pulling the linens over her head, wholly embarrassed.

Garren chuckled. She peeked from beneath the covers to watch as her husband took a pair of black trousers from the wardrobe and pulled them up over his hips. As he moved to the alcove, the morning rays glinted off the highlights of his sleep-ruffled hair and his face looked as though golden glitter dusted his chin. Jocelyn watched the rippling muscles beneath the smooth skin of his back as he turned to the mirror.

Strop, strop.

The sound made Jocelyn turn to find Ivan sharpening a straight-edge razor on a length of leather. Handing the blade to Garren, the servant went to the wardrobe and pulled out a white linen shirt.

"Your post is below, milord. I brought it with me from London."

"Ah, excellent." Garren lathered his beard with soap.

Clearing her throat, Jocelyn interrupted the conversation, bringing both men's gazes to her.

"Excuse me, but? . . ."

"Oh, I'm so sorry, milady," Dulcey said as she blew into the room. "I woulda been up sooner, but *someone*"—she glared daggers at Ivan—"took the water I heated for ye, and I had to heat some more." She bobbed her head to indicate the room next door. "I put it in the next room."

"Uh, well," Jocelyn hedged. Did they expect her to just jump out of bed in her birthday suit? Garren turned back to his mirror, and Ivan continued his perusal of the clothing in his master's wardrobe.

"Oh, Lady Jocelyn, I'm so sorry. Wait right there, I'll fetch yer robe." Dulcey hurried through the door joining the rooms. A moment later she returned, bringing a burgundy velvet dressing gown.

With Dulcey's help, Jocelyn managed to don the dressing gown without exposing so much as a bare shoulder. Together, they hurried to the privacy of Jocelyn's room to ready her for the day, closing the door behind them.

A little later, a light knock sounded as Jocelyn slipped on her shoes.

"Shall I wait to escort you down to breakfast?" Garren called from outside.

"No, you go ahead. I'll be down in a few minutes."

Dressed in black pants and white shirt, Garren sat at the dining room table, a cup of tea at his elbow, the London paper in his hands. His eyes ran over the words, but his mind was seeing Jocelyn as she'd been in bed this morning, responding to his touch, straining toward him. He recalled the soft warm comfort of his bed and that of the woman who had occupied it, and for a moment, he struggled with the urge to race back upstairs and curl up with her on the down-filled mattress.

The door opened, and Jocelyn came in wearing a soft lavender dress trimmed in deep purple ribbon. The color turned her eyes to a glittering mauve. Her blond tresses were swept up and held by a matching ribbon, a few tendrils escaping their confinement to play about her temple. Standing, Garren held her chair, unable to stop himself from caressing her shoulder as he moved to take his seat beside her.

"You look beautiful this morning, love." She smiled in thanks, a blush coloring her cheeks. He sensed some discomfort, but didn't understand it. Again, he found himself puzzled by her reaction.

Spalding came in with tea. Pouring a cup for Jocelyn, he asked, "Will ye be having your usual, milady?"

"Good morning, Spalding." She nodded her

head. "That would be fine." Taking the linen napkin resting before her, she shook it out, placing it over her lap.

"Very good." He bobbed his head and disappeared through the door, returning a few moments later with two covered plates. He placed one before Garren and the other before Jocelyn. With a flourish, he removed the covers.

"Will there be anything else?"

Garren glanced at Jocelyn's plate. "Is that all you're having?"

Following his gaze, Jocelyn looked at her plate. A thick slab of bread and a sliced apple were arranged before her.

"Yes." She frowned. "What's wrong with it?" She moved her gaze to his plate, heaped with eggs, sliced tongue, bread and butter.

"There's nothing there to sustain you."

"I don't think I could handle all the fat and calories you have there." She grimaced, a little shiver shaking her shoulders.

"The what?" Garren's brows drew together in confusion.

"Never mind." Jocelyn shook her head. "This is what I normally eat, and I'm doing fine."

Her lips curved into a soft smile, and Garren felt the pull of his attraction. She filled his mind and ah, how she filled his bed! His sudden urge to carry her upstairs surprised him. He should be exhausted after last night, but here he was thinking of starting all over again.

He watched her pop a bite of apple between her rosy lips, chewing daintily. He swallowed, his desire making his trousers uncomfortably tight.

Pulling himself together, he clamped down on

his wayward thoughts and brought his mind around to the day ahead.

"What will you do today, love?"

"Mrs. Cowan will probably have me consult with Cook over the menu." She took a sip of tea. "Not that Cook pays a bit of attention to anything I say." She shrugged.

Garren chuckled. "While you're occupied with the menu, I've some estate business to tend to. It seems Baskins was called to another of my holdings, so it may take me some time to review the ledgers. Mayhap I'll take you for a drive later. Would that suit?"

"Sure." Jocelyn dabbed at her lips and smiled at him.

Garren puzzled over her response. From where did she hail? Mayhap he would broach the subject during their ride. For now, he must concentrate on the estate.

When his plate was empty, he pushed back his chair, leaving the paper that lay forgotten at his elbow. "I'll send word around when I'm free." He kissed her upturned face then strode from the room.

Jocelyn sagged in relief. Garren hadn't said anything about last night. No sly innuendos, no taunts. Nothing. Was that good? He didn't seem unhappy with her. In fact, he seemed quite pleased. And she had caught that gleam in his eyes, the one reminiscent of this morning's. She touched her forehead where Garren had kissed her. A warm feeling filled her.

She glanced at his empty place and the paper lying there curious, she reached out and pulled it to her. Jocelyn scanned an article promoting the

English war effort, reminding the people of the sacrifices of men like Horatio Nelson. She shook her head amazed to be witnessing the history she'd learned in college.

She set aside the paper and, taking a last sip of tea, pushed back her chair.

Leaving the dining room, Jocelyn went in search of Mrs. Cowan, humming softly.

She spent the first hour with the housekeeper, reviewing the duties of the servants. The next hour she spent with the cook, attempting to change the menu to one with more vegetables and less meat. The only thing she accomplished was to gain a promise of carrots served without butter and honey.

The butler entered the kitchen just as she was leaving.

"Spalding, would you send something to drink to Lord Spenceworth? He's been poring over those books for quite a while now. He needs a break."

"Of course, milady. I'll see to it."

"Great." Jocelyn left the kitchen before the man could react to her twentieth-century response.

As she walked, she considered her limited success so far with Cook. Would she ever convince the man to prepare a simpler menu? Oh well, she thought as she climbed the stairs to her room, Garren seemed in good health. Maybe the diet wasn't as bad as she thought. Still, *she* wasn't taking any chances.

Knowing instinctively that Garren would raise the roof if he saw her in a shift and pantaloons racing up and down the stairs, she decided against her aerobics. But she could, at least, do some exercises. Once in her room, she stripped down to her shift and began her morning workout.

* * *

Garren stared at the parchment he'd found in an old ledger in the top drawer of his desk. The writing didn't resemble any from the old books, and it most certainly wasn't Baskin's hand.

He spread the paper in front of him. Concentrating on the content, he gasped as he realized it was an unfinished statement of profit. Who had begun this? And why was it folded in this ledger? Mayhap it was from his grandfather's man in London. But the snowy whiteness of the parchment proved his conclusion wrong. It was obviously new, not the forgotten project of someone from a time past.

Glancing down to the bottom of the page, he found an odd note. *Reverse signs of accounting equation.*

What the deuce did that mean? And who had written it? He puzzled over it a moment longer. It was plain that he'd have no answers until Baskin returned, it was best to put it away until the man could answer his questions.

Placing the paper aside, he closed the ledger and opened a more current one, his gaze straying every now and again back to the parchment. With a shrug, he resolved to concentrate on the task before him. The sooner done, the sooner he could spend time with Jocelyn.

His gaze shifted, again, to the mysterious page and he grumbled in frustration. Taking the statement, he folded it and returned it to the old ledger, then placed the book back in the drawer. Now he could get some work done.

Some time later, a knock interrupted Garren's calculating.

"Come." He set his pen aside, rubbing the

bridge of his nose. Spalding entered, followed by a servant carrying a tea tray.

"Milady sent you some tea, milord. She said you would be needing a rest from your work." The butler nodded to the servant, who put the tray on the corner of the desk and left.

His heart tripped at the sweet consideration his wife showed. To have his comfort seen to, not by a servant, but by his wife, drew a smile from his lips. Glancing at the tray, he noticed only one cup and frowned.

"Will Lady Jocelyn not be joining me?"

Spalding shook his head. "Nay, milord. She's busy above stairs."

Spalding poured a cup of tea. Handing it to Garren, he took a step back from the desk.

"And how did her interview with Cook go?" He sipped his tea, glancing at the butler. At the response, Garren blinked. Surely that wasn't the beginning of a smile on his staid butler's face.

Spalding cleared his throat, returning his face into its customary mask. "The usual, milord."

Garren inclined his head, taking another sip of his tea.

"Milady and Cook argued a full half hour on the merits of sauces on vegetables, sir. Milady prefers hers steamed without sauce. Cook claims they'd to be too bland, sir. Any discerning palate would rebel at such mean fare."

Garren chuckled. "And who won this battle?"

"I fear 'tis still unresolved, sir."

"And how shall I find my dinner tonight?"

"No doubt there will be two preparations of the vegetables, sir. One steamed without sauce, the other cooked with sauce."

"Mayhap I should have a word with Cook." He looked up inquisitively at the old servant.

Spalding shook his head. "Nay, milord. If I might suggest?"

"Yes?"

"I believe milady and Cook enjoy their daily sparring." Moving a step closer to the desk, Spalding lowered his voice. "He quite hums after milady leaves each morning. I've heard him say that most ladies of her station wouldn't concern themselves with the details of diet—and at the very least he appreciates the respect she shows him. He quite admires her, sir."

"Well then, I shall maintain my silence."

"Very good, milord. Will there be anything else, sir?"

"Nay. I've a bit more work to do here. Would you ask Cook to pack a basket and have it ready in an hour?"

"Yes, milord."

Once Spalding left, Garren turned back to his ledgers. It was a tiresome job, but once done, he could spend the afternoon with Jocelyn; there were so many memories from his childhood here that he wished to share with her.

The time passed quickly, and as Garren left the library, Mrs. Cowan was just coming down the stairs. At her appearance, Garren recalled a question he'd had while he was working.

"Mrs. Cowan?"

"Yes, milord?" The elderly woman stopped before him.

"I see that my wife ordered seven gowns." Mayhap there were more coming and the bill had yet to be submitted, he thought.

The housekeeper nodded. "Oh, aye. She fussed something terrible about every one."

"Particular, was she?" He arched an eyebrow.

"Oh, milord, ye've no idea. Complained about

the gowns, the undergarments and the shoes. And the fit she threw over her riding costume...." The housekeeper threw her plump hands up in exasperation.

Alarmed, Garren demanded, "What was wrong?"

"Well, milord. She said she didn't need a gown for every hour of the day. That it was bad for her health to be squeezed into a corset. That bum rolls made her look like she carried a basketball—whatever that is—on her backside." Mrs. Cowan's face had turned pink.

"She said she wanted a pair of *pants* to ride in, not a skirt." Folding her arms, the housekeeper looked totally scandalized.

He raised his eyebrows at her pronouncement. Pants was it? Whyever would she want those? Still, it was not a question he would ask the housekeeper.

"So just how many gowns did my wife order?"

"Oh sir, 'tis such a disgrace." The housekeeper kneaded her hands. "She would only accept seven, and I was lucky to talk her into that many. She said she needed only one evening gown, five day gowns, and the riding habit. Said she could sleep in her shift." At that the poor woman turned a deep shade of scarlet, her gaze dropping to her feet.

Garren was silent. Did his wife think he could not afford to clothe her properly? He frowned, glancing to the stairs. He wondered if mayhap she thought seven an extraordinary number. She was, after all, used to having much less. But surely she could see he could easily buy twice that number.

Mrs. Cowan's quiet voice reached him.

"I'm so sorry, milord. I just didn't know what to

do but as she wished. She's such a bright young woman. Learned comportment quick-like, but if ye pardon my criticism, she's a mite hard to convince of certain things."

"Aye, Mrs. Cowan. That she is." He excused the housekeeper with a brief, distracted nod and climbed the stairs. Well, she certainly didn't have any designs on his money if she wouldn't even have gowns made for herself. It would seem his silver was safe.

But what of his heart?

Chapter Thirteen

Bright sunlight warmed her skin, and Jocelyn pulled a long breath of clover-scented air into her lungs, marveling at how pure it was. She wondered how Nelwina found the twentieth century. Had she found happiness there?

The gig bumped over the rutted road and thoughts of Nelwina fled as Jocelyn gripped the side of the vehicle to keep her seat. In the jostling, she found herself pressed intimately against Garren from hip to knee. The heat of his leg permeated the cloth of his trousers and the layers of her clothing, reminding her of another time when clothing hadn't hampered the touch of their skin. And of later, of the friction as their bodies . . .

She shook the rest of the thought from her mind. A blush stung her face and she glanced at Garren, half-afraid he could hear her thoughts.

He watched the road ahead, his strong capable

hands handling the ribbons, deftly maneuvering the carriage around the worst of the ruts. He must have felt her gaze, for turning a brilliant smile on her, he gave her a lazy wink before returning his attention to his driving.

He pulled off the road, heading for a shady area beneath some trees a short distance away. Stopping there, he jumped down, offering Jocelyn a helping hand. He pulled a throw and a basket of food from under the seat, took her hand, and led her to a level spot with a beautiful view of a pond.

Shaking the blanket out, he set the basket nearby, offering his hand to help her sit.

Settled on the throw, Jocelyn hugged her knees to her chest.

"It's beautiful here." She gazed at Garren's profile. Totally masculine—that was the only way to describe it, she thought. Strong, determined, and absolutely bewitching.

"Yes. This is one of my favorite spots on the estate." He turned, smiling at her. "When I was a boy and visiting my grandfather, I would sneak down and swim here. Naked." He waggled his eyebrows.

Her breath caught in her throat. She pictured him, not as a young boy, but as a man, swimming in the pond with her. No clothes hampered their movements as the silky caress of the water flowed over and around them. She savored the contrasting warmth of his body as he held her, his hands dancing over her in love play. Her senses hummed in response to her imaginings. Her nipples tightened and a slow, sensuous warmth seeped into her.

Reluctantly, she drew her mind away from the scene, giving herself a mental shake. What was wrong with her? She hadn't thought of anything else but him since this morning.

She directed the conversation to a safer channel. "Did you spend much time at Spenceworth?"

"Nay, only a few weeks here and there. I was away at school, mostly, and after that, I spent my time in London." Garren reached over to a patch of clover next to the blanket. Plucking a stem, he placed it between his lips.

"Did you always live in Ramsgil?"

Jocelyn jerked her gaze from his face, turning to stare at the still blue water of the pond. The urge to tell him the truth warred with her common sense. The need to share her burden was so strong that she nearly wept. But how could she? Garren would never seriously consider her claim to be from the twentieth century. She had no proof.

"Jocelyn?"

Garren's voice interrupted her deliberation, and she made her choice. *Tell him what you can. Stay as close to the truth as possible,*

"No. I was born and raised in South Carolina." She waited. How would he take that news?

Snapping his fingers, he chuckled. "I've been trying to place your accent. While you have a familiar accent, some of your word usage is very unusual."

"Yes, well." She hedged, wondering what other response she could have made.

"Did you wear trousers there?"

"What?" That was hardly the question she expected.

"Trousers. Mrs. Cowan told me you wanted a pair. For riding."

"Yes. Sidesaddles don't give a feeling of security. You know?"

He laughed, shaking his head. "No, I wouldn't know. Never had to use one, myself."

"Well, you should try it. They are not very comfortable, I can tell you that."

"You mean you rode astride in America?" He pulled the clover stem from his lips.

Jocelyn searched her memory, recalling the fair her parents had taken her to when she was six. She'd proudly sat on the little pony as the attendant guided it around in a circle. Yes, she'd ridden astride.

"Yes."

Garren stared at her, amazement widening his eyes.

This was getting into dangerous territory, Jocelyn thought, and she asked the first question that popped into her mind.

"Why did you buy me?"

He flinched at her question, color brightening his cheeks.

"Father didn't enlighten you? I would have expected him to."

"No, he didn't."

Jocelyn waited. Garren's hesitation stretched on.

"Well?" she prodded.

"I fear you'll be angered when I tell you." He flashed her a boyish smile, a little sheepish.

Jocelyn couldn't help the answering smile that curved her own lips. "I'll get over it."

"It was an ultimatum."

"An ultimatum? What do you mean?"

"I was to be married within a month, or Father said he would find a wife for me." A pained expression drew his face tight. "Or worse, he would disown me."

Jocelyn drew back, shaking her head. "I can't believe *he* would do that, Garren. Why would you think he would?"

"Father felt it was past time I attended to my responsibilities and settled down."

"That's hardly reason to threaten you with a forced marriage."

"That's not the whole of it." He looked into Jocelyn's eyes before continuing. "There was a wager."

"A wager?"

"Aye, involving a widow, one who had lost her husband not six months before."

His regard wavered, and Jocelyn knew exactly what that wager must have entailed. A widow. Jocelyn thought a moment. Was that what Charles had rambled on about? His sister and Garren?

"Melody?"

"Yes." His brow wrinkled. "But how did you know?"

"Charles." With determination, she forced the image of Garren with another woman from her mind. She wouldn't be in this time forever. There was no point in getting possessive of a man she had married completely by accident.

She tried to smile reassuringly. "He was rambling on about his sister and how . . . oh, never mind. Suffice it to say, I know the gist of what happened. I gather your father found out about it and didn't take the idea too well, huh?"

"That would be quite an understatement." Garren looked out at the pond, twirling the clover between his fingers. "We'd discussed my wedded state before; however, this time he would accept nothing but that I marry and become respectable." He shrugged. "I looked over the crop of ladies in London, but could find none of interest. I was nearing the end of my month when I saw you in Ramsgil."

"But why buy me? You didn't even know me."

"Do you think I would have known my bride?" His gaze met hers. "You looked so forlorn and confused there on that block. I did the chivalrous thing, offering you a better way of life. In return, I met my father's demand." With a shrug, Garren smiled. "Everything worked out nicely, don't you think? You are happy here, aren't you?"

Was she, Jocelyn wondered? After a fashion, maybe she was. She'd adjusted to most of the things about eighteenth-century living, but that wasn't to say she didn't long for modern conveniences and comforts. A nice hot shower was one. A pizza and a cold soda. Peanut butter and jelly. Sneakers. Oh, the list could go on.

"Jocelyn?"

She gazed at Garren's face. His furrowed brow bespoke his anxiety at her delayed response. Still pondering an answer, she watched as Garren's anxiety turned to surprise and then anger.

"I would think you'd prefer living at Spenceworth to Ramsgil, or even the Colonies." He tossed the clover aside and stood up, glaring down at her.

She fumed. If he only knew what a step back living in his world was for her. And that remark about the Colonies—well, she just couldn't stand that one.

"The Colonies?" She jumped up, arms akimbo. "Excuse me, but it's America to you. We declared our independence in 1776. Remember?"

"I do beg your pardon, love. I didn't realize you were so sensitive about it. After all, it's been some twenty years." Garren took a step back.

"Sensitive?" Jocelyn leaned forward, jutting her chin out. "How would you like to be called an Italian? At one time England was under Roman law. Or doesn't that count?"

Garren's eyes widened, his brows furrowed, and he cocked his head. "Where did you come by your education?"

Her mind reeled. He could change gears faster than a NASCAR driver. And he could neatly steer the argument in any direction he chose. She took a deep breath and rolled her eyes. "School."

"You attended school?" He watched her closely.

Her mind fumbled with American history. Didn't they have schools in the late eighteenth century? Surely they must have.

"Well, yes." She hesitated, her anger cooled at the direction of his questions.

"What did you study?"

"Math, English, history. The usual." She shrugged. Sauntering over to the water's edge, she stood there looking at a reflection that wasn't really of her. Today had been an emotional roller coaster and Jocelyn felt drained, wanting nothing more than to get off the ride. But she couldn't. At least, not yet. Or maybe never.

She bit her lip, fighting the tears of fear and frustration that welled behind her eyes.

Garren watched her walk away, her expression a jumble of emotions. Her shoulders drooped and he cursed himself. He wouldn't fool himself by claiming to love Jocelyn, even after last night and this morning. But somewhere deep inside, it hurt to see this abject sadness weigh on her. And he was the cause.

From experience, he knew the Americans were frightfully proud of their independence. He certainly knew enough not to test one's patience. He didn't know what had come over him. Why had he goaded her as he had?

She was just a wife he'd bought, a way to continue his life without his father breathing down his neck. It shouldn't matter to him if she were happy here. But it did. The thought brought him up short.

Granted they were magic in bed, and he found her quick wit and biting sarcasm entertaining—but certainly that wasn't reason enough to be so desperately concerned with her happiness. So why was he?

He was just being a good and proper husband, he decided. That was all. No good husband would allow his wife to wallow in misery.

He moved quietly up behind her, lightly touching her shoulder.

"Jocelyn?"

She turned her head, offering him a glimpse of her profile, before she turned back to the pond.

"Come back to the blanket and have a little something to eat."

She remained silent. Garren clenched his teeth. What did she expect him to do? Get on his knees and beg forgiveness?

He thought a moment. Yes, that was no doubt exactly what she expected. Well, she could bloody well stand here all day then.

He turned to leave, but his conscience pricked him. She was right. He would be mightily insulted to be called an Italian. He was *English*, pure and simple. With a huff, he accepted his offense. He had offered insult to her and her country, and she deserved an apology.

Taking a breath, he kept his hands at his side and said, "I apologize, Jocelyn. You are correct. I would no more accept being called an Italian than you would a Colonial. Will you forgive me?"

She turned to him, tears shimmering in her eyes, a smile quivering on her lips. He reached out to her, and a moment later, his arms wrapped around her. She trembled in his embrace.

"Love, don't cry. I'm sorry I upset you so." With his arm around her, he steered her back to the blanket. "Come, let's have something to eat. Cook went to a deal of trouble packing this basket. If it comes back without being touched, I fear our meals for the next week will be meager at best."

Jocelyn sat on the throw, wiping at her eyes and avoiding Garren's gaze. He set about pouring a cup of wine and arranging a plate for her, all the while trying to amuse her by chatting about childhood pranks he'd played.

Every once in a while he caught her looking at him. She would lower her gaze and move her food around on her plate. With determination, he maintained the one-sided conversation. Gradually, the tension left her shoulders and he caught a hint of a smile.

"When I was seven, Grandfather took me to visit Lord and Lady Danley. They had a marvelous garden with a fish pond. Though I was told I was not to try to catch the fish, I did anyway. As luck would have it, I actually caught one. The problem was, I didn't know what to do with it. I never considered putting it back. Instead, I went to the stables and hid it in my Grandfather's coach."

He laughed, recalling his grandfather's face five days later as they rode to London. "I have never again seen a person contort his face as my grandfather did. The smell was atrocious."

Jocelyn's laughter brightened the afternoon.

An hour later, they packed up the basket and returned to Spenceworth, the comfortable atmosphere restored.

*   *   *

Their days fell into a routine. Jocelyn spent her mornings with Cook and Mrs. Cowan. Baskin had sent a message that he would be away at least another week, so Garren spent his time tending to the estate business.

But by the end of a week—as much as he'd found his time with his new wife delightful—he could no longer put off a trip to London. His father had sent an urgent note giving his regards to Jocelyn and begging Garren's presence in Parliament. Assuring his bride he would only be a few days, he set off, missing her even before Spenceworth was out of sight.

Chapter Fourteen

"Mary, don't you dare answer that door," Melody, Lady Paxton, ordered her maid and watched the girl scurry back toward the kitchen. Peering from behind the heavy draperies in her salon she caught a glimpse of a frustrated Master Jeffries. Melody swore beneath her breath. She owed the merchant for shoes and hadn't the coin to pay.

Yesterday, the dressmaker had refused to make two gowns she had ordered unless they were paid for in advance. It wouldn't take long before everyone knew of her financial distress. It was time to utilize the only leverage she had.

Charles had informed her just this morning that Garren had returned to London without his wife. Now was the perfect opportunity to take her revenge—and solve her financial difficulties.

She stayed by the window until the merchant left.

"Mary." The young maid appeared at the salon door.

"Yes, mistress." She bobbed in a curtsy.

"Have Harold ready my carriage. And tell him we'll be leaving by the back way. Then come up and help me pack a few things."

"Yes, mistress." Melody watched as the girl rushed off. It would take her the better part of a day to reach Castleside. Once there, she would put her plan into action. First, though, she needed to get a letter written.

Leaving the salon, Melody mounted the stairs to her room. At her desk, she withdrew a piece of parchment. Dipping her quill in the inkpot, she paused, gathering her thoughts before writing the brief missive. She sprinkled sand over the paper and folded it, placing it in her reticle. Before closing the purse, she checked the coins at the bottom and stuffed a hanky in beside the parchment.

Mary entered a few minutes later.

"I'll need clothing for three or four days." Pulling a bag from the back of the wardrobe, the maid began carefully packing the garments Melody chose.

"Now, take that down and be sure Harold puts it in the carriage." As her servant left, Melody pulled a black cape from the wardrobe. Putting it on, she tied it at the neck and left the room.

When she exited through the back door the carriage, along with Harold, stood waiting. "Castleside, Harold. And as discreetly as possible."

"Aye, madame." Harold tugged at his cap. The carriage pulled away just as the door closed, tossing Melody against its faded cushions.

"Watch it, you idiot. I wasn't settled yet." It seemed her pesky driver was always doing that. She swore, every time he had the chance, the man would pawn his chores off on others or do a half-hearted job. Still, with what she paid, she could expect little better.

The sky had darkened from twilight to an inky black as Melody stepped down from the carriage, her body aching from being constantly jostled. Harold had complained at her haste, but she had flatly refused anything more than one change of horses and a brief stop along the way.

"Harold, climb down here and see to a room for me." Melody watched as her exhausted driver descended. As an afterthought, Melody added, "And find a spot in the barn there for yourself." She nodded her head in the direction of the large building set behind the inn.

"Aye, madame."

Melody watched him enter the establishment, shoulders slumped, feet dragging. What was the matter with the man? Couldn't he see she was exhausted? It fatigued her more just to watch his lazy posture. She made a mental note to correct him.

Her thoughts were interrupted by Harold's approach.

"Yer room is ready, madame. I asked that he have a serving girl wait on ye. I'll just see to the horses now, if ye've nothing more ye want me to do."

"What about my bag? Do you expect me to carry it myself?"

Harold mumbled an apology. "I'll bring it around directly, madame." He climbed slowly up on his bench, and steered the horses into the barn.

Melody entered the inn, wrinkling her nose at the smell of wood smoke, ale and unwashed bodies. Lord, how she hated the lower classes. One could always tell them by their stench. A man of middle age, somewhat cleaner than the others, approached her, bobbing his head and gripping the soiled white apron tied at his overlarge waist.

"Me daughter's just seeing to yer room now, and the wife's fetching a tray fer ye, milady. If ye'll follow me, I'll lead ye to the best room we got."

Melody followed him up the rough stairs to a hallway. The landlord opened the second door on the right and waited for her to enter. His daughter bobbed in a curtsy, her ruddy cheeks flaming a bright red as she nearly toppled over, trying to edge closer to the door.

"I brung hot water in the pitcher, there, yer ladyship." She pointed to the wide ledge of the room's one window. "Ma'll bring up yer dinner real quick like. Do ye need me to help ye with yer clothes?" The girl cast a longing look at the fine material of Melody's black traveling suit.

"That won't be necessary. Direct my man to my room when he comes in with my bag."

Heavy footfalls heralded the arrival of the landlord's wife. Puffing her plump cheeks out, the woman entered the room bearing a dinner tray. Placing it on the three-legged, scarred table that sat beside the door, she offered a toothless grin. "Brung all the best for ye, milady."

Eyeing the tray critically, Melody responded in a sarcastic tone. "Yes, I can see. That will be all." She herded them out the door, slamming it shut before they could say another word.

Stepping over to the window, Melody dampened the towel left next to the pitcher and wiped the travel grime from her face and hands. She would be so glad to return to town. How she hated the country and the people who infested it.

She moved the only chair in the room closer to the table and picked at the food. She hated common food, too, but she was hungry. The bread, while coarse and brown, was at least warm and fresh. She avoided the bowl of steaming, what was it, stew? She knew she'd never keep it down. Taking a taste of the liquid in the cup, she found it was a sweet ale, really quite good, she thought grudgingly.

"Lady Melody?" A light knock interrupted her dinner. "I brung yer bag," Harold called from the other side of the door.

"Come in." She turned from her meal as Harold entered. "Well, it took you long enough. Put the bag over there near the bed." He did as she bid him and left with a slight bow.

Melody rose late the next morning. She'd slept fitfully, due to the lumpy mattress and rough linens. She should have thought to bring her own, she mused as she tidied herself. The serving girl came up, bringing a breakfast tray.

"Have my man come up immediately."

"Aye, yer ladyship." The child left the room to do her bidding.

A few minutes later, Harold knocked on the door.

"Come in, Harold." Melody pulled a coin and the folded paper from her reticle. "See that this is delivered to Lady Spenceworth, at Spenceworth Hall, immediately."

"Yes, madame." The words were spoken in one long drawn-out sigh as Harold took the note from Melody. He hurried downstairs and she rubbed her hands in anticipation. She hoped the sorry servant didn't botch this up.

The smell of damp leather and rain hung inside the carriage as it sloshed its way toward Castleside, leaving Spenceworth behind. Rain beat a tattoo on the roof, and thunder drowned out all conversation.

Jocelyn held the carriage strap in a death grip, trying to avoid being thrown against Dulcey. They had been tossed around the interior like bolts in a coffee can, and there wasn't a spot on Jocelyn's body that wasn't bruised.

She was miserable and feeling pangs of guilt for the discomfort of Dulcey and the poor driver struggling to get them to Ramsgil. But she had to get there. She had to return to her own time. No matter how wonderful Garren had been, she had to return—and before something irrevocable happened.

She hadn't given enough thought to pregnancy. This morning, she had again with the onset of her monthlies. With the first cramps, it had all come crashing down around her. If she were to become pregnant, there would be no choice for her; she would have to remain in Garren's time. There was no way she could desert their child. Even if Nelwina was a wonderful woman, Jocelyn couldn't abandon her child for another woman to carry, give birth to and raise.

No, she had to leave and now—while Garren was away—was the perfect time. And her knowledge that the time was right seemed confirmed by the appearance of this thunderstorm. It had sprung up on their journey and seemed to mirror the heartbreak of leaving that tore her apart.

She tried picturing her small apartment, with its balcony overlooking a courtyard with a few scraggly bushes and a fountain that hadn't seen water in the two years she'd lived there. Her little kitchen, so cute, with her Mr. Coffee Jr., and her microwave that was just barely big enough for her diet TV dinners. Everything was small and compact, just right for one person. Her.

The carriage slowed, pulling Jocelyn from her thoughts. Glancing out, she recognized Castleside. They were almost there.

"Dulcey, tell Thomas to take us to Ramsgil."

The maid gave her a startled glance.

"Milady?"

"Please, Dulcey. I know just the place I need to go."

The girl nodded, thumped on the roof, and then poked her head out and gave Jocelyn's directions to the driver.

Dulcey settled back inside against the cushions, her hair windblown and damp from the rain. Another flood of guilt swept Jocelyn.

Yes, she'd be glad to get back to where she belonged.

The carriage rumbled along and Jocelyn kept repeating to herself, I'll be glad to get back. It was the only way to keep at bay her other thoughts.

And suddenly with a crack of lightning came clarity.

"Like hell, I will," Jocelyn mumbled. The tiny twentieth-century city apartment no longer held any charm for her. She hadn't had coffee since this whole thing happened, and she didn't miss it. And the TV dinners she had thought were so great paled in comparison to Cook's wonderful dishes.

And she'd become accustomed to the quietude of the country. No horns blaring, phones ringing, televisions blasting. No shaking windows from the bass reverberating from some teenager's car.

Jocelyn had adjusted to this life, and now that she thought about leaving, sadness pulled at her heart. She would miss it and the people. Mrs.

Cowan and her efficient ways, the smile that always seemed to light her eyes. Spalding and his ramrod straight posture. Never would she see him a little tipsy, dancing on the table, she'd had such hope he would someday soften just a little. There would be no more shouting matches with Richard Warrick, no shared jokes. No more stern looks from Garren, no soft words in the dark of night, no tender touches or gentle kisses. No searing passion or blazing anger. No food fights in the dining room. No more making love.

No more love, period.

When had she started crying? Wiping at the tears running down her cheeks, she swallowed the dismal wail that threatened to undo her.

"Stop!" The word screeched from Jocelyn's lips, startling Dulcey.

"What, milady?"

"Dulcey, make him stop! We have to go home."

"But, Lady Spenceworth—"

"Dulcey, don't you see? I can't leave Garren."

"Ye were leaving milord? But ye just said as ye were going to buy ribbon." Her maid looked terrified.

"Never mind that. How do I get the driver to stop?"

Dulcey beat on the roof with her fist, her confused gaze filling Jocelyn with an hysterical joy.

The carriage slowed to a stop, and a moment later the door jerked open. "What is it? Is something wrong?" The driver leaned into the dark interior.

"No, nothing's wrong. Just turn around and take us back to Spenceworth."

"But, milady—"

"Please, just take me home. This was all a mistake."

"Aye, milady, but the horses be tired."

"Can we get fresh ones at Castleside?"

"Aye. It'll take near an hour to get back to Castleside, what with the weather and roads worsening."

"I know, and I'm sorry to be putting you through this. Maybe we should stay the night at Castleside and return in the morning?"

"Aye, milady. I'll find a wider spot to turn around in, then we'll head back."

The door closed; the carriage rocked and then started forward. Several minutes later, Jocelyn felt the vehicle sway to the side as it made a wide sweep and began to turn around.

Suddenly, it tilted to the right and began sliding sideways. Jocelyn heard the shouts of the driver and Dulcey's whimpers of fear. A gust of wind battered the coach as it bumped against something and then teetered and fell. Jocelyn's head slammed against the side of the coach. Her world tumbled over and over to the sound of Dulcey's screams.

With weary steps, Garren climbed the stairs to the front door of Spenceworth, thankful he'd gotten home before the storm broke. The gray clouds darkened the sky and a strong breeze swirled around him. A piece of white paper, caught between the wall and top step waved like a pennant as the breeze built to a wind.

Bending down, he pulled the parchment loose just as the front door swung open. Stuffing the paper into his pocket, he straightened and turned to face his butler.

"Milord, 'tis good to see you home again."

"Ah, Spalding." Garren walked passed the servant. "Ivan will be along. See that Cook gets something warm for him to eat."

"Aye, milord." The butler closed the door and headed for the servants' hall.

"Where is Lady Jocelyn?" Garren glanced in the library and back to the man.

"Lady Jocelyn left this morning to buy ribbons and trim."

"Oh. Then she should be back soon. I'll wait to dine when she returns."

"Very good, milord."

Moving to the library, Garren asked, "Has Baskin returned?"

"Aye, milord."

"Tell him I'll meet with him in the morning, then."

Spalding nodded. "Will there be anything else, sir?"

"Aye. Have a bath readied for me."

"Yes, milord." The servant left, and Garren mounted the stairs.

In the chamber he shared with Jocelyn he shrugged out of his coat, draping it on a nearby chair as he went to the small secretary Jocelyn had placed in the corner near the window. He smiled. She'd insisted on her own little space, not wanting to clutter his desk with her inventories and menus.

He picked up a menu, reading the carefully penned notes. Their meals had certainly taken on a different flavor since her arrival. She'd finally conquered Cook, and their meals were light, yet filling. He smiled as he scanned the crisp simple letters of her hand writing. Frowning, he studied it. Why did that hand seem so familiar?

A knock at the door drew his attention away.

Virginia Farmer

"Yes?" He placed the paper back on the desk and turned around.

"Yer water, milord." Servants brought in buckets of water, filling the large tub. Towels and soap were placed on the table before they left, closing the door after them.

Garren lifted his jacket from the chair, preparing to hang it up when the crackle of paper reminded him of the folded sheet from the steps. Drawing it out of the pocket, he opened it.

5,000 pounds will ensure your secret. Meet me in Castleside.

He read the lines twice before they made sense to him.

"Spalding," he yelled, panic filling him. With jerky movements, he pulled on his jacket again, rushing from the room.

In the hall he bumped into the butler as the man answered his summons.

"Milord, what's happened?"

"Who delivered this missive?" Garren shook the note in Spalding's face.

Following Garren down the stairs, Spalding answered, a hint of reproach in his voice. "Milord? There's been no note delivered since you left."

Garren felt himself blanche. If no one had delivered the note . . . had Jocelyn left it? No, surely not. He had already determined that she was no thief. Then, had she gone to protect his secret?

In the library, Garren went to the chest containing the estate cash. Flipping back the lid, he swore when he found it empty.

"Damn it." He turned to the butler hovering in the doorway. "When did she leave?"

"Milord? Oh, Lady Jocelyn? Around eleven, I believe. She and Dulcey left in the carriage."

"Have a mount saddled—and be quick about it, man."

Clouds scudded across the night sky, revealing a bright half-moon. A fresh wind playfully rippled through the trees, creating a natural symphony of rustling leaves and humming branches, but Garren only noted the absence of rain.

Uncertain where the meeting was to take place, Garren stopped at Castleside's blacksmith shop and enquired after the Spenceworth carriage. He was in luck, the smith had noted the carriage's crest.

"Passed right through town at a smart clip," the man answered, wiping his hands on his apron.

"You're certain it was the Spenceworth carriage?"

"Aye, milord. 'Twould be hard not to notice it."

With a grunt, Garren turned his horse back to the main thoroughfare. He focused on the road ahead, blocking out the niggling question . . . why hadn't Jocelyn stopped?

He sped off down the road.

Around every bend in the road, he expected to come upon the carriage. For over half an hour, his hopes were dashed.

Finally, when the road curved and he saw moonlight glinting off a lone carriage wheel and the horses standing in their tracers beside it, a wave of relief washed over him. It was followed by the chill of foreboding.

"Jocelyn?" Garren's right foot touched the

ground even before his horse had stopped. Running to the wheel, Garren sucked in a breath, fighting the panic that filled his mind.

A whimper near a cluster of bushes caught Garren's attention. Rushing toward it, he prayed Jocelyn wasn't hurt too badly, but by the looks of the carriage he was surprised anyone had survived. The whimpering grew louder, and Garren parted the brush. In the moonlight, he saw a muddy, scraggly Dulcey, shaking and crying.

"Dulcey, are you hurt?" The authority in Garren's voice brought a stop to the maid's whimpers.

"Oh, Lord Spenceworth. It were so bad. It was raining so hard and the wind and the thunder . . . scared me so much. I . . ."

"Dulcey, can you get up?" Garren interrupted Dulcey's anxious dialogue.

With Garren's aid, Dulcey crawled from the brush and stood on shaky legs.

"Jocelyn?" Fear caught at Garren's voice as he made a circuitous route of the rolled carriage.

"Milord." A feeble call lured Garren from his search for Jocelyn. "Here, milord. 'Tis Thomas, the coachman."

Garren followed the sound of the voice and saw Thomas limping toward the coach, his arm cradled against his body.

"Have you seen Jocelyn?"

"No, milord."

Blindly, Garren returned to the coach, slipping down the muddy embankment. "Jocelyn. Jocelyn. Can you hear me?" His voice broke with emotion. There was no evidence of his wife outside the carriage. Garren hoist himself up on the door, peering into its interior. A narrow ribbon of moonlight lessened the cavernous darkness inside the carriage.

"Jocelyn?" The smell of damp earth rose up as he eased himself down. Gingerly feeling his way into the overturned vehicle, Garren finally touched a cool, clammy arm.

"Jocelyn?" His voice shook with relief. "Everything will be fine. I'll get you out of here. Do you hear me?" Garren heard only the rattle of Jocelyn's labored breathing. As he knelt down, the cool, soft dampness of mud seeped into his pantleg.

Cradling his disheveled wife on his lap, Garren stared at her face. Her pale cheeks were marred by dark streaks. Hesitantly he brushed at them, praying it was dirt and not blood. His shoulders slumped in relief as his fingers encountered cold, grainy mud. He gently smoothed tangled strands of hair from her forehead, his hand stilling on a lump on her temple. "Jocelyn, love, can you hear me?" Garren's frantic words were snatched away as a sudden breeze swirled around in the carriage.

Placing his fingers against her neck, he felt a faint pulse. Worry furrowed his brow as a shiver shook Jocelyn's shoulders. Garren tightened his embrace, trying to share his warmth with her.

Forcing the worry from his mind, Garren called out to the coachman. "Thomas?"

"Aye, milord."

The thud of the coachman's footsteps came closer.

"I'll need you to help me with Lady Jocelyn."

It seemed to take hours to get her free of the carriage. Thomas's injuries hampered the endeavor, but finally, his wife lay on the empty roadside, her head pillowed in Garren's lap.

She needed a doctor, warmth, and dry clothing. Gazing around, Garren realized that none of those things was available. His mind frantically searched for a solution.

Thomas and Dulcey stood back, huddled together. From the grimace on Thomas's face, the pain in his arm and leg had worsened; and Garren knew the man couldn't ride for help. And Dulcey would never make it, even if she could ride. He needed a wagon, or a miracle.

The tinkling of bells carried on the evening breeze. It took a moment for the sound to penetrate Garren's frustrated mind.

"Ye'll be needing me, then."

Garren stared mutely as a small woman approached, leading a swaybacked horse drawing a wagon. She chuckled, a rasping sound that came from the back of her throat.

Leaving the horse on the road, she strode to Garren's side and peered down at Jocelyn. "Up with ye now. Don't ye worry none, I'll be seeing to the lady. Just follow me."

Garren stared at the odd woman a moment. "Who are *you*?"

"Hilda." She moved back to the horse and started down the road again. "Well, are ye coming or no? Mind ye bring yer horses along."

"Where are you going? I need to get a doctor for my wife." Garren rose, Jocelyn cradled in his arms, and followed the woman. Thomas snagged the reins of Garren's mount and the carriage horses, and he and Dulcey followed.

"To a nice spot. Ye need a nice hot fire and something warm, both inside and out."

"And she thinks there's dry wood to be found, now, after the storm?" Garren muttered, glancing down at his unconscious wife. Wrinkling his brow, he placed his lips on her cool forehead.

"Please hold on, love. I'll get help." Jocelyn didn't respond to his whispered words.

Hilda turned the horse off the road, heading

into a stand of trees. After a few minutes, they came to a small clearing. Pulling the wagon off to the side, Hilda called to Dulcey, "Ye'll find some dry wood beneath them trees. Fetch it, child."

Dulcey glanced at Garren; he nodded his consent.

Hilda disappeared into her wagon, reappearing with her arms laden with blankets. Making a pallet, she directed Garren. "Lay her down here. Wrap up in the other blanket while I tend to Jocelyn."

Garren gently placed Jocelyn on the bed of blankets. "How did you know her name?"

Kneeling next to Garren, Hilda covered her. "Later. Ye'll know all ye need to later."

"But—"

Hilda gave him a reproachful look. "Don't ye have a care fer yer wife? I said, *later*." Her sharp words drove Garren back.

Her back to the center of the clearing, Hilda called out, "Thomas, help Dulcey to start a good fire, now. When I've seen to yer mistress, I'll see to yer arm."

Thomas flashed a startled look to Garren. Garren shrugged. "You'd best see to it. And then you and Dulcey should wrap up in blankets and get warm."

"Fetch me some water from the small barrel on the side of the wagon. There's a cup hanging next to it." At Hilda's orders, Garren turned his gaze in her direction. "Aye, *you*." She nodded at him. "Get me the water."

Before he could rise, Dulcey appeared next to Hilda, the cup of water in her hand.

With a reproving glare at Garren, Hilda thanked Dulcey and set to work cleaning Jocelyn's face. Silently, the old woman rose, heading for her wagon. From beneath the seat she withdrew a small box. Opening it, she brought out a small jar and returned to her patient.

After dabbing a pungent ointment on Jocelyn's temples, she adjusted the blankets and returned the jar to the box.

The fire crackled, emitting a welcome warmth as Garren sat near it beside Jocelyn's unconscious form, watching Hilda tend Thomas.

"Don't seem to bad." Taking a square of material from her box, she created a sling for his arm. "Nothing broken, just pulled in the wrong direction. Ye'll mend."

Retrieving the box, Hilda returned it to its place beneath the wagon seat and headed back to the fire.

She plopped down on the other side of the fire and motioned to Garren. " 'Tis time we talked."

At Garren's hesitation, she clucked. "Dulcey, sit with yer mistress and see that she stays covered."

Dulcey took Garren's place as he rose and went after Hilda.

"She'll be fine."

"And how do you know this?" Worry sharpened Garren's words.

Hilda chuckled. "I know a lot of things."

"I'm sure you do." Garren mumbled. In the morning, no matter what he had to pay, he'd use this woman's wagon to take Jocelyn to the nearest doctor. She alternately shook and thrashed from fever.

"Yer wife isn't who she seems to be."

Garren jerked his gaze from Jocelyn to Hilda. Just what did this woman know? Was *she* the blackmailer?

"Tell me, Hilda, can you write?"

"Now what would I be needing to write?"

"A note, maybe?"

Hilda cackled, the dry sound rubbing against Garren's taut nerves. "A note." The cackle died to a chuckle. "A note," she repeated, her laughter rolling forth again, filling the small clearing.

"It's hardly that funny." Garren's annoyance dripped from his words.

"Ah, me fine sir, ye're looking in the wrong place fer that. I can't write. Never had a yearning to. No, I'm a helper—of sorts."

"Pardon me? And just what does that mean?"

Ignoring Garren's questions, Hilda continued, "As a helper, I know many things most don't. Strange things."

Garren felt decidedly uncomfortable with the woman's ramblings. She was nothing but a crazy old woman with a wagon. Well, he'd put up with it just to get Jocelyn the real medical help she needed. God grant him the patience.

Hilda elbowed Garren in the ribs. "Ye should be payin' attention to me. If ye love Jocelyn there, ye'll open yer mind and listen."

He jerked to attention. This is just a crazy woman, he reminded himself.

"And ye can just stop thinking I'm crazy. If ye're too stubborn or stupid to listen to me, fine. But it's yer happiness and Jocelyn's well-being ye'll be missin'."

Could the woman read his mind? And what had she said about Jocelyn's well-being? Mayhap he should listen, just in case, to the old crone.

"I don't take to the word crone. I'm in me prime." Hilda straightened her shoulders, thrusting out her nearly flat chest. It reminded him of a wet sparrow preening.

"So don't be cursing me with that word," the woman finished.

229

Garren sucked in a breath. She *could* read his thoughts. Ridiculous.

"Are ye ready to listen now?"

"Yes, fine. Tell me your story."

"Did ye never notice how strange the woman was?" She nodded toward Jocelyn. "Did ye never think there was something, not really wrong with her, just real different?" Hilda paused a moment.

Garren didn't respond; he just waited for her to continue.

"Did she never do things that didn't fit? Or say things that were strange? Not just odd, mind ye; men think all women's thoughts be odd."

Garren mulled her words over. He could cite several instances when Jocelyn had either said or did something he didn't comprehend. Like her costume at the ball. Who would have thought up something like that? Or what about what Mrs. Cowan had told him about her fit on the floor of the bedroom. Jocelyn had called them "ab crunches." They were strange words he'd dismissed at the time.

"And that's just the beginning."

"What do you mean? Is there something I should know about her?"

Hilda chuckled, "Oh, there be lots ye don't know."

"Tell me."

"Will ye be listening with an open mind, then?" She tilted her head, studying him closely.

"Yes." Garren shifted uncomfortably beneath her scrutiny.

"Hmm. Well, if ye're sure."

"I'm sure." He bit back the frustration welling inside him as she paused.

"Yer wife ain't from this time."

Garren shot to his feet, furious that he'd been

baited. "I don't know what game you're playing, but it stops right now." He jabbed his finger toward the ground. "I won't listen to any more of your demented rambling."

"Ye just remember what I told ye. She ain't of this time. Her world be much different than this one. And she has yet to make a choice between hers and yers. Remember me words when the nightmares begin, and listen carefully. Ye'll learn a lot."

Garren glared at the woman, then turned and strode over to Jocelyn, relieving Dulcey.

"Get some sleep, Dulcey. Tomorrow may prove to be more difficult than today."

"Aye, milord. Do ye think she'll be alright?" The maid pulled her blanket tighter around her shoulders.

"We can only pray."

Garren curled up in his blanket behind Jocelyn, a prayer on his lips as exhaustion claimed him.

Sunlight flickered through the trees. Garren opened his eyes to a new morning. Jocelyn lay curled in his arms, fever radiating from her small body. The events of last evening descended on him.

Pushing up, he gazed around the clearing. Thomas and Dulcey, wrapped in blankets, slept across from the ashes of the fire. Though his horses remained tethered to a bush at the outer reaches of the clearing, there was no trace of Hilda or her wagon.

Garren jumped to his feet. "Thomas. Dulcey. Wake up." Garren's loud whisper failed to reach either of the two servants.

Striding quickly to them, he nudged the coachman with the toe of his boot. "Thomas, wake up."

Thomas focused bleary eyes on Garren. "Aye, milord?"

"Where's Hilda? When did she leave?"

Confused, Thomas rose. "She's gone?" He glanced around the clearing as he rubbed at his sore arm. "Dulcey, did you hear the old woman leave?"

Scrubbing the sleep from her eyes, Dulcey followed Thomas's gaze. "No, milord. I didn't hear anything all evening."

"How the hell could the woman leave without waking any of us?" Garren ran a hand through his hair.

"How will we get Lady Spenceworth home, milord?" Thomas's worried question echoed Garren's own.

Kneeling down at Jocelyn's side, anxiety tightened Garren's chest as his hand caressed her burning brow.

"The road is well-traveled. Mayhap we'll find help there. Thomas, bring the horses." Garren picked Jocelyn up and headed out of the clearing.

Not very much later, a familiar carriage lumbered by. Garren's father stuck his head out the window, looking back at the foot travelers. With a shout to the driver, the vehicle stopped.

"Garren! Is that you, son?"

"Aye, Father." Garren shouted, increasing his stride.

Richard was out of the carriage, walking toward Garren. His brow furrowed as he recognized his son's burden.

"What's happened to your wife?"

"Father, how did . . . how came you here?"

"I was coming to drag you back to London. You're still needed and you should never have left. Then I met a strange woman, who claimed I must ride here. What's happened?" Richard held his hands out, silently offering to take Jocelyn, and Garren lost all pretense of calm as his father neared.

With a shake of his head, he moved abreast of his father's carriage door. Richard opened it, and standing to the side, he waved Garren in.

"There was a carriage accident."

Richard glanced at Thomas and Dulcey, then looked Garren up and down. "I take it you weren't involved?"

Garren settled Jocelyn on the seat inside, straightening the blanket and tucking it under her chin.

"Thomas, you and Dulcey ride up with Henry." Richard sat across from Garren and Jocelyn. "Has she come to yet?"

Creases of worry etched Garren's forehead. "No. I'm worried, Father. Her skin is so hot and dry; first she shivers and then she's burning to the touch. I've got to get a doctor for her."

"We'll get her to London. She'll need the best we can find, son." He reached across, his hand gripping Garren's wrist reassuringly. "She's a strong woman. She'll be fine with proper care."

Chapter Fifteen

"Where the bloody hell is the chit?" Melody thumped her fist against the worn seat of her carriage. "Surely she should have come this way by now."

Frustrated, she lifted the leather from the window. "Harold? Have you seen nothing?"

The coachman moved to the side of the carriage, rain dripping from the brim of his hat. With a shake of his head, he responded, "No, milady. There's been no coach come this way."

"And you're sure this is the only way it would come from Spenceworth?" She narrowed her gaze on him.

"Aye, milady."

"You're certain the note was delivered?"

"Aye, milady. I spoke with the ... er ... messenger when he returned. He assured me that the note was at the manor."

"Well, where the bloody hell is she, then?" Frustration transformed Melody's question into a shriek.

"Milady? I'm certain, I don't know." Harold tugged at his hat, taking a few steps back.

"Well, it's useless to stay here any longer. Take me back to the inn. I suppose we'll have to stay another night, but tomorrow by noon, we'll return home."

"Very good, milady."

The carriage shifted as Harold took his seat. Melody fumed. Now what was she to do? Her mind searched frantically for a solution, for a way to make Garren pay for his callous treatment of her. Pursing her lips, her eyes narrowed, and she concentrated on the problem. She had time yet, but not much.

She looked so small in the bed of Garren's London house. Her skin was alternately bright pink with fever, then translucent white. He sat in a chair pulled near the bed, Jocelyn's limp hand held in his. The doctor had come and gone, telling Garren nothing more could be done for her. Time would heal the wound on her head but he didn't know how long it would be before she'd awaken.

But what if she never woke? What if he lost her? A twinge in the area of his heart made him catch his breath.

She'd come to mean so much more to him. What had ever made him think he could keep her at arm's length? Garren shook his head. Whatever had made him think he *wanted* to?

She had changed his life, filling it, making it complete. There was a purpose to his days, a direction to his future. Now Garren understood what his father felt when his mother died. He hoped Richard found love again. To be bereft of it left a person empty and incomplete.

His thoughts turned to the mystery of the note. During the past few hours, Garren began to ponder who had sent the note and why Jocelyn had not stopped in Castleside. Even if she were only buying ribbon, she could have found some there. It didn't make any sense.

A tortured groan from Jocelyn interrupted his thoughts. With the palm of his hand, Garren smoothed away the moisture dotting her face.

"Shh, love, you're home. Everything will be fine." He tucked a tendril of damp hair behind her ear. "Just rest." He didn't know if his wife heard him, but it calmed him to say the words.

Garren remained at her side as she sank into a deeper sleep. Sliding down in a chair, he rested his head against its wooden back. Closing his eyes, he allowed his mind to wander from one memory to another until at last he came to the meeting with Hilda.

What exactly had the old woman meant about Jocelyn not being of this time? And why was he even wondering about such an odd statement from an even odder woman? But for some reason he didn't understand, he couldn't dismiss it.

Exhausted both physically and emotionally, Garren's lids slid closed and he slept.

As the first rays of dawn streaked through the windows, Garren was awakened as Dulcey brought in fresh water.

"Milord, how is milady?" The maid replaced the bowl on the table. Garren stretched the kinks out of his spine and glanced over at his wife. Her breathing was deep and regular. Though still pale, her complexion didn't carry the flush of

fever. Gently placing his palm on her forehead, he
sighed in relief at the feel of cool, dry skin.

"I believe the fever has broken. If only she
would awaken."

"Aye, milord, 'tis what the staff is praying for."
Dulcey's eyes glistened with unshed tears. "Shall I
bring ye a bit of breakfast, milord?"

"That would be fine, Dulcey. Would you have
some hot water sent up as well?" He rose from
the hard chair.

Dulcey bobbed a quick curtsy. "Right away,
milord." She left, quietly closing the door.

Garren's relief at Jocelyn's improvement was
nearly euphoric. He stepped before the window,
rubbing the back of his neck. If only she would
open those beautiful gray eyes, he thought. Then
all would be right with his world.

Well, he amended, maybe after she answered
some questions, all would be right.

It was quite suddenly that Jocelyn awoke, moan-
ing at the brightness of the room and the pain in
her head. A man, dozing in a chair next to her,
jerked to attention at the noise and for a confused
moment stared at her stupidly before some real-
ization dawned on him.

"Jocelyn, love. You're awake." The smile on his
face was comical. Her sleep-drugged mind
refused to recognize him.

"Who . . ." His smile disappeared.

"You don't remember me? Garren, your husband?" Misery flooded his brown eyes.

She'd just had the strangest dream and, awak-
ening, felt an odd sense of disappointment that it
was over.

Jocelyn's gaze scanned the face of the man
before her. Yes, he was familiar. She thought

another moment. Garren. Yes, of course . . . but then . . .

Jocelyn took in his clothing, the bedroom. And the dream became reality. Elation crowded out the disappointment.

Bringing her gaze back to Garren, she whispered, "Yes, but what happened? I feel like I've been run over by a semi."

"A what?" His brow furrowed in confusion.

"A . . . oh, nothing. What happened?"

"You don't remember?"

Jocelyn concentrated, piecing together events she recalled. Her decision to leave Spenceworth before circumstances prevented; the howling storm; a frightened Dulcey, and then . . .

"The carriage turned over, oh, lord." Turning her gaze to Garren, she reached a trembling hand to him.

"Yes, but you're fine." He took her hand, squeezing it in reassurance. "Nothing broken, just a nasty bump to your head."

Noticing the stubble on Garren's cheeks, Jocelyn raised her fingers to rub it. "How long have I been asleep?"

"Two nights now."

"Oh." She glanced past Garren. "How are Dulcey and Thomas? Were they injured?"

"Just a few bumps and scratches, but they're fine." Garren smoothed Jocelyn's hair with gentle fingers.

"Good. You should get some rest, Garren. You look exhausted."

"I will, but you should do the same thing."

"Hm, yes." The word faded as Jocelyn's eyes closed. She let a sigh escape as she drifted back into happier slumber.

* * *

Four days later, Richard entered the library, taking the seat opposite his son's desk. "How is Jocelyn today?"

Garren glanced up from the paper before him.

"She's fine. Though she's still a little weak."

"Are you still trying to puzzle out why she left Spenceworth?"

"I'm certain this is what set her off, though I haven't wanted to mention it to her." Garren slid the note across his desk to his father. He'd been reluctant to bring his father in on this, either. Garren didn't know where it would lead, but he needed someone else to help him reason it out.

While Richard picked up the note and read it, Garren continued.

"I've questioned the coachman. Just before they reached Castleside, Jocelyn ordered him to Ramsgil."

Garren ran a hand through his hair. "What I don't understand is where she put the money. The estate money box was empty, and Thomas said she carried nothing more than a small reticule."

His father glanced up from the note.

"The money, you say?" He pushed the parchment back to Garren. "Didn't Baskin inform you?"

His placed the note aside, still puzzling over Jocelyn's actions. "Of what?"

"Your money's been deposited with a goldsmith."

Garren looked up, confused. What was his father saying?

"Jocelyn made quite a fuss when she discovered the cash. She bade Baskin make the deposit."

Garren's attention was diverted from Jocelyn's actions.

"By whose authority?" Garren fought to keep his voice down.

"I heartily endorsed her. She was quite astute in pointing out the benefits."

"Who gave her leave to even look into it?" He leveled a glare at his father, knowing the answer.

His father leaned back in his chair.

"By *my* leave." Richard's jaw flexed. "After all, you'd simply abandoned her to your estate—it seemed fitting she might look after it. She is a noblewoman and obviously was capable of such a task."

Garren fumed silently. His hand curled around the parchment, drawing it into his fist.

Garren's mind reeled. Lowering his gaze, he tried to understand how Jocelyn would come by such knowledge. His gaze flickered over the menu she'd insisted on preparing for this evening's meal, though she now rested upstairs for her effort.

He frowned. The writing was familiar, and he struggled to recall where he'd seen it before. Remembering the other menu at Spenceworth and the certainty that he'd seen the writing there someplace else he looked away, concentrating. Idly, he noticed the ledger sitting off to the side.

"Bloody hell." He pulled the menu closer.

Yes. That was the same handwriting as on the paper in the old ledger at Spenceworth. He was sure of it.

"Garren?" At his father's demand for his attention, he raised his gaze.

"What?" He spoke the word abruptly, irritated.

"I asked if you knew anything in Jocelyn's past that might be referred to by this blackmailer?"

Garren gathered his composure. Was there anything in her past?

Oh, no. Only the fact that she's a commoner and I purchased her. But was there something else, too? She had neatly sidestepped his questions the day of the picnic.

"Garren?"

He jerked his gaze up from the desk, leveling it on his father and wondered how best to tell the man what he knew. He stared down at the strange letter and absently smoothed it out.

Garren felt his father's regard and looked up. Richard glanced at the note resting on the desk. His eyes narrowed, transfixing Garren in his chair.

"What the bloody hell have you done this time?" The low rumble of his father's voice was ominous.

Garren straightened his shoulders.

"Bought and married a commoner." He shrugged. Well, he'd said it. Now, he had but to weather the—

"Christ and all His saints!" His father shot to his feet, his chair crashing to the floor.

Storm, Garren finished.

"*Bought* her?" The windows rattled with Richard's voice. "Whatever possessed you to *buy* a wife?"

"Is there a difference between purchasing one with coin or with one's name and fortune?"

"You can be bloody well sure there is."

"Yes?"

Richard shook his head. Garren watched as his father struggled to capture that difference, to explain it. The silence stretched as his father's gaze met his.

"There is no difference, Father."

"But where? Where could you possible buy a wife?"

"Ramsgil."

Richard walked back to his chair, righted it and sat down heavily. "Excuse me?"

Garren took a deep breath before telling his father of the events of that day at the village green.

"You can't mean that Jocelyn is really a commoner?" Richard leaned over the desk toward Garren when the story was finished.

"Aye, Father." Even as he said it, Garren wondered if it were true.

Garren shifted in his chair.

"Nay." Richard shook his head. "I can't fathom it. She is a lady through and through. Well, a bit outspoken, but I attributed that to being a Colonial."

"I'd not let her hear you using that term. She becomes quite outraged." Garren swallowed the inappropriate smile that tugged at his lips.

"From your description, you saved her from a life of drudgery." Richard frowned. "She is beautiful . . . But I still don't understand why you felt the need to purchase a wife."

"The ultimatum."

"Oh, no. You'll not be laying this at my doorstep, Garren." Pushing to his feet, Richard paced to the hearth, his gaze on the glowing embers.

"I'm not laying it anywhere. I happen to be quite pleased with my choice. If given the opportunity, I'd do it all again." Garren leaned back in his chair, more than a little surprised at his own words.

Yes, damn it, he'd do it all again.

"I still can't believe Jocelyn is common. She's far too intelligent and well-educated." Richard eyed his son.

"There's a mystery here. When I asked of her background, I came away with nothing more than that she was educated and from South Carolina."

"Do you think someone in Ramsgil has discovered her mystery and hopes to profit from it?"

"I doubt that. Look at this parchment; it's not something you'd find in a village in northern England." Garren rubbed the expensive stationery.

His father turned to Garren, taking his seat again. "If she is from South Carolina and educated—which is obvious—then her family must be deep in the pockets. So how did you find her in a village being sold?"

"Exactly." Garren splayed his hands on the wooden desktop.

"Shall I see if I can glean any information?"

"Aye, Father, but be discreet. Whatever it is, it can't have been her fault. I refuse to believe Jocelyn has done anything truly wrong. Mayhap something embarrassing, but not criminal."

"I'll see to it."

After his father left, Garren sat, fingering his wife's menu, his mind wading through unanswered questions. If what his father thought was true, then why had she come to England and married beneath her station? Was she running from something? Or had she done something to bring about social ostracism?

But why would she leave him? She had not been headed to Castleside. Was she suddenly afraid of bringing disgrace to the Warrick name?

That had to be it, he thought. Nothing else made any sense.

But what of all those odd words and phrases she used? *Mock sale. Calories. Train. Sure. Semi. What about them?*

Unbidden, Hilda's words came to him. He shook his head, he couldn't credit anything the crazy old woman said. He wouldn't. Jocelyn was the only one who could set things to right.

It had been four days since her fever had broken. Though she still tired easily, she was much better. She would be well enough to answer his questions tonight after dinner.

"Come, have a glass of wine with me before retiring; it will help you sleep." Garren cupped Jocelyn's elbow, guiding her to the library.

Jocelyn spared him a quizzical look. "I haven't had trouble sleeping. But I'll sit with you if you like."

Entering the library, Garren headed to the sideboard where a decanter of wine stood, the fire in the hearth creating spectra as its light danced across the cut crystal. Jocelyn settled herself in one of the chairs before the fireplace. Garren, wine in hand, took the seat next to her.

"Are you tired?" Garren took a sip, setting his glass on the table between the chairs, and turned his gaze on her.

Jocelyn took a deep breath and met his gaze with a smile. "A little." He'd been remote during dinner. Though he tried to cover it, Jocelyn saw the odd tightness of his lips.

There was silence. Tension electrified the air.

A moment passed. She glanced his way. Her smile dissolved at his frown.

"What is it, Garren?" She couldn't stand the strain between them.

"Father was here while you were resting." He gazed at her over his steepled fingers.

"Oh, I'm sorry I missed him." Her nerves tightened, her stomach drew up in a knot.

"He told me of the deposit with the goldsmith."

Was that all? She exhaled her breath, surprised that she'd been holding it.

"Heavens, I'd forgotten all about that. And you're just now finding out about it?" She leaned forward. "I'm so sorry. I just assumed Baskin had informed you."

" 'Tis not what concerns me." He brought his hands down.

"Oh?"

"What concerns me is where you came by your knowledge of accounts."

Surprised, she opened her mouth and then snapped it shut before she could blurt out that she was a tax accountant.

She calmed herself, grasping one thought.

"What do you mean? Goldsmiths aren't uncommon. Most people know of them."

"Aye, but most women can't prepare a statement."

Jocelyn just stared back at him, wondering how he knew of her capabilities.

Exhaling, her husband paused and picked up a piece of paper from the table. "You have a very distinctive hand." He held up the menu she'd prepared.

She inclined her head, wondering. *So what's that got to do with accounting?*

"Jocelyn, I found a statement you started in an old ledger."

The blood rushed from her face, leaving her a bit lightheaded. Her hands shook as she gripped the arms of the chair.

Oh Lord, now that, she thought, panicked. What was she to do now? Confess? Tell him she was an accountant from the twentieth century?

Yeah, like he'd believe that one.

He threw her another curve.

"What brought you here?"

Jocelyn sighed in resignation. It was time Garren found out.

"A block of wood." Her head began to throb. Whether he believed it or not, she had to tell him the truth. Since waking from the accident, she realized she'd made the right decision to stay. She loved Garren and couldn't see life without him.

But did he love her? Or was she to be rejected yet again? She risked losing him and ending up in Bedlam when he heard the truth, she thought.

"Pardon? Did you say a block of wood?"

The look on Garren's face almost made her laugh.

Almost.

"Oh, Garren." She sighed again. "You're going to find this really hard to believe. I know I did."

Then she began her tale. With each bit of information she told him, his eyes opened wider.

Garren stood up and began pacing. "Are you saying Hilda was on the green that day?"

Jocelyn nodded. "She tugged on my skirt and told me that the woman who'd taken my place was having a worse time than I." She shrugged. "I didn't understand what she was talking about. Before I could question her, she'd disappeared into the crowd. I didn't see her again until the night Charles kidnapped me."

Garren felt her gaze as he paced upon the carpet before the hearth.

"You realize how preposterous this all sounds?" He stopped and turned to her.

She nodded again, her gray eyes filled with unshed tears.

He braced himself, fighting the urge to take her

in his arms and soothe away her distress. He
needed to understand, not comfort her.

"Garren, don't you remember in the inn? When
you told me to bathe?" Jocelyn's words rushed
out. "Remember when I screamed, and you came
in and I demanded to know what had happened
to my body?"

He stared at her a moment, recalling the abject
fear and confusion on her face that night. "Aye."
He nodded.

Jocelyn pushed to her feet and stood before
Garren.

"I should be five feet, nine inches tall and weigh
around one-thirty-five. My hair should be short
and dark brown. My eyes should be green."

Garren shook his head, finding it hard to believe
what she was saying. He wanted to believe her,
but he needed some sort of proof. It was all too
much, even prepared as he had been.

"What of 'reverse accounting equation?'" The
notation at the bottom of the statement still puzzled him. He'd questioned his receiver general,
but the man had given him an odd look before
explaining, in more detail, the workings of Garren's accounts.

"It's a way of remembering which accounts are
credit balances and which are debits." Jocelyn
sat. Folding her hands in her lap, she lifted her
wary gaze to his face.

Garren stared at her. She actually sounded like
his accountant. He shook his head.

"You see,"—she dashed a crystal tear from the
corner of her eye—"in the twentieth century,
assets are debits, liabilities and equity are credits.
Total credits must equal total debits to balance.

247

But in the eighteenth century, they're just the opposite."

Bloody hell, Garren thought rubbing his temples. He had the beginnings of a headache. He wasn't certain, but he thought his man had told him nearly the same thing, minus the twentieth-century part, of course.

"But how did you get *here*?" He still couldn't grasp the idea of time travel.

She shrugged. "I don't really know." A lone tear escaped, sliding slowly down her cheek. "One moment I sat down on a block of wood, the next I was being yanked on top of it, in the middle of the sale. And not even in my own body."

"This isn't your body?" He swept his hand to her.

She shook her head, smearing the tear from her cheek.

"This is utterly outrageous, you know?"

Jocelyn nodded, staring down at her hands, fingers interlaced, their knuckles white. "You should have experienced it from my vantage point."

Garren gazed at her bent head, trying to do exactly that, but he had a devil of a time just accepting the idea of time travel.

And he was still confused about the note and her flight from Spenceworth. "But what of the note?"

"What note?"

He walked to his desk and retrieved the paper. Handing it to her, he paced back to the hearth.

"Garren?"

He turned his gaze from the fireplace to his wife.

"Well?" He watched her brow furrow in confusion.

"I don't understand. Is someone trying to blackmail you?" She held the note out to him, her red-rimmed eyes confused.

"No, Jocelyn. That note was delivered to you and is the reason you left Spenceworth. I found it where you dropped it." Her frown deepened. "Didn't you?" He wondered now if the note actually had been meant for him.

She shook her head. "No. I never received this."

"Then why did you leave?"

He watched as she drew in a deep breath, dropping her gaze back to her hands.

"I was leaving you." He barely heard her words, so quietly did she speak.

"You were leaving me?" His heart lurched. "But why?"

"I couldn't stay. What if I become pregnant?" She glanced at him, twin tears etching watery paths down her cheeks.

Garren flinched. She didn't want to bear his children?

"But then, I realized that I . . ." Jocelyn paused. What was she afraid of? That he would turn from her?

"But then what?" His voice was strained his anguish tearing him apart.

"But then I realized that I . . . I love you." His wife held her breath and closed her eyes.

For a long moment, Garren didn't say anything, just watched her. She gripped her fingers tighter. Then she opened her eyes and tried to look resolute. "But, I guess the best thing is to try to get back where I belong."

His heart thudded in his chest. Did it really matter where she was from? He loved her too. Whether she was from the twentieth century or not, whether she was mad or not, and whether this was her body or not. It didn't matter to him. What mattered was her happiness. And she obviously wanted him.

"You *are* where you belong." In three rapid strides Garren was before her. Kneeling, he lifted her chin, cradling her face in his hands as he dried her tears with his thumbs.

"I'll hear no more of this. You're my wife, and there's an end to it." Another tear escaped, rolling sadly down her cheek.

"But—"

Garren captured the tear with his finger. "No, Jocelyn." He shook his head. "You belong here, with me." Misery clouded her gray eyes.

Confused, he searched her face for the reason for her unhappiness. Couldn't she tell he would not, no, he *could not* bear to part with her? Or was it the thought of having his children?

"You don't want children?"

His heart thudded painfully. Until this moment he'd not given much thought to children, but now it seemed of utmost importance that Jocelyn be the mother of his brood. He craved a little girl with blond hair and gray eyes, and her mother's laugh.

Another crystal tear slipped free. Jocelyn raised her gaze, moisture brimming in her eyes, liquefying their gray depths into molten silver.

He studied her countenance. She awaited something, he thought. Her look was guarded—as if expecting pain, or rejection.

He realized in a moment of clarity that she didn't know how he felt. A smile pulled at the corners of his lips before stretching across his face.

Jocelyn tipped her head to one side as he grinned, and tears ran in rivulets down her cheeks.

"I love you," was all he said.

Garren's simple declaration evidently destroyed her control. As he stood up, bringing her with him in an embrace, she sobbed, an uncontrollable release of pent-up emotion that shook her frame.

Chapter Sixteen

In the darkness of their room, Garren stripped their clothing off and settled Jocelyn against him in the wide bed.

Her sobbing had subsided, leaving only an occasional hiccup in her breathing. She lay curled in Garren's embrace, the bed linens draped haphazardly over them.

"You do believe me, don't you, Garren?"

Did he believe her? No. Not entirely. She was surely mistaken. But lying like this with her, it seemed unimportant, at least for the moment. But the moment would pass, he told himself, and he would have to deal with this.

" 'Tis very hard." He nuzzled her hair, inhaling the clean smell of sunshine. She'd spent time today in the garden, he thought.

"I know." Jocelyn shifted, moving back against him. He swallowed a groan. He didn't want to talk right now. His wife was too enticing, and the subject too far-fetched. Slipping his hand up from her waist, he captured her breast, allowing the weight to settle in his palm.

"I . . ."

A surge of satisfaction raced through Garren's veins as she caught her breath.

"Garren?"

"Yes, love?" The tip of her breast firmed, poking the center of his hand, sending jolts of fire to his loins.

She fidgeted.

His hardness settled against the smooth skin of her bottom, and a groan escaped from his compressed lips.

What did he care where she came from, who she was running from? Or even whether she was mad as he'd first thought. He gave a rueful shake of his head. Jocelyn was no crazier than any other woman, he thought.

"You *don't* believe me, do you?" The desolation in her voice cooled his ardor.

Crisp evening air brushed his heated skin as Jocelyn shifted onto her back, distancing herself both physically and emotionally from him.

"I wish there was some way to convince you," she said. The darkness shrouded them, but Garren knew by the tone of her voice that there were more tears in her eyes.

He longed to ease her mind, and his own, for that matter, but her story was too unbelievable. Even with Hilda's admonishments. He was a man who believed in reality, and neither her story nor the old woman's claims were grounded in that.

"I see," was all he said. Garren moved closer, reaching for her. She was stiff and unyielding.

"Jocelyn, you've been through much lately. Please rest."

Taking her in his arms, Garren held her until she relaxed, having given in to fatigue. Breathing her sweet scent, he wondered exactly what tomorrow would bring.

The morning brought Jocelyn out of bed early. Slipping into her robe, she quietly left Garren sleeping and headed to the garden in the rear of the house. She needed to think, and exercise always helped her clear her head and sort things out.

Leaving the house through the door to the garden, Jocelyn moved along the winding path. It was obvious to her that Garren hadn't believed her explanations about how she'd got here. She needed something to prove she was from another time. But what?

She sorted through ideas, discarding one after another. Everything she thought of was only hearsay. She had no proof. Garren wouldn't believe any of her descriptions of the future, so what did that leave?

She paused in her meanderings as a thought hit her.

She snapped her fingers. "Of course. I'm in the past," she said to the shrubs and turned around, walking quickly back. "I'll just tell him of the past." She stopped. "But what? What good will it do to tell him things that have already happened?" Her shoulders slumped as she entered the house, her mind whirling through the maze of her problem.

Passing the hall table, Jocelyn's attention was caught by a tidy stack of mail, at the bottom was an old newspaper.

Stopping abruptly, she tapped her forehead with her index finger. "That's it!"

Quickly she took the paper and unfolded it.

Scanning, she found an article about a trial in which Admiral Jervis testified. Glancing at the paper, she noted the date: 28 June. She needed to know what today's date.

She smiled. *Oh yes!* She wiggled her eyebrows. *Thank you, Dr. Townsend!*

The "Nelson Maniac," as he had been referred to in college, had turned his English history class into an in-depth study of Admiral Horatio Nelson. Excitement bubbled in her veins. God willing, she would give Garren something to think about.

Climbing the stairs, Jocelyn composed her words as she entered the room she shared with her husband.

She sat on the bed and gently shook him.

"Garren?" Her voice rose with anticipation.

His sleepy, brown eyes opened, squinting against the morning light.

"Hmm, love?" He reached for her, pulling her down next to him. "What are you doing up at this hour?" He closed his eyes.

"Walking in the garden." She jostled his shoulder. "Garren? What's today's date?"

His eyelids slid up and he quirked an eyebrow.

"The 30th of July." Garren yawned. "Why?"

Jocelyn took a moment to search through bits of information, wondering how to begin. It would be best to ease into this, she mused.

"Have you kept up with Admiral Nelson?"

He patted her arm. "Love, I believe he's a rear-admiral."

"Hmm. But he'll be an admiral, when all is said and done."

Garren nodded tiredly. "No doubt you're right. The man has shown himself to be a brilliant naval officer."

"Yes." Warming to her subject, she sat up, plumping a pillow behind her. "But Jervis got most of the credit for the battle of Cape St. Vincent."

Garren pushed to a sitting position. "And what makes you say that?" Bracing himself against the pillows, he eyed her closely. "Sir John is no less intelligent and talented in military maneuvers."

Jocelyn smiled. "Yes, but wasn't it Nelson who single-handedly took on the largest ship in the world? He broke from the line, and it was his daring that gave the English the edge, even though they were outmanned."

Garren gave her a long, considering look.

"How do you know anything about that?"

"I told you, I'm from the twentieth century. I studied Nelson in college." Jocelyn left the bed and walked around the room, her mind culling facts she'd thought long-since forgotten.

"It was a shame about the loss of his eye. That was three years ago, but it doesn't seem to have hampered his career."

Turning around, she smiled at the confused frown on Garren's face.

"But then, the loss of his arm was even worse."

"Ah, but he didn't lose his arm." Garren folded his arms, flashing a benevolent smile at her.

"Ah, but he did," she mocked him. "In the battle of Santa Cruz." She walked to the foot of the bed. "But then, it just happened less than a week ago, so you wouldn't know it yet." She smiled.

His charitable smile vanished, and a blaze of suspicion lit his eyes.

"How do you even know there was an assault on Santa Cruz?"

"I told you, Garren." She held her hands out to him in supplication. "Don't you see, I couldn't know any of this if what I said wasn't true." She thought about adding other details, like the failure of the mission, but the sudden suspicion clouding Garren's eyes made her halt.

He cocked his head to the side. "You could be a spy."

"For whom?" Her hands flew into the air. He was really trying not to believe her, wasn't he?

"The French."

"You mean Napoleon?" With an indelicate snort, she continued. "I wouldn't give that overbearing little man the time of day, let alone information on the English. Besides, even if I were a spy, which I'm not, how would I know of Nelson's injuries? I've been here with you. I've had no contact with anyone. And you know it."

Placing her hands on her hips, she issued her challenge. "Say you what. See if you can find out anything about Nelson. If I'm right, then you'll know I'm telling you the truth, hard as that might be to handle. If I'm wrong, and I know I'm not," she shrugged. "Then you can send me off to Bedlam."

"Jocelyn, don't even joke about that." He ran a hand over his face.

"Please, Garren, do this for me."

A knock came at the door.

"Please?"

Garren gave a tired nod just as Dulcey entered to dress Jocelyn for the coming day.

Leaving Jocelyn in the care of the household staff, Garren climbed into his carriage, instructing the driver to take him to his father's house.

Replaying their conversation from that morning, Garren worried that Jocelyn's accident had, in some way, affected her mind. He pushed aside the idea of Jocelyn being a French spy. He knew she'd had no contact with anyone outside his staff since Lady Tinsbury's ball. So how could she know so much about Nelson?

He rubbed his temple. Nothing made any sense.

Curiosity, more than anything, drove him to seek out his father. He didn't think about Jocelyn being right, or how he'd react, or what it would mean. He simply didn't believe her prediction would come to pass.

The carriage stopped amid a jingle of harnesses and snorting horses. Garren alighted, climbing the few stairs to his parents' home.

As he entered, Richard stepped into the entry hall.

"Garren. How are you, son?" Richard nodded toward his library.

Following his father into the room, Garren responded, "Fine."

"How is Jocelyn?"

"Much better." Garren sat in a large leather chair opposite his father's desk.

"I would like you and Jocelyn to join me for dinner tomorrow night. Do you think it's too soon for her?"

"Whyever are you having a dinner party? Most of the ton won't arrive in London for another week."

"It won't be a true dinner party, Garren. Lady Elizabeth arrived today, and I thought it would be pleasant to have a small dinner *en famille*, so to speak."

Garren stared at his father, wondering what to make of his father's comment. *En famille?* Could it be that his father had finally decided to wed Lady Elizabeth?

"Is Jocelyn sufficiently recovered to dine with us tomorrow night?"

"Us?" Garren raised a brow. "Us?"

Richard shuffled the paper before him, absently glancing over the print.

Ah, so that was the way the wind was blowing. And about time, too, Garren thought, fighting the urge to grin like an idiot. He watched his father for a long moment, waiting for the man to elaborate, but Richard remained silent.

"Aye." An uncharacteristic flush rose on his father's face, and the chuckle Garren had fought to control slipped out.

Shooting his son a peevish glance, the great bear of a man pushed the paper he'd been fidgeting with toward Garren.

"Have you seen this?" Richard handed him the London paper, effectively closing the subject of Elizabeth. "Malmesbury reports that every courtesy is being offered to him by the French. Mayhap a peaceful solution can be found. I told you that you should have come back to Parliament."

Allowing the change of subject, Garren sat back, ready to discuss the war and all its implications. "The French are just stalling."

"Aye, but we are at their mercy. England doesn't have the heart to continue this war."

"What of Nelson?" Garren stretched his legs before him. He asked the question out of concern, not because Jocelyn bid him do so. But he knew he was only trying to convince himself and doing a poor job of it.

"Still in the Mediterranean, I believe. Mark my words, we've not heard the last of him. He's fearless and completely loyal to England."

"No, we've not." At least according to Jocelyn, Garren thought. "Is he due back soon?"

"Who can tell? I should expect this whole fiasco will be over shortly."

"But at what cost?" Garren sighed. There would be no news of the man today. It was no surprise, he supposed, not if he gave as little credit to Jocelyn's prediction as he should. For a moment, maybe he'd wanted to believe her. . . .

Mayhap it would be best to retire with Jocelyn to Spenceworth. The quiet solitude of the country might be enough for her to regain her mental health.

Standing, Garren moved to the door. "I'll return and get Jocelyn. We'll see you tomorrow evening then."

"I'd advise you to ask her view." Richard smiled. "She has a mind of her own and will take it amiss if you think to dictate to her." He chuckled.

"Yes, Father. I'm only too aware of her independence."

Jocelyn looked up as Garren entered the library, and her heart fell to her feet when she saw Garren's face.

"There's no news, is there?" She shook her head. "I should have realized that it would take more time. In my time, you can actually see a war as it happens, no matter how far away." With a sigh, she added, "Kind of sick, isn't it?"

Garren just stared at her. She flinched at the pity she saw reflected in his gaze. What had she expected? Here she was, talking about things he couldn't possibly understand. She should just keep her mouth shut.

"Father's invited us to dine with him tomorrow night. Do you feel up to it?"

Jocelyn smiled. "Of course. Really Garren, I'm much better. The headache is gone. I'm my old self again."

His glance was guarded and he gave her a nod. "If you're certain."

"It will be just the three of us?"

"And Lady Elizabeth."

"Ah." Jocelyn smiled.

"And what does that mean?"

"That I saw the looks that passed between the two of them at her ball. Now *there*'s a couple who belong together."

He chuckled. " 'Tis evident to you, also?"

The tension of a moment ago evaporated, and Garren's shoulders relaxed.

She flashed a smile at Garren and nodded.

"I've an appointment now, love. I'll see you at dinner."

Jocelyn stood up and walked to Garren. Stretching on her tiptoes, she planted a kiss at the corner of his lips.

"I'll be here." She smiled as he left, and his guarded look was replaced with one of bemusement.

Jocelyn adjusted the skirt of her silver tissue dress, settled the matching shawl on her shoulders, and pulled up the elbow-length gloves.

Garren glanced at her in the low light of the carriage. "You look lovely tonight."

Garren wore black evening clothes. A black waistcoat embroidered with silver thread set off the snowy white shirt he wore beneath a close-fitting jacket. His neckcloth was tied in an intricate knot; a diamond stickpin winked in the light cast by the carriage lanterns.

"Thank you. So do you."

He smiled. "I look lovely?"

"Well, maybe lovely isn't the word." She laughed. Eyeing him closely in the waning light, she said, "No, I think 'hunky' is better."

His eyebrow rose, and Jocelyn mentally shook herself. Ever since she'd told Garren where she came from, she'd been freer with her modern language. And she shouldn't be. The last thing she wanted to do was disconcert him. Beginning this moment, she would be as careful as she had been before the accident.

"You look very handsome," she amended, smiling brightly.

The carriage slowed to a stop and the driver opened the door. Garren alighted, turning and offering his assistance to Jocelyn.

The door to the Warrick manor was opened by a bent white-haired butler.

"Good evening, Hobbs." Garren greeted the servant. Taking her hand, he pulled his wife forward. "This is my bride, Lady Jocelyn."

Hobbs peered at Jocelyn, then glanced at Garren, giving him a wink. "Very good, milord." With great pomp and ceremony, Hobbs took Jocelyn's shawl and showed her and Garren into the salon.

"The Earl and Countess of Spenceworth." Jocelyn choked on a chuckle. The words had seemed to explode from the servant's nose.

"Lord, Garren, does the man think we're royalty?"

Garren laughed. "He does love ceremony."

Richard greeted them as they entered, taking Jocelyn's hand and tucking it into the crook of his arm. "And how is my daughter faring?" He flashed her a smile. "Are you completely recovered, my dear?" He gave her fingers a paternal pat.

"Yes, completely."

Jocelyn recognized Elizabeth Tinsbury immediately. The duchess smiled, her gaze traveling quickly over Jocelyn before resting on Richard. If ever love could shine in someone's eyes, it did in Elizabeth's.

Jocelyn glanced up at Richard, only to realize his gaze held Elizabeth's, an intimate smile playing about his lips.

The moment of silence grew too long, and with a little start Elizabeth shifted her gaze to Jocelyn, breaking the spell of a moment before. Giving the duchess a quick wink, Jocelyn watched color suffuse the lady's cheeks. The woman smiled quickly and, turning away, took her place on the settee.

Richard's deep voice relieved the strain. "You recall the duchess of Tinsbury?"

"Of course." Jocelyn smiled. "It's good to see you again."

"I'm glad to see you well." Elizabeth returned Jocelyn's smile. "Come, sit here with me." The noblewoman patted the spot next to her and Jocelyn joined her. "Will you be attending the Harpers' ball?"

That morning, Garren had mentioned an invitation, but he hadn't said whether they would be going. And she hadn't thought of pursuing it; she had other things on her mind.

A shiver shook Jocelyn's shoulders as she recalled her last ball. "I don't know. After the last one, I'm not sure I want to."

The duchess nodded, placing her hand over Jocelyn's. "You can't know how sorry I am about the entire debacle."

"It wasn't your fault." Jocelyn shrugged off the woman's concern. It was done and over with, no sense in dredging it up again.

"Still . . ." Elizabeth glanced down. "I wanted

Richard to go after you, too, but he said Garren had raced off and was sure to find you."

"I'm fine, really."

Raising her gaze to Jocelyn's, Elizabeth smiled. "Good." She paused. "This one is not a masked ball." With a little squeeze, she removed her hand from Jocelyn's and gave her a shy smile.

"Well, that's good to know." Jocelyn chuckled, and Elizabeth joined in. "I won't be standing close to any doors, either."

Elizabeth laughed lightly. "I should stay with the dowagers, if I were you. No man is brave enough to charge their ranks."

Dinner was announced and Richard escorted Elizabeth in, while Jocelyn took Garren's arm. A rich cherrywood table, close to fifteen feet long, presided over the dining room.

They sat in an intimate arrangement, Richard at the head of the table, with Elizabeth on his right, Jocelyn on his left, and Garren seated on Jocelyn's left. White, tapered candles flickered in the silver candelabra, casting a warm glow on the diners.

Richard's staff first served a rich cream-based soup. Jocelyn barely gave a thought to the cholesterol and calories as she dipped her spoon in the thick concoction, savoring the flavor on her tongue.

"So, we'll be seeing you at the ball, then?" Lady Elizabeth directed her question to Garren.

Garren glanced at Jocelyn before answering. "Aye, if Jocelyn feels up to it, I think we will attend."

"Jocelyn, I have the most wonderful seamstress if you need a new gown. I could bring her by tomorrow afternoon, if you like."

Jocelyn glanced at Garren, her mind skimming

over the clothing Mrs. Cowan had sent. Did she really need another gown?

"A wonderful suggestion, Lady Elizabeth." Garren must have seen the look on Jocelyn's face. "Will you be available tomorrow afternoon, wife?"

She shrugged. "I hadn't any plans."

"Excellent." Richard drew the topic to a close as the entree was served.

The conversation ebbed and flowed as the meal progressed, and Jocelyn found she had won a true friend in Elizabeth. The older woman was warm and open, telling Jocelyn tidbits of gossip about the ton. Not that Jocelyn knew who Elizabeth was talking about, but some of the stories were quite humorous.

When dessert was served, Jocelyn looked at the creamy substance, then glanced at Garren. He smiled and, arching an eyebrow, he lifted his spoon.

"Garren! Don't you dare."

Her gasp drew the attention of Richard and Elizabeth.

"Ah, so you remember?"

Heat blossomed in Jocelyn's cheeks. She remembered only too well their last experience with this dessert.

"What?" Richard glanced between Jocelyn and Garren, a bemused smile on his face.

"Dessert." Jocelyn and Garren said in unison.

Richard frowned in confusion. "And what else would it be?"

"Nothing." Jocelyn took a spoonful. "It's wonderful."

"Is this the first time you've tasted syllabub?" Elizabeth queried innocently, at which point, Garren and Jocelyn broke into peals of laughter.

"I believe it is." Garren offered between chuckles.

"Usually, we wear it." Jocelyn laughed so hard tears streamed down her cheeks. Each time they looked at each other, she and Garren laughed even harder.

"I beg your pardon? Did you say *wear?*" Elizabeth's eyebrows arched high, her eyes rounding with disbelief.

Still giggling, Jocelyn nodded.

Elizabeth's brow furrowed and she shook her head. "But how does one wear syllabub?"

"And *why* would one want to?" Richard added stuffily.

Garren's chuckles eased some and he replied. "It's just something married couples do, Father."

Chapter Seventeen

"Thirty-one." Jocelyn counted, exhaling as she brought her torso up from the floor. With Garren away this morning on business, she had decided to catch up on her exercises.

"Thirty-two," she puffed. He'd hovered over her for the three days since the dinner at his father's. This was the first chance she'd had to work out, and she didn't see the fact that they were at Garren's London accommodations as anything of a hindrance.

"Thirty-three."

Only seventeen more crunches and she'd be finished, all in enough time to bathe and be dressed before Lady Elizabeth and her seamstress arrived.

"Thirty-four." The muscles of her stomach tightened, the familiar burn giving Jocelyn a surge of satisfaction.

"Thirty-five."

"Jocelyn?" The deep masculine voice startled her.

Twisting around, she watched as Garren rushed to her side, a worried frown creasing his brow.

"My God, are you hurt?" Kneeling down, he grasped her shoulders, pulling her close to his chest. "Jocelyn, speak to me."

"I'm fine. Just doing a few exercises." She cuddled close to him, enjoying the smell of clean linen and Garren's special masculine scent for a moment before remembering her not-so-tidy self.

Pushing away from him, she stood. "I didn't expect you back so soon."

Garren studied Jocelyn's face a long moment before his gaze traveled down her scantily clad form. A moment of confusion overwhelmed him before he glanced sharply up at her.

"What the bloody hell is beneath your shift?"

Jocelyn raised the hem. "Knickers." She grinned as color washed over Garren's face.

Coming to his feet in a rush, he ran his hand through his hair. "What?"

"Knickers. Bloomers." Her grin broadened. "I made them myself." Letting the material fall down around her calves, she proudly folded her arms over her chest.

He stared at her legs a moment before allowing his gaze to meet hers. Her grin was infectious, and without realizing, he too smiled.

"What were you doing on the floor and dressed like this?"

"Garren." Jocelyn tried for patience. After all, she realized, he still didn't believe that she was from the twentieth century. "I was exercising. And I do it in this because it's more comfortable." She patted his arm as she passed him on her way to her bed and the robe draped over its post.

Shrugging into it and tying it at her waist, she turned around.

He eyed her closely. "Mrs. Cowan mentioned some sort of fit you'd had once. Is this what she meant?"

Jocelyn chuckled. "Poor thing. I tried to explain to her that I was fine."

His eyes narrowed, his jaw tensed, and Jocelyn wisely chose to change the subject.

"What brought you home so soon?"

Garren shook his head and handed her a piece of folded parchment. "A messenger intercepted me on my way to meet Father."

Scanning the contents, her breath hitched in her throat when she finally made sense of the writing.

"I'm supposed to meet Queen Charlotte?"

"You're to be presented to Her Majesty," Garren corrected.

"Lord, the queen." Jocelyn muttered, smoothing a loose tendril of hair from her face.

Garren gave her a sidelong glance and turned to leave. At the door he stopped. Turning around, he said, " 'Tis a good thing Lady Elizabeth is bringing the seamstress today; you'll need a new costume for the presentation as well as the ball. Remind her that she has only five days to complete the ball gown."

Jocelyn nodded. "Fine." Her mind wasn't on Garren's instructions, but on the absurd notion of meeting a queen who had been dead nearly two hundred years.

He opened the door, stopped, and turned back to her. "And Jocelyn?"

She looked up from the paper. "What?"

"Remove those bloody knickers. They're indecent." The door closed with a click.

Dropping the note on the table, Jocelyn ran to the door and jerked it open.

"Garren?"

He stopped at the stairs. "Yes?"

"Are you leaving again?"

"Yes, love. And no more exercising, hmm? 'Tis hardly ladylike to thrash around on the floor." He waggled his eyebrows. "Especially without one's husband!"

"Garren!" Shocked, Jocelyn glanced down the hallway and back at him. "Behave!" But her reprimand was ruined by the involuntary chuckle and saucy grin she gave him.

Garren maneuvered his mount through the busy streets of London by rote, his mind on his wife and her exercising. What a fetching picture she presented in her shift and knickers. He grinned, hearing again the outrage in her voice as he left the house. Did she realize how seductive her laugh was? Or what her smile promised? His body reacted to his recollections, and he shifted uncomfortably in his saddle.

His memory reached a little further back, and the lightness of a moment ago receded as he recalled the panic that had flooded his veins when he had come upon her on the floor. Mrs. Cowan had described the exact scene to him at Spenceworth, but he had dismissed it, thinking his housekeeper had overreacted. But seeing it with his own eyes, he could understand the woman's reaction. What need did a woman have for this exercise? Men wanted—nay, expected—a woman to be soft and fragile.

But Jocelyn was that, he thought, despite her exercising. What then was the need? Unless it had something to do with the twentieth century. His hands tightened on the reins, causing his horse to sidestep and toss its head. Now he was starting to believe her!

Abruptly brought back to the present, Garren relaxed his grip and turned down a less crowded street to the coffeehouse where he was to meet Richard. Earlier, he'd met with some members of Parliament at his club, and he was anxious to discuss the details he'd learned of the war effort with his father.

" 'Tis amazing we still have a navy." The duke commented shortly after Garren joined him.

"I still say that if there had been less hesitation on the part of the officers, morale would be much better." Garren shrugged. "Of course, better provisions would help, too."

Garren and Richard lapsed into silence, each enjoying the coffee served to them.

Putting the cup down, Garren look at his father. "Any word about Jocelyn's family?"

"Nay." Richard shook his head. "I've sent a note off to a business associate in the Colon . . . America." He gave Garren a rueful grin. "But it will take another two months at least to get word back." Leaning forward a bit, Richard lowered his voice. "I've not found anyone with knowledge of any Tanners. If there were anyone searching for her here, the people I know would have that information." Richard sighed. "We'll just have to wait for information from America."

Another two months of uncertainty, Garren thought.

"Don't worry, son. We'll get to the bottom of all this."

Garren snorted. "Well, we'd better do it soon. I'm to present Jocelyn to the queen."

271

"Bloody hell." Richard looked up in alarm. "You'll have to come up with something, my boy. Chances are, George will be there. And unless he is in one of his moods, he's bound to ask after her people."

"I know." Garren moaned.

Half an hour later, weaving his way through the patrons of the coffeehouse, Garren stopped when his forearm was gripped and a feminine voice purred, "I've not congratulated you on your marriage, Garren."

He stiffened, recognizing Melody's voice. Turning around, he faced her with a cool nod. In a frosty tone he replied, "Thank you. If you'll excuse me." He started to turn away, but Melody's nails dug into his arm through his coat, stopping him.

"Don't you dare turn away from me," she snarled, casting a furtive glance around them.

"Melody, kindly unhand me. You're making a scene."

"You have yet to see what I can do."

"And I really don't wish to." Garren eyed her with contempt. "Now let go."

Melody's perfect complexion mottled, her lips thinning. "I could ruin you, Garren. You should be careful what you say to me."

"You tried that once, and look where it got you." Garren shrugged out of her hold. "Now, good day."

"You'll regret this, Garren. I swear it. I'm not a woman to be turned aside."

Outside, Garren took a deep breath, and with a shake of his head, flipped a coin to the lad holding his horse. On the ride home he turned his thoughts to Jocelyn and her tantalizing undergarments, dismissing the encounter with Lady Paxton.

* * *

"I think the blue." Lady Elizabeth cocked her head to the side, her gaze darting from the green to the blue silk draped over Jocelyn's shoulder.

Jocelyn nodded to the seamstress. "And the green for the ball." She glanced at Elizabeth.

"Ah, yes." The older woman's eyes rounded with surprise. "I'd nearly forgotten about the ball." She laughed. "With all the stir over being presented, it slipped my mind."

With Dulcey's help, Jocelyn dressed.

"I should like to get started straight away on your gowns, milady." The seamstress gathered up her books and cloth samples, preparing to leave. "I would like the first fitting in two days." Glancing up at Jocelyn, she added, "If that will do?"

"Oh, yes, of course." Disappointment colored Jocelyn's tone. She had a million questions to ask Elizabeth about the presentation, and she didn't know when she'd get another chance. But her friend solved the dilemma.

"I'll have my carriage take you home, Elise, then return later for me." Elizabeth smiled at Jocelyn. "Mayhap we should discuss the protocol. You might want to practice your curtsy, too."

Jocelyn heaved a quiet sigh of relief.

"Wonderful." Jocelyn slipped on her shoes. "In the salon, then?"

Lady Elizabeth followed her downstairs, giving directions to the appropriate servants. The butler escorted them downstairs, and Jocelyn and Elizabeth went to the salon.

A few minutes later, settled with tea, Lady Elizabeth told Jocelyn what to expect at court.

" 'Tis a great deal of ceremony to it all. The queen will be announced, and when you can see her from the corner of your eye, you should drop into a formal curtsy."

Jocelyn frowned.

" 'Tis one we'll practice." Patting Jocelyn's hand, Elizabeth smiled. "You'll do fine. I shouldn't be surprised if the king joined the queen. He so adores his wife and daughters."

"Oh, Lord." Jocelyn moaned, fighting the urge to slump back in her chair.

"Don't worry. The king seldom engages in conversation at presentations, especially with a woman."

Jocelyn bit back her bristling reply. How could Elizabeth just accept that kind of treatment? How could she, herself?

Elizabeth leaned closer and confided in a hushed tone, "Men seldom have anything worthwhile to say, anyway." She smiled at Jocelyn and sat back, sipping her tea.

"All men?" Jocelyn arched an eyebrow at the older woman.

"Well, on occasion, Richard has been known to say some rather intelligent things." She laughed. "Catches me quite by surprise!"

"Surely you don't mean that?"

A sigh escaped Elizabeth's lips and she placed her cup in its saucer, her gaze going to the window behind Jocelyn. "No, of course not. Richard is one of the few men who doesn't speak to me as if I were a pampered pet."

"You love him, don't you?" Jocelyn hadn't meant to say it out loud, especially seeing Lady Elizabeth's cheeks redden.

"I'm sorry, I shouldn't—"

"You're right, of course." The older woman focused on Jocelyn, a smile playing about her lips. "I do love Garren's father. Richard was the strong shoulder I relied upon after my husband died." With a little shrug, she turned her attention back to her tea. "I think I must have always loved him. Mind you, I loved William, too—but there was always a corner of my heart that Richard held."

"You've known him that long, then?"

Elizabeth looked at Jocelyn. "My, yes. Since we were children. Richard and William were very close. I was always tagging along, trying to be included in the boys' adventures." She raised her eyebrows. "Not that they would have any of it. Well, at least not until I was older." She smiled.

"Why aren't the two of you married? I mean, a blind person can see the way he feels just by the way he looks at you." Jocelyn sat on the edge of her seat, watching Elizabeth's lovely face glow with an inner light.

"Richard was waiting for Garren to settle."

"Well, he's settled now."

Elizabeth nodded. "Yes, he is, isn't he?" She grinned. "And Richard is suddenly shy."

Jocelyn snorted inelegantly. "I seriously doubt that. I think he's afraid."

"Of me?" Elizabeth placed her hand dramatically on her chest.

"No." Jocelyn shook her head. "He's afraid you'll come to your senses and say no."

Both ladies laughed.

"He has nothing to worry about. I never intend to come to my senses when it comes to Richard."

The clicking of her heels against the polished wooden floor echoed Melody's frustration.

"Damn Garren Warrick! He should never have shunned me like he did. And then to turn away

275

from me today. Well, he'll regret those actions. All of them."

Charles stood silently near the hearth, guardedly watching his sister's mounting anger.

"You're sure of your information, Charles? Garren paid Haslett for the woman?"

Charles nodded mutely, his eyes never leaving his agitated sister as she moved back and forth.

"Next week Garren will be humiliated before the queen. When we bring it before Her Majesty that one of the nobility has *purchased* a wife from a commoner . . . Well, things will look very bleak for the haughty Earl of Spenceworth. And I'll finally have my revenge of him."

Melody turned, leveling a glare at Charles. "You'll not muddle this, will you brother?"

Charles's Adam's apple bobbed nervously in his throat. When he answered, his voice was nothing more than a croak. "No, but—"

"But what?" Charles's shoulders hunched at Melody's strident voice. When she raged like this, the smarter man simply let her have her way. Crossing Melody now could be painful; but if her plan failed, he would bear the brunt of her anger and frustration. He couldn't see what defaming Garren would do, other than cause the man to be ostracized and maybe pay a fine. It still left both him and Melody nearly penniless. But to point that out now would be a grand mistake.

"But what if they don't believe us? After all, Garren has many friends. Won't we need proof?"

"Charles." Melody's voice was fraught with frustration as she stopped before him. "*He'll* need proof that he didn't."

Charles didn't relish the idea of standing against Lord Spenceworth with nothing more than his word as protection. He wanted something more substantial.

"Would it not be better to have Haslett here to identify his wife and Garren?"

Surprise widened Melody's eyes. "Charles, you're absolutely correct. If we have Haslett here, he can vouch for our story. He will identify Garren as the man who purchased his wife."

Melody's pacing began anew. "Yes, we have to find the man and get him here. Do you think you can convince him to come to London?"

"No doubt. But how will I get him before the king?"

Melody smiled coolly. "I've still a few friends who will help me. You just get the man here."

"Me? Why not send your coachman for him?" Charles certainly didn't want to go after the man. The thought of sitting in the same carriage with the filthy commoner turned his stomach.

"No, Charles, I believe it would be best for *you* to escort him here. If you bring him the day before, he can stay in the stables. That way we know he'll be here."

Charles knew when Melody had that stubborn look in her eyes that it would be useless to argue with her. He'd just make the man ride up top with the driver. Even that wouldn't ease the long drive, though.

Charles entered the smoky tavern, his walking stick raised above the filthy floor. Squinting against the gloom of the room, he recognized Haslett sitting at a table, a mug before him. Stepping up to Haslett, Charles used the end of his stick to nudge the man.

"Eh, what ye want?" Haslett's voice cut short Charles's patience.

Haslett turned from his ale to look at Charles. "Oh, sorry, govna. Though ye was someone else."

"Yes, quite. I would have a word with you outside." Charles turned and left the inn, expecting Haslett to follow. He wasn't disappointed.

The door thudded shut, and Charles took a deep breath of fresh air. He hated the stench and smoke of the common houses these people frequented, and there was nothing to compel him to stay the night in one. He would simply have Haslett in London a day earlier than Melody required.

Haslett caught up with him and walked a spell, silently, beside him.

"Well, what did ye wont with me?"

Charles turned his gaze from the yard in front of the inn to Haslett, and cringed. Did the man never bathe? His hair hung in greasy hanks, at least three days' growth of beard stubbled his face, and the odor from the man turned Charles's stomach. He pulled a kerchief from his coat pocket and held it to his nose as he moved upwind.

"I've come to take you to London."

"What?" Haslett's surprise stretched his eyes wide. "Ye want me to go to London with ye?"

"Yes."

"Why?" Suspicion dulled his bloodshot eyes.

"You recall selling your wife some time ago, do you not?"

"Aye, what of it? It were legal-like."

"Just so. Do you remember who you sold her to?"

"Gentry is all I know." Haslett stopped walking. "I told him she were a handful. I won't give him back his money. Sold her fair and square, I did. She's his problem now."

"He's not looking for his money back."

"Then what do ye want with me in London?"

"Would you recognize the man if you saw him again?"

"Aye, his kind be hard to forget. Why?"

"That's all I want you to do. Identify the man."

"Why?"

"That's not your business."

"What's in it fer me?"

Charles cursed under his breath. Of course, the man would want money. But how little could he offer him and still get the man to London?

"Half crown, food and lodging." Surely, sleeping in the stable would equal or surpass where Haslett now slept.

"Ye'll be paying me now, then?"

"Hardly. You'll get your money when you've identified the man."

Haslett scowled, turned his head, and spit a stream of saliva into the dirt at his feet. "Jest remember that, govna. I'll collect my money— make no doubt about that."

Charles shrugged, eager to get back to town. "Now, my carriage is over there." He nodded to his right. "We must leave immediately."

Haslett looked at the shiny black conveyance. "Ye want me to ride to London in that?"

"Yes, what's wrong with it?"

"Nothing, govna. I just never been in such a fine carriage."

You've likely never been in any carriage, you lout. "No, you'll ride up top with the driver."

Charles strode to the vehicle. "Hey, govna, what's yer name? Ye never told me."

Ignoring the question, Charles opened the door and climbed inside. A few moment later, the carriage started back to London.

* * *

The ride was most uncomfortable. Charles pondered Melody's plan and wondered how if Haslett would be more hindrance than help. No telling what Melody would do if this scheme of hers didn't work. Her fits were becoming more difficult and frequent. Sometimes he wondered at her sanity, and this obsession with Warrick had begun to worry him. He knew there had never been any hope of the man marrying his sister, and while he was horrified for his sister, he was surprised that she had not yet accepted her fate.

A cloud of foreboding drifted over him. Mayhap he should have kept his mouth shut about Garren and his wife.

They reached London late that evening. Charles directed Haslett to the stables.

"You'll stay there for the night."

Grumbling at the cheap lodgings, Haslett nonetheless followed the driver.

Charles continued on his own room some three blocks away, looking forward to a long night's sleep.

Chapter Eighteen

Jocelyn, closely followed by Dulcey, traversed the streets of London and was appalled at the smell and squalor around her. Even though she was in the better part of town, there was no comparison to the London of her time.

She stopped at a corner, allowing a cart to turn in front of her, and looked across the street. A man dressed in dirt-caked clothing seemed vaguely familiar. A carriage passed, obstructing her view of the man; and when it was gone, so was the man. Jocelyn shrugged and continued on.

In the process of choosing a new pair of gloves some time later, Jocelyn gasped as the man's identity finally hit her.

"Haslett." The word careered through her mind. A foreboding weighed her heart.

What is he doing in London?

Surely it wasn't that unusual for a villager to

281

come to the capital. It was, after all, a free country. He could come and go as he pleased. And he hadn't shown any signs of recognizing her. Just because he was also in London didn't mean anything . . . did it?

No, she shook her head, *it is nothing more than coincidence.*

But still, the feeling of impending doom darkened her day and she became anxious to return to the country.

In a hurry, suddenly, Jocelyn finished buying her gloves.

"Come Dulcey, we should be getting home." She pulled at the maid's arm, nearly dragging her down the street to the Warrick carriage.

"Where in the bloody hell is that man?" Melody leaned closer to Charles, her eyes flashing in uncontrolled anger.

"Calm yourself, sister, I'll find him."

"You'd best do that, or everything will be lost."

Charles wanted to point out to her that everything was already lost. The merchants weren't going to forgive her debts because she brought shame to the Warricks. No, she was doomed to debtor's prison, and if he wasn't careful, he'd be accompanying her. She seemed beyond reason now, and Charles knew it. If he allowed Melody to do this, he would be as much at fault as she—but how could he talk her out of it?

Melody's narrow gaze pinned him to the floor. She knew him too well. "Don't tell me, Charles. You're trying to find a way out of this, aren't you?"

"Melody, it won't serve any purpose, except to satisfy your thirst for vengeance. It won't pay the merchants off. It won't bring us back into society. Don't you see this?"

"Shut up!" she screamed, covering her ears to block out his words.

"Melody, I can't let you do this."

She flew at him, her fingers arched like claws, aiming for his face.

Fury lent her strength and, as Charles put his hands up to protect his face, she toppled them both to the floor. He felt a stinging scrape, and then the welling of blood trickled down his cheek. Pushing his enraged sibling away, he stumbled to his feet. Mopping at the blood on his cheek with a handkerchief from his pocket, he hurried to the door.

"You'll have to find someone else to do your dirty work, Melody, for I shan't be a party to your downfall."

Melody spun around. "Fine, you bastard. I can accomplish this without your aid. No doubt, you'd have made a mess of things anyway."

The front door slammed as Charles left.

In the hall, Melody shouted, "Mary, send the coachman to me at once!"

"You'll never guess who I saw today." Jocelyn shifted in her chair, watching Garren at his desk. She'd struggled with how to bring up the subject of Haslett the remainder of the day. Even though she'd convinced herself that she was overreacting, she still felt compelled to tell Garren.

Garren looked up from his papers, a smile of indulgence curving his lips. "Who?"

"My old husband."

The smile died on Garren's lips. The room stilled. The fire ceased its crackling, the clock ceased its ticking, and Jocelyn held her breath. A look of concern flashed momentarily on Garren's face.

"And did you speak with him?" His voice was controlled.

"No. I wasn't about to get close to that man. Personal hygiene isn't his strong suit. Besides, he didn't notice me."

"Exactly where did you see him, love?"

"Across the street from Elise's shop." Jocelyn locked her fingers together in her lap.

"Hmm." A frown marred Garren's brow, and he lapsed into silence.

After a moment, Jocelyn's nerves got the better of her.

"Garren? What are you thinking?"

"Nothing, love. 'Tis not so unusual for someone to come to London, and you said he didn't notice you." He gazed at her. "There's nothing to worry over."

Garren gave a smile that didn't make it to his eyes. "Are you nervous about meeting the queen tomorrow?"

Taking his cue, Jocelyn changed subjects, though she wondered what Garren wasn't telling her.

"A little. Elizabeth told me that the king might even be there."

" 'Tis a possibility. George has been known to come to such things."

"George the Third. Don't they call him Mad George?"

Annoyance wrinkled Garren's brow. "Of course they don't. Whyever would he be called that?"

Standing, Jocelyn inclined her head—looking like a kid with her hand caught in the cookie jar. "Well, I think it would drive me a little crazy if I had to run this country. I mean, it's not exactly a walk in the park, you know?" Obviously anxious to change the subject, Jocelyn moved to the door.

"I think I'll dress for dinner." She flashed him a smile and left.

"She says the strangest things," Garren said to the empty room. King George was one of the hardest working monarchs in England's history. Mayhap, to a woman, the king appeared a bit odd; most didn't give a thought to what the man did, or the burden associated with his responsibilities. But Jocelyn's attitude was certainly a surprise.

Drawing his thoughts from his odd wife, he pondered the news of Haslett's arrival in London. Was something behind this appearance? Well, he thought with a shrug, there was little he could do now. Whatever the man was up to, Garren felt sure he'd know soon enough.

The carriage rocked to a halt before Richard's home, but before the footman could open the carriage door, Garren's father stepped outside. With a deep sigh, Garren realized there would be no private word with Richard, and he worried anew. Something was afoot and he could feel it.

"Ah, Garren. Didn't want to risk arriving late." Richard approached and climbed into the carriage. "Jocelyn, you look lovely." He smiled.

"Thank you." She smiled back nervously.

"Garren?" Richard held out a parchment. "I came across this in my desk and thought you should have it."

Garren took the parchment, unrolled it, and glanced over the writing. It was his marriage certificate. He recalled the stunned expression of the vicar when Jocelyn had signed her name. Gazing at her signature, he smiled. Would it always seem a little childlike?

Rolling the document up, he tucked it inside his coat pocket.

"Thank you, Father."

Garren sat back, enjoying the banter between his wife and his father as they drove to the Queen's house.

The hall was crowded with overdressed ladies and pompous dandies. Jocelyn tightened her grip on Garren's arm and wished again that she was back at Spenceworth. A long red carpet stretched straight to a pair of empty, heavy, ornate chairs. Candles heated the room beyond comfort. The powdered and perfumed nobles themselves emitted a burning odor, mixed with the smell of unwashed bodies. Jocelyn stifled the urge to pinch her nose.

At the open archway of the room, a man dressed in velvet and holding a long staff appeared. He thumped three times, and the crowd quieted. He thumped again, three times.

"George the Third, by the grace of God, of England, Scotland and Wales, King. Head of the Commonwealth, Defender of the Faith."

Thump, thump.

"Her Royal Highness, Queen Charlotte." The man stepped aside.

King George, with Queen Charlotte on his arm, proceeded down the red carpet. Eyeing those on either side of the aisle, he slowly made his way to the thrones. Each person bowed or curtsied as the royal couple passed. Catching a glimpse of the queen in the corner of her eye, Jocelyn dropped into what she hoped was a graceful curtsy. *This is stupid, he's just a man who's going slowly nuts*. But nonetheless, she kept her eyes downcast, waiting for him to pass.

Garren gave her arm a gentle tug, indicating that the royal couple had proceeded past.

Jocelyn paid no attention to the sounds

around her. Instead she wondered again, why all the hoopla? She tightened her fingers on Garren's arm.

Garren glanced at her, then leaned closer.

"Garren, I still don't understand why the queen wants to meet me," she whispered in his ear.

"You're a new face and married to one of His Majesty's lords. It's a natural curiosity," Garren whispered back, offering her an encouraging smile.

Moments later, Jocelyn and Garren stepped onto the red carpet. Jocelyn took a deep breath and concentrated on putting one foot in front of the other and not tripping over her skirts. She didn't want to disgrace Garren.

As they walked the interminable distance, Jocelyn felt the muscles in Garren's arm stiffen. Glancing up at him, she noticed the whiteness around his lips. Turning her gaze in the direction his was focused, she saw a dark-haired woman staring at Garren from the center of the crowd. A smirk lent an ugly line to her face. The woman's gaze was filled with hatred as it traveled over Jocelyn. Confused, Jocelyn looked back at Garren and pressed her fingers into his arm. He glanced down at her, " 'Tis Melody." His words were a bare whisper.

As they neared the king, Jocelyn turned her thoughts from the woman and her hateful looks to what would happen next.

Garren stopped and bowed; Jocelyn dropped into the lowest curtsy she could. Placing her fingertips in Garren's extended palm, she rose.

"Ah. My Lord Spenceworth. We see the rumors weren't exaggerated."

"Your Majesty." Garren bowed.

" 'Tis the bride he bought!" The screech of a

female voice amid the onlookers drew the king's attention from Jocelyn and Garren.

Jocelyn's heart swelled with dread inside her chest, and she glanced over her shoulder to see Melody taken in hand by two guards. It was then that she noticed a man standing near Melody. Though he was cleaner and in finer clothes, it was still Haslett. Anxiety churned in her stomach. *What is this all about?*

"Who is that woman?" The king slapped the arm of his chair in anger.

The man with the staff leaned over. "Lady Paxton, Your Majesty."

"Bring her forward. We would know her reason for interrupting us."

At a nod from the king's attendant, Melody and Haslett were led forward. Melody dropped into a deep curtsy while Haslett stood, slack-jawed, before belatedly recalling himself and bowing.

"What is the meaning of this outburst?" His Majesty leaned forward, his eyebrows drawn together in a frown.

Melody rose from her curtsy. "This man sold his wife to Lord Spenceworth." Pushing a frightened Haslett before her, she coached, "Is this the man to whom you sold you wife?"

Haslett's gaze traveled from Garren, to Melody, to Jocelyn, and finally to the king. He nodded.

The king stared at Melody. "Madame, are you accusing Lord Spenceworth of buying this commoner's wife?" Disbelief colored his words.

"Yes." She pointed at Jocelyn. "She's nothing more than a village woman from Ramsgil."

"Is this true?" The king directed the question to Garren.

" 'Tis him that I sold her to. For sixpence." Haslett found his tongue.

The crowd snickered.

"Silence!" The king glared at the man. "Lord Spenceworth, is this true?"

"I sold my Nelwina to him." Haslett nodded emphatically.

"Silence! We say!" the king roared.

"Your Majesty, this is my wife, Lady Jocelyn Spenceworth. I know not who this Nelwina woman is," Garren offered.

"He's lying. He bought her on market day in Ramsgil. Tell His Majesty," Melody nudged Haslett.

Thumping his hand on his thigh, King George shouted, "By the rood, woman, hold your tongue!" To Haslett, the king demanded, "Do you say that the Countess of Spenceworth was your wife?"

Jocelyn held her breath. Haslett might bring their world down with one word. As he eyed her up and down. Catching his gaze, Jocelyn gave him her best superior glare. He dropped his eyes and shuffled his feet.

"Well, man? Speak up." Haslett jumped at the king's command.

"Well, yer Majesty, I can't be sure. Ye see, my Nelwina stood strong on her posterns. Not skinny like this 'un." Haslett squinted at Jocelyn, his gaze focusing on the curls resting over her shoulder. "Nelwina's hair were lighter and 'tweren't nary a curl in the lot of it." He glanced back at the king. "I just don't know, yer Majesty. Can ye make her say something? My Nelwina's voice could strip the bark off trees."

The king's eyebrows arched and he flicked a negligent wrist in Jocelyn's direction. "If you please, Countess."

She glanced at Garren, receiving a slight nod.

289

"As you wish, your Majesty." She turned to Haslett. "The rain in Spain stays mainly on the plain."

The king's eyes rounded and he blinked several times. Queen Charlotte giggled.

Well, what was she supposed to have said?

"Nay, yer Majesty." Haslett shook his head. "My Nelwina don't know nothing about rain or Spain or such. This here's a real lady. No, I guess she's not my Nelwina."

The king turned his glare on Melody. Then, to Garren he said, "What say you, My Lord Spenceworth?"

"Your Majesty, if I may?" Garren reached inside his coat pocket and withdrew the parchment.

"Of course, Lord Spenceworth, if you can bring some sense to all of this." His Majesty waved his hand in the air.

"Yes. I would offer you the marriage contract, signed by both myself and my wife. If you will note, my wife's name is Jocelyn Tanner, not Nelwina Ham. Lady Paxton is mistaken." Garren passed the parchment to the king's attendant.

"There is no mistake! This man"—Melody swung her arm in Garren's direction, her voice increasingly shrill—"has broken the law, your Majesty. You *must* do something."

"Do you think to tell us what We must do, Lady Paxton?" The king's face had turned red with anger. "We know, quite well, how to govern."

Turning from her, he glanced at the parchment his man handed him. "It would appear everything is in order." With a stern look, he continued. "To slander a member of the House of Lords is a most serious charge, Madame. The Earl of Spenceworth would be within his rights to bring charges against you." King George arched his eyebrows in question as he glanced at Garren.

Garren shook his head. "No, your Majesty. I rely on your judgment."

"Lady Paxton, you should consider yourself most fortunate that our Lord Spenceworth is willing to overlook your behavior. However, we cannot. You will remove yourself from court and never darken our doors again." The king nodded to the guards.

Four guards escorted a fuming Melody and a confused Haslett out amid the titters and guffaws of the crowd.

The pompous man in uniform banged his staff on the floor three times, and the assembly quieted.

"And now Lady Spenceworth, we congratulate you on your marriage. 'Tis good to see one of our nobles happily wed."

"Thank you, your Majesty."

"And how do you find London?"

"Very well, but it stinks." Jocelyn bit her lip. Why did the truth always have to escape?

King George's eyebrows lowered, and he stared disconcertingly at her. "We have found that one who complains usually has a solution to the problem."

In the ensuing silence, Jocelyn swore she could hear the candles burn. She thought a moment, but a problem of this scope was too much for her. "Yes, your Majesty. I'll hie myself back to the country, where the air is clean and the population smaller."

The king slapped his knee, a shout of laughter bursting from his throat. "Well done, my lady, well done, indeed."

Turning his gaze to Garren, he continued. "Don't look so stricken, sir. You've a wonderfully forthright wife. We caution you, however, to garner some control of her, or she'll have you dancing attendance on her."

"Yes, your Majesty." Garren bowed stiffly. Shooting a fierce glare at Jocelyn and taking her elbow, he guided her away.

Jocelyn glanced at Garren as she unpinned her hair and began brushing it. He sat in bed, his bare chest glowing in the firelight, anticipation shining in his eyes. She shook her head. So far she'd been pretty lucky, and by keeping track of her body's rhythms, she hadn't become pregnant.

Until now.

For the next few days she must not surrender to Garren's loving. But from the gleam in his eyes, she had her work cut out for her.

Maybe the best course was an open, honest discussion.

She extinguished the candle on the mantle and crawled into bed. Garren immediately turned toward her. Tucking her against him, he moved his hand across her waist, then toward her breast.

Covering his hand with hers, Jocelyn stilled his exploration.

"Garren, we need to talk."

He nuzzled her neck, his lips searing a path to the sensitive area behind her ear. She squirmed away.

"Garren." She arched away from his questing lips. "We can't."

He arched an eyebrow. "Mayhap you can't, but

292

I assure you, love, I can." He grinned and made another move for her neck.

"No. You can't." She pushed to her feet, and strode to the fireplace. In order to get him to listen, she had to remove herself from his clutches.

"Jocelyn? Is something wrong?" He sat up, bracing a pillow behind him.

"It's just not a good time."

"Is it—"

Jocelyn blushed. "No, it's not that time."

"What, then?" His puzzled frown gave him a boyish appeal.

"I just . . . I just can't afford to get pregnant." There, she'd said it.

"You don't wish to have children?" Disappointment deepened his frown as he folded his arms over his chest.

"It's not that I don't want children." She glanced away, then taking a deep breath, she continued. "Until you believe I'm from the twentieth century, I can't take the chance of getting pregnant."

Garren was puzzled. What did his believing or not believing have to do with children? He loved her whether she was mad or not.

"Don't you see? If I have to return to my time and I'm pregnant, I'll leave this body." His gaze followed the sweep of her hand, lingering on the thin folds of her nightgown. The sleeveless garment exposed the smooth skin of her arms and neck. Soft fabric fell over the fullness of her breasts, and his gaze caught on the peaks pushing against the material. Garren swallowed, fighting the urge to rush to her, take her into his arms, and kiss her uncertainty away.

293

With reluctance, he pulled his gaze and his mind from her body to look into her eyes.

"Why would you have to leave?"

Tears brimmed in her eyes, and Garren swore beneath his breath. He'd done it again. When would he learn?

The subject was too sensitive, apparently.

"I can't stay if you don't believe me." Jocelyn dashed a tear away. "What kind of marriage would we have if there weren't trust between us?"

He sighed. He had no response. Indeed, trust and belief *were* paramount in a marriage; they were the very foundation. But what she asked of him was too much. No one with any sense would believe in time travel.

But the woman he loved did.

Maybe for her, he could find a way.

"News should come soon about Nelson. You will believe me then, won't you, Garren?" Jocelyn wrapped her arms around her waist, the pleading in her voice reflected in her gray gaze.

"Come, love. 'Tis late. This will all come out right in time." He patted the empty place beside him.

Her shoulders slumped, and with dragging steps, she came to bed. He shushed her objections when he pulled her close, wrapping his arms around her and tucking her head beneath his chin.

Long after her breathing became deep and regular, Garren stared at the firelight flickering on the ceiling. He could not wish for Jocelyn to be right, for then Nelson would have to suffer; but he wanted with all his heart for their marriage to be long and happy. He sighed softly. The obstacle of her claim stood between them and happiness. Could she not give up her silly tale?

But what if news came of a wounded Nelson? What would be his response?

He shook his head . . . nay, 'twas too bizarre to contemplate.

Chapter Nineteen

"Are you certain you wouldn't like to dance, Jocelyn?" Garren stood next to her, his hand on her shoulder.

Jocelyn looked up at him from her seat, and smiled, shaking her head gently.

Garren returned her smile. She hadn't danced since Lady Tinsbury's ball, and he suspected she doubted her ability to recall the intricate steps.

The music swirled around them, and Jocelyn seemed content to watch the beautifully gowned women and well-dressed men move by. And Garren was content to watch his wife.

"Garren?"

He looked down at Jocelyn and followed her glance to the doors leading in from the gardens.

His father strode through the open doors, a wide smile lighting his face as he looked at Lady Elizabeth and patted her hand that was tucked into his elbow. The lady met his smile with a shy one of her own and blushing cheeks.

"I believe Father has finally asked Lady Elizabeth to marry him." Garren grinned.

"And it appears she said yes," Jocelyn chuckled.

"I had thought there would be an announcement at dinner the other night." Garren watched his father escort Elizabeth to the dance floor.

"I would have thought they'd come right over to tell us." Jocelyn watched the happy couple, wishing to share their joy.

"Father will want to do that in private. You know how he feels about family."

"Should we host a dinner for them?" Jocelyn could have kicked herself for the suggestion the minute it left her lips. She knew nothing about putting on a dinner party in this day and age. But Richard and Elizabeth deserved the attention.

Garren turned his gaze on her, a smile tilting his lips, his eyes alight. "That would be perfect. Mayhap a small one, with a few of their closest friends. We'll have them draw up a guest list in the next day or two."

"Garren, I'll have to have your help with this. I know nothing about planning something like this."

He smiled, patting her hand. "I'm here for you, love."

"I suppose we'll have to let them in on the secret of flinging syllabub, now." She grinned up at him.

He chuckled.

Jocelyn rose from her seat, placing her hand on his arm. "Why don't we get something to drink?"

Leaving the ballroom, Garren guided her to the refreshment table set up in another room. He took the cup of punch offered by a servant and handed it to Jocelyn. As they moved away, they passed a group of men clustered at the end of the table.

"Quite a press tonight, isn't it?" a small, rotund man commented, mopping at his brow.

"And this is just the beginning of the Little Season," another offered.

" 'Tis the war. Everyone's trying to lift their spirits," a third put in. "Especially now that Nelson's returned so badly wounded."

Garren felt Jocelyn's hand squeeze his arm as he stopped, his gaze riveted on the speaker.

"Nelson's returned, you say?" the first man asked.

"Aye. And most grievously maimed. I can't think what this will do to his career."

"What happened?" the second member of the group asked.

Garren held his breath. A shiver of apprehension slid down his spine.

"Had his right arm shot off." The man shook his head. "Such a shame, and at a time when England so needs a lift. To have our hero suffer so. Well, I can't tell you what it might do to public support of the war."

Garren's frantic gaze collided with Jocelyn's calm one.

"Garren?" Her eyes filled with concern.

"You knew." Shock lowered his voice to a low whisper.

With a sad nod of her head, she glanced around the roomful of people, then steered him to a settee in a quiet corner.

"What of Nelson?"

"Sit, Garren." Jocelyn patted the spot next to her. His gaze on her face, he sat, his mind grappling with the news.

"I can't tell you that, Garren." Her gaze dropped to her lap. "If I tell you one thing, it could lead to others, and who knows what kind of trouble that could bring."

Anger seethed within him. After what they'd just learned, she owed him answers. Did she expect him to smile, pat her hand and say, "Yes, dear. It's quite all right that you're from the twentieth century. Quite normal."

His hand gripped hers, stopping her attempts to comfort him. "Jocelyn, you must tell me."

She shook her head, tears brimming in her eyes. "I can't. Garren, please. Let's just go home."

Abruptly, he rose, pulling Jocelyn to her feet. She would tell him nothing; he could see it in the set of her chin. He was trying to deal with this the only way he knew, by garnering more information. And she was his only source.

His fingers tightened on her upper arm. He resolutely tamped down the guilt that rose when she flinched as his fingers dug into her flesh. Maintaining his hold, he threaded his way around the people loitering in the room until he located Lord and Lady Harper.

After a hurried farewell, they waited silently while their carriage was brought around. Garren handed her up into the dark interior. Confusion, fear, and anger warred within him. Waging a silent battle to gain control, Garren held in all his hurtful words that were screaming to be released.

His withdrawal from her was more than physical, it was emotional. Jocelyn hugged herself, fear sending chills through her body. Her fiancé in the twentieth century had withdrawn like this, too, but in the madness of planning a large wedding, she'd missed it until it was too late.

Would Garren leave her, too?

A heavy silence settled over them, relieved only by the steady clip-clop of the horses' hooves as they traveled the London streets.

Jocelyn understood only too well what Garren was experiencing. Hadn't she gone through just such denial and shock in Castleside? What could she say to him?

Tears clogged her throat; misery pressed in on her heart.

In the darkness, she squinted, attempting to see Garren's face. She was so scared.

Maybe she should try to return to her time. Look what she was putting Garren through. And it would be this way every time he asked her for details of the future.

Oh, she could tell him some, but sooner or later either she or Garren would slip, speaking of things that had yet to happen. She had no idea what it would take to change history. Something that seemed small and inconsequential might alter the chain of events. The thought set her to shaking.

No. She shook her head. *If I stay here I have to put my past aside, wipe out any knowledge of the future. And Garren won't help me forget.*

The carriage slowed to a stop, and a moment later the door opened. Garren exited first, then turned to help her down. They climbed the steps together, but once inside, Garren closed himself in his library.

Jocelyn stood in the hall, staring at the shut door, her heart heavy with his rejection. Fighting back the tears, she climbed the stairs to their room.

Garren would never accept her now. She realized that, until this evening, he had accepted her without believing her. Now that he believed her,

300

he couldn't accept her. And she couldn't stay without both.

Tears of frustration welled in her eyes as she opened the door to their room. Standing just inside the threshold, Jocelyn knew she couldn't sleep in this haven she'd shared with Garren, not when she now planned to leave him.

Rushing to the bed, she snatched the nightrail draped over it and left the room. Walking quickly down the hall, she entered a guest chamber.

She'd get a few hours' sleep and then, before the household rose, she'd set off for Ramsgil. If she had to sit on that stump of wood for a week, she would.

She *had* to return.

Stripping off her ballgown, Jocelyn draped it over a chair. Her hands trembled as she slid her nightgown on over her head and climbed into a cold bed. Curled on her side, she felt her heart splinter. She surrendered to the sorrow she'd held at bay, crying until the pillow was wet with her spent tears.

Then she slept.

Garren took a bottle from the cabinet. Not bothering with a glass, he tilted the bottle up to his lips, taking in a long pull of fiery liquid.

The whiskey seared a path down his throat before pooling in his stomach. Shaking his head, he wondered how he would ever reconcile himself to Jocelyn's past.

Or was it her future? He snorted, then took another long drink.

If she was from the future, then, as of now, she had no past. He frowned. Was that right?

Dropping into a leather chair, he combed his fingers through his hair. Hell, she didn't even exist yet. So, who was that upstairs?

Eyeing the bottle of amber liquor, he tilted it to his lips again.

Any doubt he might have had about her claim had vanished tonight at the ball. When he combined the old woman's words with all the odd things Jocelyn had said and done when he first met her, then added in Nelson's injury, there was no other explanation. He *did* believe her. And it what was driving him crazy.

He believed the unbelievable.

Taking another swallow of whiskey, Garren stretched his legs out, bracing the bottle against his stomach.

His thoughts marched to the next problem—that of her silence about the future. How dare she demand his trust when she would not give hers? It sent flames of indignation though him. Bloody hell! He was her *husband*. It was her *duty* to tell him what he wanted to know. He snorted. Did she truly believe he could change history?

Surely she could tell him things that wouldn't affect the future. Something about fashion, or music, or literature? It didn't have to be political.

Hell and damnation. Why was he needing to know? He either believed her or he didn't.

Taking one last sip, he put the bottle on the floor near his chair. He'd rest a minute and then go upstairs and talk to Jocelyn. He'd tell her he didn't need to know any more—that he loved her, and it didn't matter. His eyes drifted shut.

Jocelyn came awake with a start as a rumble of thunder shook the panes of glass in the window. Rubbing her puffy eyes, she swung her legs over the side of the bed. The sky had just begun to lighten as she slipped on her gown from last

302

night, regretting she hadn't thought to get something more appropriate to wear for today. With a shrug, she slid on the thin, matching slippers and quietly stole from the room.

As she inched nearer to the closed door of the chamber she'd shared with Garren, Jocelyn's heart thudded painfully in her chest, tears blurring her eyes. Lightning flared around the house, followed by a crack of thunder. As she choked back a sob, she moved on, taking the stairs rapidly to the hall below.

At the foot of the staircase she stilled, listening intently for any sounds; but it was still quite early, and the house remained silent. Only the wind sounded.

Spotting one of her capes on the stand by the door, Jocelyn snatched it and made her way to the back of the house. She huddled in the warm folds of her cape as she hurried to the stables, just as another burst of thunder echoed and lightning exploded through the sky.

Well, she thought, Hilda had told her that lightning storms could be magical. She was about to test that theory.

Praying she could remember how to saddle a horse and be gone before anyone found her, she inched open the door to the stables.

Do you really expect Garren to try to stop you, she thought? More likely, he'll be relieved you're gone. Biting back a cry, Jocelyn struggled with despair as she moved through the stables, her slippers making barely a sound on the hay-strewn floor.

Eyeing the horses in their stalls, Jocelyn chose the smallest: a plump, dappled mare. The horse watched Jocelyn struggle with the saddle and

303

blanket. After a few abortive attempts, she finally managed to get the animal ready, glancing over her shoulder at the slightest noise the entire time.

Outside, she brought the mare to the mounting block. Stepping up, she stuffed her foot into the stirrup and swung her leg over the mare's broad back. Her mount sidestepped and tossed its head as fat raindrops plopped all around them.

Nudging the horse, Jocelyn headed away from the house, and made her way to the north road out of London. The tears she'd fought to control were now blending with the raindrops falling faster on her face.

A pounding commenced, and Garren opened one eye and moaned. Closing it, he pushed himself to a straighter position, and rubbed at the crick in his neck. Another pounding had him holding his head, groaning with agony.

"Milord?" A servant's voice was low and hesitant.

He opened his eyes to see his butler before him, a frown pulling the man's brows together.

"What the bloody hell is wrong?" he mumbled, even the patter of rain on the windows paining him.

"Milord," Stevens clenched his hands together. "The stableman reports that a mare is gone, and Lady Jocelyn is not in residence."

Garren glared at the hapless servant. "Of course she's in residence, man. We leave *today* for Spenceworth."

"Begging your pardon, milord, but Dulcey went to awaken milady and found the room empty, the bed unused."

"Bloody hell!" Garren lurched to his feet, holding his head when it felt fair to falling off.

Where the hell could she have gone? He ran a

hand through his hair, forcing his weary mind to think. She knew no one other than his father and Lady Elizabeth in London. Surely, she wouldn't be banging on their doors at this early hour.

So where had she gone?

Stepping around his chair, Garren knocked over the empty whiskey bottle on the floor, drawing both his and the butler's attention.

Stevens had the effrontery to raise an eyebrow. Had Garren's head not hurt so badly or his stomach not pitched and rolled, he would have given the man a good dressing down. But as it was, he had to work to pull his mind from its maze of pain.

Think, man. Think. Where would Jocelyn go?

Ramsgil, of course.

He gasped. When she'd left him before—and in the rain, he noted absently—she'd headed to Ramsgil. That was where all of this had started. Mayhap that was where she thought she would find her way back to her time.

No, his mind screamed. She can't leave! Somehow he would make this right.

Garren rubbed his hands wearily over his face. Rain pelted the windows, drawing his attention. "Have the carriage readied. I go after my bride."

He just prayed he would be in time.

Glancing at the clock on the mantle, he saw it was just seven. She couldn't have been gone long, he thought. He just had to hurry.

He flew to his room, climbing the stairs quickly, his head pounding with each footfall. Within his chamber, his valet waited, a cup of noxious liquid in his hand. Ivan had seen Garren through more than one bout of drinking; his cure, though almost as bad as the disease, worked quickly and well.

Grimacing, Garren took the proffered cup and

gulped it down. He washed his face and dressed in warm clothing.

"I'll need blankets," he instructed the butler as he descended the stairs.

He shrugged into his greatcoat and made his way out the door to the waiting carriage, cursing the rain that would hamper his journey.

The rain shifted from a soft gentle mist to a hard driving deluge. And Jocelyn rode, unprotected, in its midst. Garren stuck his head out the window. Unmindful of the rain drenching him, he saw Ramsgil up ahead.

Hell and be damned! He could have made better time afoot.

He rapped on the roof and the carriage stopped. Bolting out the door, he jumped down and landed in the middle of the puddle of muddy water. Unmindful of the damage done to his boots and clothing, he broke into a run toward the cluster of buildings circling the village green.

A wave of relief swept over him when he saw a forlorn figure huddled in her sodden cape, on the block of wood in the village center. Wet strands of hair were plastered to her face. Water dripped from the hem of her clothing into her thin, muddied shoes, and a shiver shook her.

Oh, Jocelyn. *What have I done?*

Walking toward her, Garren felt fear grip his stomach. What if he couldn't convince her to stay?

He straightened his shoulders. If he had to bodily carry her away to Spenceworth, then so be it. But he would not allow her to leave him.

His steps slowed. But no, hadn't the old woman, Hilda, told him Jocelyn must make the decision herself? His shoulders sagged.

The rain turned into a gentle shower, and Garren wiped away the moisture on his face. What could he say to help her decide to stay?

"Jocelyn?" He stretched his hand out to her.

Her red-rimmed, silver gaze traveled from his hand to his face and back to his hand. She shook her head. Strands of wet hair slapped against her cheeks.

She watched him warily as he joined her on the block.

Brushing the wood with his hand, he asked, "Is this how you'll return?"

"Yes." Her whispered word was so full of despair he nearly cried for her.

Closing his eyes against it, he fought against the tide of emotion strangling him. He cleared his throat.

"Before you go, tell me what your real name is." Since the scene with the king, he'd wondered if the name she used was indeed her own or one she had made up.

She gave him a confused look. "Jocelyn Marie Tanner."

"Truly?"

"Yes. Why?" Her delicate brown brow arched.

He chuckled. "I gave Haslett sixpence." He raised his brows. "Your last name is Tanner. . . ." He waited for understanding to light her gaze, but she remained confused. "A sixpence is known as a bender or a tanner."

She smiled sadly and shook her head. "I know what you're implying, Garren, but it's just a coincidence."

He reached for her hand, desperate to convince her. "I have another question for you."

She cocked her head to the side, allowing his hand to cover hers.

"Haven't you changed history already?"

Jocelyn frowned.

"By being here?" Her eyes widened as he continued. "Mayhap your presence is part and parcel of history. Granted, an unrecorded part, but still a part."

He watched the play of emotion cross her face. One moment it was surprise and then, total concentration as she weighed his logic.

"I hadn't thought of that." Her voice quivered, but hope bloomed in her eyes.

What Garren said made sense, Jocelyn thought. Maybe it *was* all part of history. After all, there were things in ancient Egypt that could not be explained easily. And she had no intention of passing along technology. As if she even could.

She looked deeply into Garren's eyes. Love was reflected in their warm brown depths. She understood his reaction last night; he had needed time and space to come to terms with who she was and where she came from.

And he had come for her.

Fresh tears stung her eyes at what she saw shimmering in his gaze.

He loved her.

A moment of pure elation held her still as she accepted it, allowed it to fill her heart and warm her soul.

Right or wrong, she could not leave him. And she wondered now how she'd ever thought she could. There was nothing for her back home. Home was here, with the man who held her heart.

With a decisive nod of her head, Jocelyn smiled at Garren.

Lacing her fingers with his, she stood.

"Why do you insist on sitting in the rain, Garren?

She smiled. "We'll both end up with pneumonia."

His eyebrows rose in surprise. Then dropping his head back, Garren laughed to the heavens. Wrapping an arm around her, he signaled to the waiting carriage.

A bolt of lightning split the sky as the large black conveyance came forward and stopped, then thunder rumbled in the distance. Garren helped her into the vehicle, and just as he closed the door, rain pattered loudly on the carriage.

Wrapping Jocelyn in blankets, Garren held her close, the smell of wet leather and wool filling the carriage's interior.

"You're certain you wish to stay?" Garren's whisper teased her ear, his warm breath sending a shiver along her neck.

She turned to him and smiled. "Yes." He smiled back.

Suddenly, a blinding flash filled the sky outside the window. Jocelyn gasped and squeezed her eyes shut as she clung to Garren, seeking protection from the force threatening to rip her world apart. The air crackled with electricity and thunder rolled over them.

Jocelyn slowly opened her eyes, praying she wouldn't find herself clinging to a stranger on a British tour bus.

"That was bloody close." Garren's voice shook with emotion.

At the familiar sound of his voice, Joceyln sighed in relief. Following Garren's gaze out the window, she saw the auction block, fingers of smoke rising from its jagged wooden edges where the lightning had split it in half.

The tinkling of bells accompanied a cackle of familiar laughter and Jocelyn and Garren both craned their necks peering out the carriage window. A wagon, pulled by a rather swaybacked horse, rolled toward them through the smoke.

"I knew ye'd find yer happiness here and she'd find hers there." Hilda gave Joceyln a wink from her perch on the wagon.

Hilda snapped the reins over the horse's back, plodding by. With a wave of her hand, she called over her shoulder, "Ah, how I love happy endings."

Garren gripped Jocelyn's hand, drawing her attention. Their gazes met and held. Jocelyn smiled. "Oh, but I love happy beginnings better."

More Than Magic

Kathleen Nance

Darius is as beautiful, as mesmerizing, as dangerous as a man can be. His dark, star-kissed eyes promise exquisite joys, yet it is common knowledge he has no intention of taking a wife. Ever. Sex and sensuality will never ensnare Darius, for he is their master. But magic can. Knowledge of his true name will give a mortal woman power over the arrogant djinni, and an age-old enemy has carefully baited the trap. Alluring yet innocent, Isis Montgomery will snare his attention, and the spell she's been given will bind him to her. But who can control a force that is even more than magic?

___52299-3 $5.99 US/$6.99 CAN

HIGH ENERGY DARA JOY

Zanita Masterson knows nothing about physics, until a reporting job leads her to Tyberius Evans. The rogue scientist is six feet of piercing blue eyes, rock-hard muscles and maverick ideas—with his own masterful equation for sizzling ecstasy and high energy.

___4438-2 $4.99 US/$5.99 CAN

Dorchester Publishing Co., Inc.
P.O. Box 6640
Wayne, PA 19087-8640

Please add $1.75 for shipping and handling for the first book and $.50 for each book thereafter. NY, NYC, and PA residents, please add appropriate sales tax. No cash, stamps, or C.O.D.s. All orders shipped within 6 weeks via postal service book rate. Canadian orders require $2.00 extra postage and must be paid in U.S. dollars through a U.S. banking facility.

Name_____

Address_____

City_____ State_____ Zip_____

I have enclosed $_____ in payment for the checked book(s).

Payment <u>must</u> accompany all orders. ☐ Please send a free catalog.

CHECK OUT OUR WEBSITE! www.dorchesterpub.com

Starlight, Starbright

Saranne Dawson

Serena has always been curious: insatiable in her quest for knowledge and voracious in her appetite for adventure. No one understands her fascination with the heavens and the wondrous moving stars that trace the vast sky. But when one of those "stars" lands, the biggest, most handsome man she has ever seen steps off the ship and captures her heart.

His mission is simple: Bring Serena to the Sisterhood for training to harness her great mental power. Yet Darian can't stop thinking about the way she looks at him as though he is the only man in the universe. Despite all the forces that conspire to keep them apart, Darian knows that together he and Serena can tap the power of the stars.

___52346-9 $5.50 US/$6.50 CAN

THE MAGIC OF TWO
SARANNE DAWSON

Quinn knows he seems mad, deserting everything familiar to sail across the sea to search for a land that probably only existed in his grandfather's imagination. But a chance encounter with a pale-haired beauty erases any doubts he may have had. Jasmine is like no other woman he has known: She is the one he has been searching for, the one who can help him find their lost home. She, too, has heard the tales of a peaceful valley surrounded by tall snow-capped mountains and the two peoples who lived there until they were scattered across the globe. And when she looks into Quinn's soft eyes and feels his strong arms encircle her, she knows that together they can chase away the demons that plague them to find happiness in the valley, if only they can surrender to the magic of two.

___52308-6 $5.50 US/$6.50 CAN

Dorchester Publishing Co., Inc.
P.O. Box 6640
Wayne, PA 19087-8640

Please add $1.75 for shipping and handling for the first book and $.50 for each book thereafter. NY, NYC, and PA residents, please add appropriate sales tax. No cash, stamps, or C.O.D.s. All orders shipped within 6 weeks via postal service book rate. Canadian orders require $2.00 extra postage and must be paid in U.S. dollars through a U.S. banking facility.

Name_____
Address_____
City_____State_____Zip_____
I have enclosed $_____ in payment for the checked book(s).
Payment <u>must</u> accompany all orders. ☐ Please send a free catalog.
CHECK OUT OUR WEBSITE! www.dorchesterpub.com

Prince Of Thieves

Saranne Dawson

Lord Roderic Hode, the former Earl of Varley, is Maryana's king's sworn enemy and now leads a rogue band of thieves who steals from the rich and gives to the poor. But when she looks into Roderic's blazing eyes, she sees his passion for life, for his people, for her. Deep in the forest, he takes her to the peak of ecstasy and joins their souls with a desire sanctioned only by love. Torn between her heritage and a love that knows no bounds, Maryana will gladly renounce her people if only she can forever remain in the strong arms of her prince of thieves.

___52288-8 $5.50 US/$6.50 CAN

Dorchester Publishing Co., Inc.
P.O. Box 6640
Wayne, PA 19087-8640

THE WHITE SUN

STOBIE PIEL

Sierra of Nirvahda has never known love. But with her long dark tresses and shining eyes she has inspired plenty of it, only to turn away with a tuneless heart. Yet when she finds herself hiding deep within a cavern on the red planet of Tseir, her heart begins to do strange things. For with her in the cave is Arnoth of Valenwood, the sound of his lyre reaching out to her through the dark and winding passageways. His song speaks to her of yearnings, an ache she will come to know when he holds her body close to his, with the rhythm of their hearts beating for the memory and melody of their souls.

___52292-6 $5.50 US/$6.50 CAN

Dorchester Publishing Co., Inc.
P.O. Box 6640
Wayne, PA 19087-8640

A DISTANT STAR

ANNE AVERY

Pride makes her run faster and longer than the others—traveling swiftly to carry her urgent messages. But hard as she tries, Nareen can never subdue her indomitable spirit—the passionate zeal all successful runners learn to suppress. And when she looks into the glittering gaze of the man called Jerrel and feels his searing touch, Nareen fears even more for her ability to maintain self-control. He is searching a distant world for his lost brother when his life is saved by the courageous messenger. Nareen's beauty and daring enchant him, but Jerrel cannot permit anyone to turn him from his mission, not even the proud and passionate woman who offers him a love capable of bridging the stars.

___52335-3 $5.50 US/$6.50 CAN

Dorchester Publishing Co., Inc.
P.O. Box 6640
Wayne, PA 19087-8640

Please add $1.75 for shipping and handling for the first book and $.50 for each book thereafter. NY, NYC, and PA residents, please add appropriate sales tax. No cash, stamps, or C.O.D.s. All orders shipped within 6 weeks via postal service book rate. Canadian orders require $2.00 extra postage and must be paid in U.S. dollars through a U.S. banking facility.

Name_____
Address_____
City_____State_____Zip_____
I have enclosed $_____ in payment for the checked book(s).
Payment <u>must</u> accompany all orders. ❏ Please send a free catalog.
     CHECK OUT OUR WEBSITE! www.dorchesterpub.com

Shielder

Catherine Spangler

Unjustly shunned by her people, Nessa dan Ranul knows she is unlovable—so when an opportunity arises for her to save her world, she leaps at the chance. Setting out for the farthest reaches of the galaxy, she has one goal: to elude capture and deliver her race from destruction. But then she finds herself at the questionable mercy of Chase McKnight, a handsome bounty hunter. Suddenly, Nessa finds that escape is the last thing she wants. In Chase's passionate embrace she finds a nirvana of which she never dared dream—with a man she never dared trust. But as her identity remains a secret and her mission incomplete, each passing day brings her nearer to oblivion.

The Midnight Moon

Stobie Piel

Dane Calydon knows there is more to the mysterious Aiyana than meets the eye, but when he removes her protective wrappings, he is unprepared for what he uncovers: a woman beautiful beyond his wildest imaginings. Though she claimed to be an amphibious creature, he was seduced by her sweet voice, and now, with her standing before him, he is powerless to resist her perfect form. Yet he knows she is more than a mere enchantress, for he has glimpsed her healing, caring side. But as secrets from her past overshadow their happiness, Dane realizes he must lift the veil of darkness surrounding her before she can surrender both body and soul to his tender kisses.

___52268-3 $5.50 US/$6.50 CAN

Dorchester Publishing Co., Inc.
P.O. Box 6640
Wayne, PA 19087-8640

Please add $1.75 for shipping and handling for the first book and $.50 for each book thereafter. NY, NYC, and PA residents, please add appropriate sales tax. No cash, stamps, or C.O.D.s. All orders shipped within 6 weeks via postal service book rate. Canadian orders require $2.00 extra postage and must be paid in U.S. dollars through a U.S. banking facility.

Name_____
Address_____
City_____State_____Zip_____
I have enclosed $_____ in payment for the checked book(s).
Payment <u>must</u> accompany all orders. ❏ Please send a free catalog.
    CHECK OUT OUR WEBSITE! www.dorchesterpub.com